MAN OVERBOARD

How could he not forgive her? She might be young and foolish but Sophie wasn't wicked. Still, a seaman embracing an admiral's daughter, for whatever reason, might be enough to restore public flogging to the Navy's roster of crime and punishment. Beginning with the cat-o'-nine-tails being unleashed on Ben's back.

But finding it impossible to ignore Sophie Harrington's need for comfort, Ben enfolded her quivering body as lightly as he could and gently patted her back as he would to calm a babe in distress. A curious mixture of honeysuckle and salt scented her hair, the most exotic mixture he'd ever inhaled.

As Sophie's trembling body pressed against him, seeking warmth and solace, Ben became too aware of the soft fullness of her breasts. He reacted as a man who had not been this close to a woman in months might be expected to respond. A man alone at sea with a beautiful woman. Despite this being the wrong time and the wrong place, a smoldering heat took hold of him.

BOOK YOUR PLACE ON OUR WEBSITE AND MAKE THE READING CONNECTION!

We've created a customized website just for our very special readers, where you can get the inside scoop on everything that's going on with Zebra, Pinnacle and Kensington books.

When you come online, you'll have the exciting opportunity to:

- View covers of upcoming books
- Read sample chapters
- Learn about our future publishing schedule (listed by publication month *and author*)
- Find out when your favorite authors will be visiting a city near you
- Search for and order backlist books from our online catalog
- Check out author bios and background information
- Send e-mail to your favorite authors
- Meet the Kensington staff online
- Join us in weekly chats with authors, readers and other guests
- Get writing guidelines
- AND MUCH MORE!

**Visit our website at
http://www.kensingtonbooks.com**

THE ADMIRAL'S DAUGHTER

Sandra Madden

ZEBRA BOOKS
Kensington Publishing Corp.
http://www.kensingtonbooks.com

Kensington Publishing Corp.
850 Third Avenue
New York, NY 10022

All Kensington titles, imprints and distributed lines are
available at special quantity discounts for bulk purchases for
sales promotion, premiums, fund-raising, educational or
institutional use.

Special book excerpts or customized printings can also be
created to fit specific needs. For details, write or phone the
office of the Kensington Special Sales Manager: Kensington
Publishing Corp., 850 Third Avenue, New York, NY 10022.
Attn. Special Sales Department. Phone: 1-800-221-2647.

Zebra and the Z logo Reg. U.S. Pat. & TM Off.

First Printing: April 2003
10 9 8 7 6 5 4 3 2 1

Printed in the United States of America

Dedicated with love and pride to my son,
Lt. Commander Ted Dempsey,
U.S. Naval Academy
Class of '88,
who introduced me to the exciting
history and traditions of The Yard.

AUTHOR'S NOTE

Until November 1853, Cornelius K. Stribling served as Superintendent of the U.S. Naval Academy, when he was succeeded by Commander Louis M. Goldsborough.

Dulany House served as the residence of all academy superintendents from 1850 until 1882.

For purposes of this novel, I created the position of Commandant of Midshipmen for Admiral Wesley Harrington, several years before the position was actually established.

One

"Yoo-hoo!"

The first clear day in late April boasted the fresh scent of spring and the mellow look of summer. A light, salty breeze promised a perfect day for sailing.

Ben Swain's fifteen-foot sloop, *Nantucket Lady*, bobbed at anchor along with fishing boats and sailing craft at the city dock in Annapolis. Within easy walking distance of the Naval Academy, the picturesque marina edged out into Annapolis Harbor, where the Severn River met the Chesapeake Bay.

"Yoo-hoo!"

At the second call from the cheerful female voice, Ben's curiosity got the better of him. His gaze shifted from the anchor bend in his hand, up to the pier. Shielding his eyes from the glare of sun on water, he squinted, straining to see who had called him.

Oh, no. Sophie Harrington.

A deep—Davy Jones locker deep—sense of foreboding washed over Ben as he watched Sophie Harrington sashay toward the pier. She twirled her ruffled blue parasol as carefree as a schoolgirl, unaware that the prickly hairs on the back of his neck stood on end.

Ben did not scare easily. He'd been decorated for bravery in action. But as he watched the young woman in the blue gown bearing down upon him, he experienced an unsettling case of the jimjams.

He'd seen Sophie Harrington for the first time just last week on the parade ground. And while he hadn't yet met her formally, he'd certainly heard enough to know that she should be avoided at all costs. According to the stories circulating around the Naval Academy, and Annapolis in general, Miss Harrington frequently wore bloomers and had been expelled not once, but twice, from exclusive finishing schools for young women.

Rumors persisted that she owned six cats and talked to herself. While Ben usually paid no mind to gossip and had never met a lady he didn't like, he felt more than a little apprehensive about meeting this particular young woman.

"Yoo-hoo, Seaman!"

Seaman. His rank never failed to annoy him. As a man who had once commanded his own whaling ship, he'd expected to be swiftly promoted to officer status.

Could he pretend not to have heard, not to have seen her? On the off chance such a diversionary tactic would work, he speedily prepared to cast off in his small single-mast sloop. As soon as Ben had finished retying the anchor knot, he surreptitiously surveyed the dock in hopes that Miss Harrington had changed course and gone on her way.

No such luck. Apparently indifference did not deter the admiral's daughter. She marched down the pier with an audible swish of skirts and was almost upon him.

"Seaman Swain!"

Damn. It was worse than he thought. She knew not

only his rank but his name. What could she possibly want with him? Ben was out of uniform and off duty. And Sophie Harrington, the daughter of his commanding officer, was definitely off limits.

Although the girl had earned a somewhat nefarious reputation, her beauty was almost as legendary as her brazen misdeeds—and saved her from outright censure. Although Ben had seen Sophie from a distance any number of times since being assigned to the Naval Academy three months ago, he'd never come close enough to her to make his own assessment.

From the width of her skirt, it was obvious that many layers of petticoats lay beneath her blue silk walking dress. The dress, trimmed with wide flounces of ivory lace, matched her parasol. A white chip bonnet adorned with a plethora of blue flowers and feathers was tied beneath her chin with a bow of wide lace ribbon. Except for several silky tendrils that had escaped captivity, the silly bonnet all but hid her tawny-colored hair.

She swished to a stop on the weathered, wooden dock above him. He could no longer pretend to be otherwise engaged. Once again shading his eyes, Ben looked up and into a smile as warm and glorious as a tropical sun. A man could melt in the dazzling brightness of Sophie's smile.

"Good morning!" She spoke in a soft, melodious tone.

He felt a curious hitch in his throat. "Good morning, ma'am."

Lost in her smile, Ben likened it to the sort you gave to an old friend whom you hadn't seen in some time. But Sophie Harrington didn't know Ben. She was a stranger to him.

He regarded the dimple in her left cheek. No stories

he'd heard about the girl had mentioned her dimple. Completely taken off guard, Ben stared at the deep indentation as if in all of his twenty-nine years of living, he'd never seen a dimple before. He found it both charming and alarming. Sophie's dimple, perhaps her most captivating feature, came as a warning sign of mischief in the making.

Again, Ben experienced that prickly beware feeling. This time the needling sensation attacked the pit of his stomach.

Stretching down, Sophie extended a gloved hand. "We've not been formally introduced. I'm Sophie Harrington."

The boat rocked as Ben stretched forward and up in order to take her hand. "A pleasure to meet you, ma'am."

Her hand felt small in his, but to Ben's surprise, her handshake was firm. No limp, meaningless pump of politeness for this lady. Her sweet honeysuckle fragrance drifted close enough for him to understand that she came armed with a full complement of feminine weapons.

"It's lovely weather for sailing, isn't it?" she asked.

"First good day in a while," he agreed. Ben's mind raced, searching for the right words to send the young woman on her way without insulting her.

"Seaman, I'd like to learn how to sail."

Her gaze met his dead on. Aquamarine eyes, the luminescent blue-green shade of Caribbean shoals, met his. Rimming Sophie's eyes were the longest fringes of dark, upswept lashes he'd ever seen. Something close to where Ben's heart should be quivered.

Women did not sail.

"Seaman?" she prodded.

"I'm certain that your father could arrange for one of his aides to take you sailing," he said.

"You don't understand. 'Tis not a ride that I'm after. I want to be the captain of my own ship . . . so to speak. Do you know how often I've watched others sail?" she asked, before quickly proceeding to answer her own question. "Hundreds of times. Unfold the mainsail and then the jib—"

"There is a great deal more to sailing than raising the sails," Ben said, interrupting what he feared might be a long, step-by-step recitation.

Sophie aimed her amazing eyes at his. "I would like you to teach me how to sail, Mister Swain."

For the first time since meeting Admiral Harrington, Ben felt a twinge of compassion for the man. Sophie's father was a tough, by-the-book naval officer. No one questioned or argued with the Commandant of Midshipman. Except his only child, Ben suspected. According to the wagging tongues of Annapolis, Wesley Harrington's beautiful, rebellious daughter provided a constant stream of torment for him.

Ben ran a hand through his hair. If he could only come right out and say, *Go away*. But that was unthinkable. Instead, he excused himself politely. "I'm sorry, ma'am, but I can't teach you how to sail."

"Why not? You instruct the midshipmen. I'm nineteen years old. Certainly I can retain as much, or more, than an eighteen-year-old boy."

"I don't doubt that you have a great deal of intelligence, ma'am, but I have no authority to teach anyone but my students."

Her gently arched brows gathered in a frown as Sophie swirled her frothy silk and lace parasol above her head. Ben interpreted the swooshing noise as a manifestation of Sophie's irritation.

While she appeared otherwise occupied in thought, Ben studied the brazen beauty. Of medium height, her head might just clear his shoulders if he stood beside her. But her height was the only characteristic the Harrington girl possessed that could be described as average. Certainly her voluptuous figure, high cheekbones, and narrow, symmetrical nose could not be classified as average.

With a small sigh, she raised her eyes to the sky as if seeking inspiration from above. Evidently, she found it. "When you are off duty, I see no reason why you could not instruct a private student."

Perhaps he could. But the last person Ben would choose as a private student would be Sophie Harrington. He had no wish to sabotage his future even though at the present his naval career seemed stalled off the rocks. Inexplicably, he'd been transferred from his ship to this school for green boys. Worse, he saw no possibility of receiving a promotion in the line of duty as a sailing instructor. Ben's single consolation was that his whaling mates could not see him now.

"I'm afraid I have very little off-duty time," he said.

"I won't require much of your time," she replied. "I learn quickly."

"Perhaps you might find another officer to teach you to sail."

"But I want you."

In any other circumstance Ben would feel flattered that a beautiful young woman wanted him, for any purpose. He'd earned a well-founded reputation as a grog-drinking, chanty-singing, son of a whaling man—with a lusty appetite for the ladies.

"I've heard my father speak of you," Sophie continued. "You are considered the best sailor in Annapolis. Before you received orders to the academy, you sailed out of the Key West Naval Station. And while you were on patrol, you singlehandedly saved the lives of three officers who attempted to board a slaver off the coast of Cuba."

This woman knew too much.

"The admiral—I call my father the admiral, which you would understand if you lived with him—said you were from a long line of Nantucket whalers."

Did she ever take a breath?

"Father said that there are no braver sailors than whalers."

"Foolhardiness is often mistaken for bravery."

"I am confident that you are not foolhardy and that I can trust my safety to you, Seaman Swain."

If the admiral thought so highly of him, what the hell was Ben doing teaching landlubbers the rudiments of sailing, he wondered? Every hour spent showing a callow boy how to tie a lash or a bow line wasted Ben's knowledge and experience. He yearned to be out at sea, longed for the adventure he'd known all of his life.

Admiral Perry sailed to Japan. Why wasn't Ben on the frigate *Mississippi* or the *Susquehanna* traveling the high seas with Perry's force? No, instead of experiencing the excitement of exploration, here he sat, stuck in Annapolis teaching pimply-faced boys. Teaching a woman how to sail would be the absolute last, humiliating straw for Ben.

Resentment churned in his gut at the thought.

"I wish I could help you, Miss Harrington, but I'm afraid I must decline."

Sophie Harrington might be an adventure unto herself, but not one he could afford. Her lips parted for an almost soundless sigh. But in the next moment, a smile played on her lips, generous, rosy-red lips. Her eyes sparkled as if she kept a scandalous secret.

Ben felt new, true alarm.

"Please, call me Sophie. Imagine!" Lowering her voice, she proceeded to mimic Ben issuing an order. "Miss Harrington, man the mast!"

"I would never say that."

"Hoist the mainsail, Miss Harrington!"

He found her mock play both amusing and annoying. "I would never say that either."

"Miss Harrington, about ship!"

"Nor that."

The impudent young woman giggled while Ben worked to suppress a chuckle and figure out why her foolishness would make him want to laugh. Plainly, Miss Harrington was beyond his understanding.

"What would you say?" she asked, sobering a bit.

Lowering his gaze from her remarkable, but distracting, eyes, Ben rubbed the stubble on his jaw. He hadn't bothered shaving this morning. He hadn't expected to encounter a lady.

"There is only one thing for me to say, Miss Harrington. And that is good day." He offered an apologetic smile and a brief salute to soften his escape. "If I don't cast off soon, there will be no wind to fill my sail."

Ben had lingered with Sophie long enough, basked too long in the warmth of her smile, inhaled much too much of her sweet honeysuckle fragrance. Before he knew it, he would be rendered incapable of reasoning.

The academy's faculty, civilian and officers alike, had been warned away from the admiral's daughter and Ben had no desire to end his career over a woman. Besides, when the time came for him to settle, he'd be looking for an old-fashioned sort of girl, not the sort who approached strangers and demanded they teach her how to sail.

"Is it the wind, or me?" she asked. "Has my father ordered every male at the Naval Academy to avoid me?"

"If Admiral Harrington did give such an order, I'd obey his command," Ben replied, deftly sidestepping a direct answer. "I always obey orders."

Seagulls cried out as they circled above. Watermen tonged for oysters in the harbor. The peaceful setting warred with Sophie's inner turmoil. Her position as the admiral's daughter constantly curtailed her pleasure.

She'd been on her way to the milliner's when she'd stopped to admire the scenery. Her senses buzzed, coming alive with fresh enthusiasm for spring newly arrived. Sophie contemplated the azure sky, the colorful array of boats in the marina, and the ruggedly handsome sailor at work on his shiny white sloop.

As it happened, she recognized him. She'd heard about this broad-shouldered officer and knew his name. Without making a conscious decision, Sophie found herself heading in the direction of the pier . . . and Ben Swain.

Now, she attempted to banish any concerns he might have about her. "Of course you obey orders. I should not expect you to do less."

In all probability, the seaman had heard of at least one of her escapades. Some of the rumors circulating about Sophie were true, but certainly not all. She was bold enough but not brave enough to partake in some of the more slanderous activities attributed to her.

Although Annapolis was Maryland's state capital, it

remained a small town despite a seasonal swelling of the population by politicians and Naval Academy and St. Johns College students.

"If the admiral orders me to teach you how to sail, I shall be happy to fulfill my duty," Swain told her with a wry smile. His inky, indigo eyes twinkled like a born rogue.

He knew he'd never receive such an order.

And Sophie had never wrestled with the desire to rip the shirt off a man's back before. But it was all she could think about while she conversed with Ben Swain. A tear here, a shred there.

"I should warn you that my father indulges me," she bluffed. In truth Sophie could not recall the last time the admiral had indulged her.

Gazing down at Ben Swain, she could find nothing soft nor pretty about him. In fact, it was his rough edges that made him extremely attractive. Tall, broad-boned, and muscular, the sailing instructor struck a compelling figure. He radiated a swaggering, devil-take-care attitude, which she found quite disarming.

With his white linen shirt sleeves rolled up to his elbows, Sophie could follow the wandering paths of corded blue veins rising from the dark flesh of his forearms. His shirt lay opened at the collar, revealing an oddly stirring glimpse of dark, crisp chest curls.

"Do you know how to swim, Miss Harrington?" he asked.

"I've been around water all of my life. I swim very well."

It was true enough that she had been around water all of her life. Her father was a naval officer after all. It was not true that she knew how to swim, although Sophie felt fairly certain she could stay afloat.

As the breeze ruffled his thick shock of dark hair, the

seaman's sharp gaze narrowed on her in a patently skeptical manner. A look that gave her a tingly sensation. Needles and pins pierced her skin in nibbly bites.

Swain possessed the swarthy complexion of a pirate; the dark, exciting exterior of a man who had spent years at sea and survived. Given the proper circumstances, she thought he could prove to be a dangerous man. Exceedingly dangerous.

"Before you think of learning to sail, be sure you know how to swim," he cautioned. "The midshipmen that I instruct are required to pass a swim test before they step foot aboard a skiff."

"The ability to swim is not restricted to males. I am certain I could pass your test."

"My tests are rigorous."

"I am a new woman not bound by old traditions. Challenges do not frighten me."

Swain's dark brows furrowed toward the bridge of his nose. His lips tightened, narrowed but well-formed lips, she noted. Lips that aroused Sophie's curiosity. Would his hard mouth soften if pressed against a woman's lips, hers for instance?

"I will await my orders."

He met her bluff with an enigmatic smile that sent hot sparks darting down her spine. Stymied for the moment, she gazed down at the charismatic sailor, a man far different from any other man she'd ever met. Pure, bodacious masculinity seeped from his every pore, reaching out to her, drawing her to him. Sophie could not be certain if it was the twinkle in his eyes, his slightly crooked smile, or his droll way of speaking that caused the turmoil within her. Even though Swain had not moved, had not touched her, Sophie felt the spiky heat of him settle beneath her skin.

"I shall obtain the orders today," she declared with

utmost confidence. She called his bluff with another, knowing full well that her father would never agree.

"I must be on my way," he said again.

She did not notice a smidgen of regret in his voice.

"Of course."

"Good day, Miss Harrington."

Sophie felt more disappointment than she ought from Swain's stubborn refusal. Although he had said nothing disrespectful, he possessed an arrogance, an arrogant attitude. Even his smile held a swagger.

"Good day, Seaman."

He grinned then. One corner of his mouth slid up into a beguiling lopsided smile. Sophie sucked in her breath. Her feet felt numb, as if they'd fallen asleep.

Ben Swain was a man's man and a woman's desire. He would be the hero to win the heart of Sophie's heroine, Fifi LaDeux. Could there be any doubt? The seaman had been created to fulfill a woman's fantasies.

At last the feeling returned to her feet, and whirling about, Sophie hurried up the dock away from the undermining influences of Mister Swain. She would put him out of her sight, but not out of mind. Sophie's literary endeavors alone demanded she learn more about the sailing instructor.

The Naval Academy was founded on the site of Fort Severn, a nine-acre parcel of land on the eastern edge of Annapolis. The old obsolete fort stood at the tip of a wedge-shaped peninsula called Windmill Point. A circular structure, once belonging to the army, Fort Severn had been fitted with ten guns to protect the once bustling harbor. A hospital, blacksmith shop, bakery, post sutler shop, officers' quarters, and midshipmen's dormitories comprised the close-knit community within the academy grounds. Two brick walls enclosed the shore sides, and a masonry gatehouse at the end of Governor Street allowed authorized entry only.

Sophie, however, could enter and leave at will. And she left the academy frequently. Although her father and most of the officers regarded Annapolis as the dullest of towns, Sophie loved the serenity of the old city. The capital of Maryland since 1694, Annapolis had seen its fortunes diminish over the years as the shipping business shifted up the bay to Baltimore. But Sophie took pleasure in the genteel environs of cobblestone streets, quaint shops, and elegant Georgian mansions. She especially held dear a charming cottage on Prince George Street.

As she indulged in her favorite pastime of shopping, Sophie's thoughts kept returning to Ben Swain. She'd often heard her father speak of the problems promoting officers in a Navy too small for its own good. But the admiral never allowed Sophie to keep company with anyone lower in rank than a lieutenant.

Heaving a sigh, she willed herself to stop thinking about her newest acquaintance. Sophie had never experienced problems concentrating on new purchases before, but her thoughts continued to drift back to him. Unfortunately, the sailing instructor held the same backward attitude as the majority of his sex. A pity, since he was so much more striking in appearance than most men.

Sophie could see no reason why she could not sail. Innumerable times she had watched beginning sailors simply hoist the sail and direct the boat into the wind. Mastering such simple maneuvers required a bit of strength and determination, neither of which she lacked. She would show the arrogant sailing instructor that she had made no idle boast. And in the process, perhaps, give her father a reason to be proud. When all the admiral had ever wanted in life beyond his navy stripes was to have a son, Sophie had done him the ultimate disservice by being born a girl.

Her opportunity to sail came sooner than expected.

Two hours later, after leaving the milliner's shop, she strolled down the cobblestones of Pinkney Street to the dock. The *Nantucket Lady* had left its berth, but a young midshipman standing nearby negotiated to hire a sailboat for an hour.

Sophie did what anyone in her shoes would do when wishing to sail and presented with a green, uncertain boy from the sounds of him. She sidled up to the midshipman just as he had finished his transaction.

The tall, gangly boy frowned at Sophie as if he should know her, but could not quite remember her face nor her name. He surrendered to the puzzle by giving her a jerky smile, uncertain and nervous.

Intending to put him at ease, she greeted him cheerfully, and with a great wide smile. "Hello. My name is Sophie. I do not believe we have met."

He immediately stiffened, squaring his shoulders, raising his chin. "Joseph Baker, Class of 1856."

Sophie's good fortune continued. As a member of the fourth class, the boy would be greener than his upperclassmen. "'Tis a pleasure to meet you, Joseph. At ease," she added, as he appeared quite ill at ease.

"Th-thank you, ma'am." He relaxed his stance but his Adam's apple bobbed as if he had swallowed too hard.

"Do you sail?"

"Well . . ." Coloring, he shifted from foot to foot. "I've had half-a-dozen lessons but I'm not top notch yet. I need practice. Seaman Swain says that I'm too slow."

Slow was just the right speed for Sophie's first lesson. The longer it took the midshipman to hoist a sail, the more she felt she could learn.

Joseph Baker possessed a charming Southern accent and innocent hazel eyes. Sophie warmed to him immediately. His uncertainty regarding his sailing expertise did nothing to dissuade her. Between the two of them she felt certain they could manage a turn around the basin.

"Perhaps I can help. Are you going out for a practice sail now?"

"Yes, ma'am. I've just hired this vessel."

"I'd like to come with you if I might." She batted her lashes for good measure. "I'm learning to sail as well."

Sophie told herself a small exaggeration was not only necessary but permissible in the name of her art. She wished to use the sailing experience in her writing endeavors.

The boy's nervous gaze darted about the pier as if he were looking for someone to give him an excuse for not taking her along. But the few sailors and midshipmen on the dock were concentrating on their own business and completely unaware of Joseph's dilemma.

"I . . . I guess that would be all right," he allowed. "Where would you like to go?"

"We shall just sail about the harbor."

"Yes, ma'am."

With the grace of all good Southern gentlemen, Joseph helped Sophie into the small vessel. Her gown presented a problem as she made her way to the bench. She stumbled and would have fallen if the young man hadn't seized her hand until she regained her balance.

Once seated, Sophie took command. "Sail on, Joseph."

"Yes, ma'am."

"As we sail, would you mind explaining what you are doing, just as your instructor explained it to you?"

"No, ma'am."

As it happened, the boy's explanations were hesitant and sometimes confusing. Nevertheless Sophie learned a few of the basic rules and discovered in the process that, just as she suspected she would, she enjoyed sailing. The fingers of wind tingled against her face, the ribbons of her bonnet blew over her shoulder, loose strands of hair tickled her neck, and she laughed out loud.

Exhilarated by her new experience, Sophie lost track of the time. Closing her eyes, she held her face to the wind. More than thirty minutes later, the midshipman cleared his throat to gain her attention. Wearing a worried frown, he gazed up at the sky.

"We might should take her back, ma'am. Those clouds rolling in look bad."

Sophie looked about. The dark plum clouds indeed appeared ominous. White caps crowned the choppy water. As much as she disliked ending the lesson, the storm was rolling in swiftly.

"Aye, aye, sailor. Turn ho." She didn't know precisely what "turn ho" meant, but it sounded knowledgeable.

Belatedly, Sophie wondered if she could withstand the wrath of her father if he should discover what she'd done this day. The answer came easily. Of course, she had many times in the past.

"Ma'am?"

The boy's complexion had taken on a chalky cast. The gusts of wind grew stronger each minute, tossing the small sloop as if it were a toy boat in a wash basin.

She rubbed a soothing circle over her roiling stomach and forced a smile. "Yes, Joseph?"

"I don't know how to turn the vessel about."

Neither did she. She had no idea how to turn the small sailboat about. Drat.

Two

Midshipman Baker's eyes were about as wide as they could go and not pop. "I mean, I meant to say that I've never maneuvered a vessel in weather like this," he explained.

Always helpful, although not always knowledgeable, Sophie offered a suggestion. "I . . . I think you tack."

"Tack?"

"Yes?"

Joseph frowned so deeply that his dark brows united.

Fear curled in the pit of her stomach like an angry snake. A bolt of silver light slashed through the sky. Thunder rumbled in the distance. Unable to control the trembling that had taken hold of her, Sophie twisted on the bench and looked back toward the city dock. To her vast relief, a rowboat, broad in the bow, splashed through the choppy bay headed their way.

"Help is coming!" she shouted.

Determined to make certain that they were seen, Sophie planted her feet to maintain balance, stood, and removed her bonnet. Swaying precariously, she waved the flower-, lace-, and feather-bedecked confection in the air as if it were a hurricane flag.

Joseph sat unnervingly still. Apparently in a paralyzing state of fear, he nonetheless managed a death grip on the tiller as the boat bobbed about on a circular course all of its own.

Still standing, but concentrated on the rowboat drawing closer, Sophie did not see Midshipman Baker come out of his shock and spring into action. Her gaze focused on the man rowing the boat. Seaman Swain.

While she stared in dismay, Midshipman Baker attempted to turn their small skiff. Sophie felt the wild rocking motion but could do nothing to stop her fall as the vessel dipped and listed dangerously close to the water's edge.

She flew through the air with a scream. Her hat, feathers and all, took wing as well. Her last thought as she plunged into the icy abyss was that she might have gone too far attempting to satisfy her desire to sail.

A lick of lightning illuminated the darkening sky. The roll of thunder drowned out the sound of the churning bay.

Ben's anger dissolved into chilling horror as he watched Admiral Harrington's daughter topple from the hired sailboat. Seemingly suspended in air for one brief moment, she plummeted with a splash into the cold, rough water. He hoped against hope that the headstrong girl truly knew how to swim.

Gritting his teeth, he plunged the oars of his borrowed boat deeper into the water, rowing stronger and faster than he ever had before. Knowing he could handle a rowboat more easily than a sail in stormy weather, Ben had appropriated this boat from one of Annapolis's oyster men. Unfortunately, the heady stench of mollusks permeated the craft.

At the onset of the rescue mission, Ben had believed Midshipman Baker to be the only one in trouble. Sophie's presence came as a surprise. The anxious owner of the hired sailboat had not mentioned a woman setting out with the academy student.

"Help!" Joseph shouted, waving his arms over his head. "Woman overboard!"

Sophie emerged from the water sputtering. She flailed only a few feet away from the bow of Ben's leaky rowboat. With the skill earned by years at sea, he eased the boat within yards of the frightened young woman.

"Grab hold, Miss Harrington!" Ben yelled as he threw out a lifeline.

"I can't! It's too far away!"

Aghast, he watched as Sophie gulped water, sputtered, and submerged again. The admiral's daughter swam no better than Ben's anchor. He would have to dive in after her.

Sophie's head bobbed up just as Ben dropped anchor.

"My feet are . . . are tangled . . . in my skirt!" she cried, before going under once more.

Ben yanked the lifeline in and threw it out again. This time it hit Sophie on the head as she surfaced. "Yeouch!"

"Grab it!" he bellowed before he dove.

When he emerged from the numbing cold water, Sophie had a hold on the lifeline. When it slipped out of her hands, he was there to catch her. Wrapping an arm around her waist, he pulled her limp body against him.

"Don't move, just breathe," he cautioned as he side-stroked through the stormy water to the boat.

He felt the shudder that rocked her body almost as if it were his own. Ben's strokes were swift and strong, but with only one arm against a turbulent sea, it seemed an eternity before they reached the weatherbeaten old wooden boat. While Ben swung himself into the lurching vessel, Sophie clung to the sides taking in great gulps of air.

Drenched to the skin and shaking from the cold water, Ben leaned over and pulled Sophie to safety. Her teeth chattered and she trembled from head to toe. He grasped her upper arms to steady her.

She managed a weak smile. "Th-thank you. You saved my life."

Hanks of wet hair fell in her face and past her shoulders in a matted, water-kissed curtain. Thoroughly wet and torn in several places, Sophie's beautiful blue gown adhered to the generous curves of her body. Fright glazed her eyes. She swayed before him as vulnerable as she might ever be, and more beautiful than a woman had a right to be.

If Sophie had been anyone else but the admiral's daughter, he might have taken her into his arms to comfort her, to hold her until her trembling stopped and her teeth no longer chattered. Thinking better of a simple humanitarian act which might be misconstrued, he simply nodded and eased her down on the single bench.

Ben sat down beside Sophie, twisting his body to face her, intending to give some sort of comfort before taking up the oars. While he considered how to warm her without actual contact, Sophie solved his dilemma. Without pretense or pride she inched closer to him. Resting her head against his chest, she circled her arms around his waist. "I'm . . . I'm so sorry for putting you to th-this trouble. Pu-please forgive me."

How could he not forgive her? She might be young and foolish but Sophie wasn't wicked. Still, a seaman embracing an admiral's daughter, for whatever reason, might be enough to restore public flogging to the Navy's roster of crime and punishment. Beginning with the "cat-o'-nine-tails" being unleashed on Ben's back.

But finding it impossible to ignore Sophie Harrington's need for comfort, Ben enfolded her quivering body as lightly as he could and still be touching. He gently patted her back as he would to calm a babe in distress. A curious mixture of honeysuckle and salt scented her hair, the most exotic mixture he'd ever inhaled.

As Sophie's trembling body pressed against him seeking warmth and solace, Ben became too aware of the soft fullness of her breasts. He reacted as a man who had not been this close to a woman in months might be expected to respond. A man alone at sea with a beautiful woman. Despite this being the wrong time and the wrong place, a smoldering heat took hold of him.

"Help! Help!"

Midshipman Baker. How could Ben have forgotten the boy? He looked over just as Joseph lost his balance and tumbled into the water, hitting his head and overturning his hired sailboat.

"Oh, no!" Sophie cried, then started as a bolt of lightning flashed across the darkening sky. "Oh, sweet mercy!"

Ben set her down on the floor of the rowboat. If he wasn't mistaken, the boy had hit his head. "It's wet but safe here," he told her. "I'm going after Joseph."

Nodding, she drew a deep breath through parted blue lips and straightened her shoulders as if she were making ready to meet a foe head on.

Once again, Ben dove into the churning bay waters. Joseph's unconscious body lay across the upturned boat, buffeted by the wind and waves. This wasn't the first time Ben had struggled against the elements, but each time he ventured into the water, he never knew who would win. He figured nature always held the upper hand.

The current pummeled him as he swam to the midshipman. Every muscle in his body ached by the time he reached Joseph. Cupping the boy's chin in his hand, Ben made his one-armed way back to the sloop as he had done with Sophie.

As soon as Ben had finished shoving and hauling the midshipman—who at dead weight weighed a great deal more than Sophie—into the boat, he attempted to reassure his quaking female passenger.

"We'll be ashore before the storm breaks," he said.

Sophie didn't look as if she believed him. "Is Joseph all right?" she asked.

"Other than sporting a lump on his head, he'll be fine."

At that, she lifted her chin and shot Ben a tight, quavering smile.

The rumble of thunder rattled the sides of the boat.

The admiral's daughter jumped. The color drained from her face until she became so white, Ben thought she might pass out. But Sophie had pluck, he had to hand it to her. The willful young woman simply braced herself against the sides of the boat and bit down on her lip.

"I would appreciate it if you would not tell my father about this . . . this incident," Sophie shouted.

"Perhaps in the future, you'll not coax innocent boys into trouble, will you?"

"Joseph said he knew how to sail."

Still unconscious, Joseph said nothing.

"Young midshipmen think they know a lot more than they do."

"A trait they share with their instructors?"

Although her body might be soaked and shivering, Sophie's supply of pure mettle obviously had not been dampened.

"I warned you," he yelled above the storm, "but you said you knew how to swim. You told me you would be safe sailing."

"I . . . I have been known to exaggerate."

"Is that what it's called?" He spoke through his teeth as he pulled hard on the oars.

He raced against time, raced against the weather. The downpour of rain began while they were still fifty feet from the dock.

Reaching up from the bottom of the boat, where she still sat, Sophie laid a hand on his knee. Ben found himself staring into beseeching turquoise eyes. "I . . . I would be forever in your debt if you would, if you would not mention this little incident to my father."

With her gaze locked on his, he could hardly refuse her second request.

"Please, Seaman Swain."

Ben experienced a strange, painful tug at his heart. He knew he should report the . . . incident, but when Sophie cringed as another flash of lightning cracked across the sky, he realized he could not.

"I have never had the pleasure of a conversation with your father, Sophie. I see no reason to have one now. Just promise me you'll stay off the dock and any and all boats."

"I will . . . until I learn to swim."

Despite her bravado, she shuddered and hunkered down with each strike of lightning and rumble of thunder. Any other woman experiencing a similar storm might not consider boating in the future. But

Ben had learned quickly that Sophie was not like any woman he'd met before.

True to his word, he had no part in conveying Sophie's sailing disaster to her father. But as he rowed up to the dock through the pounding rain, the first figure Ben spotted among the gathered onlookers was Admiral Harrington, wet and red with fury.

"Once again you have mortified me!"

Sophie's angry father slammed his fist on the desk. The inkwell bounced and several loose papers fluttered to the polished wood floor.

"I . . . I am terribly sorry, sir."

The admiral's study was a cold, barren room in comparison with the rest of Dulany House. The stately colonial mansion on the Naval Academy grounds had been their home since the school became official three years prior. It was the longest Sophie could remember living in one place.

A bookcase and two plum-colored wingback chairs were the only furnishings. Two portraits hung on the wall behind and to either side of her father's desk, one of President Pierce and one of the Secretary of the Navy, George Bancroft. The eyes of both men seemed to be constantly staring at the occupants of the room, following no matter where one moved. Sophie thought the portraits exceedingly unsettling.

She shifted her gaze from the livid face of her father to the nearest of the two floor-to-ceiling windows flanking the fireplace. Watching the rain seemed the safest thing to do. Two hours had passed since being hustled from the downpour. Bathed, dried, dressed, and with head held high, she faced her father and awaited her fate.

She did not wait alone. Ben Swain stood stiffly beside her. Though he moved nary a muscle, she could feel the heat of him, smell the soap and citrus scent of him. Inhaling deeply, she found the essence of his aftershave the single pleasant aspect in this unpleasant business they faced together.

The admiral railed from behind his desk. Although a short man, barely five foot seven inches, he nevertheless presented a fearsome figure. Sophie did not know her father well. She had spent years at boarding schools, while he spent months at a time away at sea. He'd served with honor in both the Pacific and Home Squadrons. Sophie felt as if she and her father were like ghost ships in the night, passing, always passing. Beyond what she could feel intuitively or observe firsthand, her father remained a stranger. And that sad fact haunted her.

Sophie had been raised by a succession of nannies after her mother had died giving birth to her. As soon as she was old enough, her tyrannical father had shipped Sophie away to boarding school. Whenever she misbehaved, he threatened to send her to Saint Louis to live with his spinster sister, Edith.

Sophie felt blessed to possess a fertile imagination. If not for the characters and friends she conjured, she would have led a lonely life.

The admiral's spectacles perched against a rather bulbous nose while his dark gray gaze blazed above the rims of his glasses in a familiar fashion. Sophie had seen this look before. Numerous times. Somehow, she always managed to enrage her father when innocently seeking to broaden her horizons.

"What do you have to say for yourself, young lady?"

If it were not for the rain against the windowpanes, the sound of Sophie's thudding heart surely would fill the room. It was bad enough to be the object of her father's fury yet again, but to have Seaman Swain witness her humiliation made matters worse.

"I apologize, sir. I could see no harm in learning how to sail."

"Women do not sail." He spat the words between his teeth, his eyes glinting with anger. "Women are not strong enough to do what is required. And it is common knowledge that members of your sex are unable to keep their wits about them when problems occur. The storm you encountered is just such an example."

"But I did not—"

"You go against nature again and again."

"We would have been fine if it had not been for the storm—which did not cause me to lose my wits," she added. "Seaman Swain can attest—"

"Do not drag the seaman into this," her father growled.

"No, sir."

So often in these situations, the admiral's dark Vandyke beard and mustache reminded Sophie of sketches she'd seen of the devil—without the small nubby horns atop his head, of course. Her father's thin, meticulously trimmed facial hair seemed at odds with his solid, barrel-like proportions. Even the flattering naval uniform could not conceal the fact that Wesley Harrington's chest was as round as his waist. But Sophie kept such observations to herself.

"You are an extremely fortunate young lady. If it weren't for Swain's quick action, you might be dead."

From the corner of her eye, Sophie saw Ben Swain draw himself up into an even taller, more compelling force, but his gaze never wavered from the book-shelves behind her father.

"Yes, sir," she replied softly.

While a man in uniform always appeared more heart-stirringly handsome, Sophie had been around naval stations long enough to be able to separate the man from the uniform. But Ben Swain, pressed and polished to perfection, cut an exceptionally smart fig-ure in his navy blue uniform.

The flattering color drew attention to his riveting dark sapphire eyes. His high-collared white shirt cre-ated a striking contrast against his dark, leathered skin. Sophie thought the stiff shirt collar might well stand on its own. But the navy silk cravat softened the spot a bit.

Unadorned epaulets sat squarely on the shoul-ders—splendidly wide shoulders—of his wool jacket. Accentuating the breadth of his considerable chest, a double row of gleaming gold buttons blazed down the blue jacket. At first glance, the sailing instructor gave the astonishing impression of inherent dignity and raw male virility.

Sophie's gaze fell to the regulation narrow trousers that complimented Swain's round and firm derriere, more than any officers she knew—not that she nor-mally noticed the rear anatomical attributes of a man.

From his gleaming boots to the neat cap tucked be-neath one arm, Ben Swain did more for the navy uniform than any man in Sophie's memory.

"Sophie, are you paying attention to me?"

"Yes, Father."

"If it were not for the storm, more than likely I would never have discovered your latest indiscretion." Bracing against his stiff arms and splayed hands, her father leaned across the desk. The pinky finger of his left hand was missing, a casualty of the Mexican War. "Is that what you were thinking?"

That is exactly what Sophie thought. Screwing up her brow in what she hoped to be an apologetic frown, she took at different approach with her father in hopes of ending this embarrassing scene. She could only imagine what Swain thought of all this. And it wasn't good.

"Father, I only sought to earn your respect by learning how to sail."

He straightened, clenching his jaw before he spoke. "You do not require my respect. You are my daughter."

Oh, but Sophie did require his respect. Even more, she needed her father's love. But further argument would not put an end to this fruitless encounter. Tamping down her bubbling frustration, she lowered her gaze and replied quietly, "Yes, sir."

"Seaman Swain, one of the Navy's finest sailors, risked his life to save you. Have you nothing to say to him?"

She'd already apologized to Ben. Now her father insisted she grovel.

As Sophie turned her head toward the hero who had saved her, Swain cast a maddening I-told-you-so look from the corner of his eye. With one look, he set her teeth on edge, stirred her insides to a slow, nettled burn.

Swain's cocky attitude, unseen by her father, rankled Sophie. A mere seaman had no business behaving like a lieutenant. She looked away, over her father's shoulders and into the portrait eyes of President Pierce.

"I shall forever be in your debt, Seaman Swain." She spoke in a barely audible monotone. "You have my undying gratitude."

"My pleasure, ma'am." Ben's stilted reply echoed coldly.

Thankfully, her father remained oblivious to anything but what he had to say. He continued his measured tirade without any indication that he'd noticed the strain of Sophie and Ben's exchange.

"This is just one more situation in an endless series of situations which force me into decisions I would rather not make."

Uh-oh. Sophie didn't like the sound of that.

She glanced at Ben again. Did he truly have to be present for this lecture? Still standing at rigid attention with shoulders squared and eyes forward, he appeared to have retreated into himself. He might as well have been a statue, unmoving and unaffected. And why should he be affected? No loathsome decision her father made regarding Sophie would affect Ben.

Steeling herself, Sophie met her father's icy gaze and asked the question he had been waiting for her to ask. "What is that, Father? What decisions have you made?"

Scowling, he took two steps away, turned, and took two steps back. Deep folds of frustration lined his face. "If it were not for Seaman Swain, you might have drowned today."

"Father, I don't—"

His arm shot out as he pointed a finger at her. "Do not dare to argue the point. You behaved foolishly, sailing out on the bay when you don't know how to swim and had not a proper, experienced escort."

She clamped down on her lip. Far be it from Sophie to inform her father that Seaman Swain, the man he thought of so highly, had refused her request for instruction. Otherwise she might have been sailing safely with Swain and learning when to head for port.

"Yes, sir."

The angry admiral seemed to collect himself as he turned his somber gaze to Swain. "I commend you for saving my daughter's life, Seaman. You have earned my heartfelt thanks and esteem."

"I did what any man would have done, sir."

Sophie's father sank to his chair. He picked up the pocket compass that lay before him, regarding it as if it held the answer to a mystery. Rain no longer pelted the windowpanes. The Spartan study fell silent in anticipation of the admiral's next words. "I have made an important decision, Sophie."

"Yes, sir."

"You shall marry Captain Ferguson before summer—"

"Marry!" she cried.

"Yes."

"Before summer?" In shock, all Sophie could manage was to repeat fragments of her father's decree. A biting mixture of outrage and disbelief all but choked her.

"It's not soon enough as far as I'm concerned. You need a firm hand and the patient guidance of a good man, Sophie. Marriage will do wonders for you."

"But I don—"

"Six weeks should give you ample time to plan a small wedding."

"I'm too young to marry!" she wailed in protest. Even her lungs balked, refusing to take in air. "I do not wish to marry."

"Andrew's a good man," her father said as if she hadn't spoken. "He's from a fine family. He'll be able to keep you in style, buy you as many hats and shoes as your heart desires."

"Andrew Ferguson is too old for me," Sophie protested. "He's forty years old if a day."

"Age brings wisdom and experience," her father countered. "And a man with experience is exactly what you need. Andrew will know how to keep you in check."

"I do not need to be kept in check," Sophie bristled.

The admiral's expression grew sterner still. He slowly inhaled, his formidable chest swelling to the button-popping stage. "We will discuss this further when we are alone. Not that there is anything you can say to change my mind."

"Arranged marriages are no longer in vogue," she bit out angrily.

"You will thank me for this one day," her father declared tersely.

"I shall never marry. Never."

"You are dismissed, Sophie."

Tears she would rather not shed in front of her father and the seaman threatened to spill. "Per-perhaps I can persuade you to come to an agreement at dinner this evening."

"I shall be dining with Admiral Porter this evening."

"When you return—"

"Sophie, I refuse to argue with you any longer. Master Swain has exercised all patience. Leave us to our business. I shall talk with you tomorrow."

Again the room fell silent. Mutinous tension crackled in the air. Sophie clamped down on her lip. Whirling on her heel, she stormed from the room. And while she did not precisely slam the door behind her, the room nevertheless vibrated from the sound of a door closed with excessive force.

The admiral turned to Ben. "Forgive my daughter. Sophie is excessively willful. 'Tis the lack of a mother to blame."

"Yes, sir."

"If Sophie had been born a boy, I would have known what to do. I could have raised a boy properly. As it is, I fear Sophie's brashness and independent streak are quite masculine in nature and unattractive in a woman. I had hoped the finishing schools would cure her, but alas, she has spent too much time in the company of sailors."

Ben held his tongue. To agree with the admiral might land him in dangerous territory. As independent and willful as she was, Sophie was fortunate to have survived to this point. That she had lived to arrive at a marriageable age, he viewed as a plus. Although Ben had little respect for Andrew Ferguson, he did feel a tinge of sympathy for the captain. He expected that any man who became Sophie's husband would face unimaginable challenges.

"Am I correct that you are currently assigned to the Department of Seamanship, Swain?" Admiral Harrington asked.

"Yes, sir. I'm instructing basic sailing." Ben hesitated only a fraction of a second. "Although I think my experience and knowledge might be better utilized elsewhere."

"I agree with you, Swain. But we also need to turn out well-educated naval officers. The academy has only been officially in existence for three years. There is much to be done. We are laying a foundation here for the future of the Navy."

With his hands clasped behind his back, the admiral strolled to the fireplace, its grate piled with cold ashes. "We are in a fledgling stage and must proceed carefully if we are to succeed. It's just as important to have our best officers and sailors stationed here as it is to have them at our active bases. Robert E. Lee, the Superintendent of West Point, is watching us closely and will make note of our innovations."

"Yes, sir. And sir, I should like to take this opportunity to say that Midshipman Baker did not realize Miss Harrington was your daughter when he agreed to take her sailing with him. I've reprimanded the boy, but I don't think he should receive demerits in this case."

"I agree." The admiral grunted. "My daughter has a knack of luring innocent victims into the worst predicaments."

After just one experience with Sophie, Ben could not argue the point with the admiral. "I expect the boy might have alluded to being a better sailor than he knew himself to be," he said.

Ben held himself partially responsible for Baker's arrogant attitude. Instructors at the academy had a twofold mission, to instill unshakable confidence in the midshipmen, yet motivate each to even higher achievement.

"I understand," the admiral said, moving back to his desk.

"Midshipman Baker is in one of my classes and not doing as well as he should. To his credit, he hired the boat for a practice run at his own expense."

The admiral stood behind his chair, gripping its back. "The young man has paid for his mistake. I'm satisfied with the way you've addressed the entire incident, Swain."

"I hope to be considered for ship duty in the near future," Ben replied. He didn't belong at the academy. He belonged on the sea. The yearning for the adventure he'd enjoyed since his whaling days never ended. He possessed the soul of a wanderer and made no excuses.

"You shall be, Seaman. I have no doubt of it. But don't underestimate your work here."

"No, sir."

"When the time comes to move on, I shall give you a strong recommendation."

"Thank you, sir." A promotion would be appreciated as well but that might be too much to hope for.

During a skirmish with a slave ship in the Caribbean, he'd rescued a lieutenant and a captain, one from drowning, one from a sword. But the Navy was small and promotions scarce. As much as he wished to achieve a commissioned rank of lieutenant, he knew men who had died of old age waiting for a similar promotion. Fortunately, there was more than one way to get where Ben wanted to go.

"I have also been working on a design for a steam-driven ship that I believe would serve the Navy well in battle."

"Interesting. You're a good man." Admiral Harrington gave him a tight-lipped smile. "I believe that in you I have found the right fellow to watch over Sophie until she is safely married."

"Sir?" Ben jerked as if about to be struck by an unexpected body blow.

"I want you to see to it that my girl stays out of trouble and is at all times removed from harm's way."

"Yes, sir." His voice cracked.

"I can only entrust my daughter's well-being to a man I trust and respect."

Ben's throat constricted as if he'd swallowed burning whiskey. "Sir, I am highly flattered but I must confess that I have little experience with women. Another officer might be—"

"As of sixteen hundred hours, you will be assigned to protect my daughter . . . from herself."

There it was—the actual blow. Whomp! Damn.

Was he expected to say something? The only words swirling in Ben's brain were: *No. No! Absolutely not.*

He pressed his lips together.

"The attic room is empty and ready for immediate occupancy," Admiral Harrington said, raking a hand through his thick salt-and-pepper helmet of hair. "Or if you prefer, you can have the spare room off of the kitchen when Sophie's maid leaves. Abigail plans to depart in a matter of days."

Ben stood numbly, listening but unable to completely comprehend what he had heard.

"I expect you to station yourself in and around Dulany House," the admiral said.

"You're asking me to move into your home, sir?"

"Yes. Further, I am ordering you to make certain that Sophie does nothing to jeopardize the marriage that I have worked diligently to arrange. In addition, you must make sure that no harm comes to her before she can be wed."

"But sir, what about my students, my sailing classes?" Ben objected as forcefully as he dared.

How had he come to this, acting as nursemaid to a headstrong young woman? At the very least he should be preparing to sail with the midshipmen on their summer cruise aboard the *U.S.S. Preble.*

"You will continue to instruct, Seaman Swain. Your classes are held in the morning, are they not?"

"Yes, sir."

"My daughter never rises before noon."

Ben grasped at a last, desperate straw. "I believe Miss Harrington might resent me acting as her watchdog."

"Sophie need not know. I shall inform her that you are consulting with me on an important project. That steam-driven ship you mentioned. As far as she is concerned, you must be at my beck and call."

"Will she believe that?"

"Certainly. Have you not noticed? My daughter pays little attention to anything I say. Sophie will think I have rewarded you with a plum assignment for saving her life."

"Yes, sir," Ben replied dully.

"I'll not forget this service to me—and to Sophie—when the time comes for you to receive new orders."

A swell of mixed emotions drummed through Ben, including anger, disappointment, and sorely wounded pride. If his future depended on keeping Sophie out of trouble and fit for marriage, he was all but doomed.

Three

In the last dusky, dappled light of day, Ben sat at a stone table in the Harrington garden pondering his ill-fortune. Surrounded by budding rosebushes and stalks he recognized as the beginnings of daffodils and irises, he smoked a thick Cuban cigar. Pursing his lips, he puffed a series of perfect smoke rings. His mind dwelled on other things as he contemplated the ethereal rings that spiraled into the air above him before dissolving.

The first time Ben set eyes on the dimpled beauty, he knew Sophie spelled trouble. Before she reached the dock, he should have hoisted sail and made his getaway.

He gloomily pondered his fate, determined to come up with a plan to escape his current predicament. Swift deployment to a ship seemed the best answer. There were hours of idleness aboard ship when he could continue working on the design for his steam-driven battleship. More importantly, he could not put a safe distance between himself and Sophie Harrington quickly enough.

After too many icy Nantucket winters, Ben favored being stationed in the South. Based in Key West, he'd sailed on a frigate through the Caribbean, giving chase to the slave ships. He'd felt a keen satisfaction in putting the slavers out of business and freeing their captives. At the moment he'd give anything to return. But he could hardly demand such an order.

Ben's grim musings were interrupted by the sound of a creaking door. It came from the rear of the house, not far from where he sat. The door creaked open and then it creaked shut.

Nerves instantly at full alert, he ground out his cigar in the gravel beneath his feet. It might be the cook or one of the other day servants departing for the evening. But Ben wasn't taking any chances. He prepared to detain whoever walked through the vine-laden arbor which carved a path between the stately evergreen hedges. If Sophie Harrington was attempting to sneak off, Ben would have her back in her chamber before she could blink.

The admiral considered his daughter under "house arrest." Ben's job was to see that Sophie stayed at home.

It came as no surprise to see his commanding officer's daughter dash through the arbor. In order to gain maximum speed, she held her skirts above her ankles. Trim, attractive ankles, he noted with fleeting admiration.

Unaware that Ben watched, Sophie fled toward the back gate.

"Going somewhere?" he asked, stepping out from the shadows.

Sophie stopped in her tracks. After a single breath's pause, she whirled to confront Ben. Realizing his height alone could be intimidating, he straightened, squared his shoulders, slung his hip forward, folded his arms across his chest, hiked a brow, and leveled a glowering gaze.

"Seaman . . . Seaman Swain." Her eyes seemed to double in size. She looked lovely.

"Good evening, Miss Harrington."

Deceptively lovely and innocent.

Ben had yet to see Sophie wearing bloomers, but maybe she saved those for special occasions. His gaze locked on her startled turquoise eyes before drifting downward in a hasty, sweeping inspection. Her light brown hair, streaked with strands of gold, had been brushed to a lustrous sheen and fell in loose curls about her shoulders. A shawl-like collar of lace spread from the deep vee neckline of her pale, apple green gown. The plunging neckline afforded a teasing glimpse of cleavage, just enough of a peek to cause Ben to experience an uncomfortable warming in parts of his anatomy better left cold.

He would rather feel the effects of scurvy than be aroused by the admiral's eccentric daughter.

"Are you going somewhere?" he asked, raising his gaze to meet hers.

Without parasol, gloves, or reticule, Sophie didn't appear dressed for the street. But she'd been headed for the back gate, which opened on a narrow ally leading to the street.

Lifting her chin in a decidedly defiant manner, she replied in clipped tones, "As a matter of fact, I am on my way to see Flora Muldoony."

"Flora?" he repeated, startled. Unfolding his arms, he planted balled fists on his hips and regarded Sophie through narrowed eyes. She couldn't mean the same Flora whom Ben knew. "The Flora who works at Reynolds Tavern?" he asked.

"Do you know Flora?"

"Yes." Flora was the first woman Ben had met after his arrival in Annapolis. The fiery barmaid was a woman of the world, a very different world than that inhabited by the admiral's daughter.

"Flora is . . . she's my friend," Sophie told him in a quiet, defensive tone.

"Flora the tavern maid is your friend?"

Sophie glared at him with that uppity look again, as if to say, who was he to question her choice of friends? "It's difficult to find friends. Between boarding schools, I've been raised among men for the most part," she explained. "With the exception of a few former schoolmates and Navy wives who are scattered about the country from Virginia to the Pacific Coast, I am not on intimate terms with many women."

Ben could not deny that the Navy life was hard on women. At the same time he knew Admiral Harrington would throw him in the brig if he discovered Ben had allowed his daughter to associate with a tavern maid.

"Do you think your father would approve of you befriending a girl like Flora?" he asked carefully.

"My father dislikes most things that I do," Sophie replied. She pulled a lace hanky from the wrist of her dress as she meandered over to the bench where he'd been smoking. "He never approves."

The volumes of petticoats beneath her full skirt made Sophie's waist appear as tiny as a child's. And her gown, made from untold yards of silk, created a mesmerizing rustle as she moved.

"I'm sure you exaggerate," Ben said, although he wasn't all that certain.

Sinking to the bench, Sophie leaned into a pale yellow rosebud and inhaled. "Do you mind if I ask what you are doing in our garden?"

"Waiting to meet with your father. The admiral's given me the opportunity to work closely with him on a top-secret steam project."

"Oh?" She inclined her head, regarding him with her enormous, luminous eyes.

"Yes, I've been ordered to move into Dulany House for the duration."

"Curious." She heaved a heart weary sigh. "My father has rewarded you and punished me."

"You commandeered a sailboat and an innocent midshipman. Did you not expect to be taken to task?"

"Taken to task, yes. But punished with marriage? No!"

"The question is, who is being punished, Ferguson or you?" he quipped.

Sophie's face went pale and she stiffened on the bench as if her spine had suddenly been infused with steel. "Has my father given you leave to insult me?"

"My apologies," he said, dipping his head. He felt as dumb as a sponge. The instant Ben saw the hurt expression on Sophie's beautiful face, he'd wanted to bite his flippant tongue.

"Apology accepted." She smoothed the hanky in her hand against her lap. "Despite everything, I enjoyed the sailing. The feel of the wind on my face, the faint smell of salt, the flapping of the sail, and until the storm . . . the silence. I shall sail again."

"Not on my watch."

"What?"

"I suggest you learn to swim first."

"When the weather is warmer, I shall do just that." Sophie regarded Ben as if she were a portrait artist about to paint his likeness. He squirmed under her scrutiny, watching warily as her gaze drifted from his eyes to his nose and then to his lips.

"Something tells me that I could learn a lot from a man like you."

What the hell was she talking about? Was she flirting with him?

"If you're interested in whales or ships, I might be of some help," he allowed.

"I don't care to know about whales. I was thinking that you could teach me to swim."

"No. No. No, I couldn't." If he wasn't careful, he'd wind up facing court-martial on account of Sophie Harrington.

"Yes, you could," she declared, with a sweet smile. "A woman must be able to take care of herself."

"Maybe so, but swimming is something you should learn from someone else. A woman, at that."

"But I do not know a woman who swims, and I wish to be independent in all ways."

Here it was then. Ben knew he'd hear it sooner or later. Radical talk. Independent. Sophie had come under the spell of those meddling equal rights women, Elizabeth Cady Something and Susan B. Anthony. He wondered if he should report this subversive conversation to the admiral.

"Why do you wish to be independent?" Ben knew as soon as the words were out that he should not have asked. He didn't understand why but conversation with Sophie Harrington made him as nervous as a minnow swimming in a school of sharks.

Sophie gazed into space as if she'd fallen into a trance. "For many reasons. Most women don't think they can have their own home unless a husband provides one for them. Is that not a pity?"

Ben had stumbled on quicksand before. He knew the feeling, and knew he was on dangerous ground even though his feet were firmly planted. "But you believe differently?"

Her mouth grew soft. The expression in her eyes grew wistful. "I will soon be supporting myself. And

I'll be living in the old Bailey cottage on Prince George Street. It's for sale, you know."

"No, I didn't." Like a helpless sailor clinging to a raft as it is buffeted by a stormy sea and swept toward the rocks, Ben could see the wreck coming and felt powerless to stop it.

"Do you know the name 'Elizabeth Wetherell'?" Sophie asked.

"No."

"She's a famous author who wrote a remarkable book. You must read it. I shall lend you my copy of *The Wide, Wide World.*"

"I look forward to reading it." No way in hell.

"I wish to emulate Miss Wetherell and earn my own way," Sophie told him. She'd snapped out of her trance-like state. "I shall live in a cottage on Prince George Street and write popular novels for the rest of my days."

"You've found a house where you wish to live forever?" The voyager in Ben's soul could not fathom living in one place for an entire lifetime without ever going out to sea.

"I have moved so often, following my father from station to station. We never stayed in one place long enough for me to ever have felt at home. I refuse to move again. My home shall be here, in Annapolis."

Ben loved what Sophie apparently disliked. He found excitement traveling to other countries, meeting people from other cultures. And her solution to remaining in the small city on the bay seemed far-fetched. Perhaps he'd misunderstood. "You wish to write novels?"

She reached up and tugged at his hand, until Ben sat down on the bench beside her. He was immediately consumed in a sweet, calming cloud of honeysuckle. Her eyes sparkled as they met his.

"More and more women are writing novels. Harriet Beecher Stowe has won much fame for her book published just last year. Perhaps you have heard of *Uncle Tom's Cabin*?"

Although he did not disagree with Mrs. Stowe, notoriety is what she had won. But Ben held his opinion, issuing only a grunt, a brief noncommittal sound.

Sophie laid a small warm hand on his knee. "You must promise me that my novel writing shall remain our secret."

His knee jerked away of its own accord while Ben nodded a hasty agreement.

"I have very nearly finished writing my first book. It's called *The Romantic Adventures of Fifi LaDeux, An Unmarried Woman.*"

"Romantic adventures," he repeated, too stunned even to grunt.

"It's a wonderful story concerning an innocent French maiden who arrives in the United States from Paris."

He lowered his head into his hands.

"Some of my characters . . . well, some are naughty."

Ben really did not want to know. He shuddered to think what lay in the naughty inner workings of Sophie's imagination.

"I shall give you a copy one day."

He felt her rise. Raising his head and taking a deep, bracing breath, Ben got up as well. "I'll look forward to reading your novel."

"But now I must be on my way to the tavern. Flora provides me with a great deal of material for my novel."

"Flora?"

"Yes. And the rest comes from my own experience."

That didn't make Ben feel any better at all. "You're going to the tavern now?"

"Don't worry. I keep a heavy veil and gloves in the gardening shed over there. It's my disguise for whenever I venture to Reynolds Tavern. I have not been recognized yet."

He doubted that very much.

After flashing a bright smile, Sophie turned on her heel and headed briskly toward the shed.

Ben followed, thinking of how to delay her—no, stop her—short of using force. "When do you write your novel?" he asked.

She shot him a mischievous smile over her shoulder. "My father believes I sleep until noon, but in truth I write in the morning. Fifi's adventures are based on Flora's experience with a dash of my own. 'Tis like baking a cake by adding a mixture of ingredients."

Some cake. Ben could only imagine the results of such an incredulous collaboration. He shuddered.

"The problem is that if I am to avoid marriage to Andrew Ferguson, I must finish my novel quickly. Tonight may have to be my last meeting with Flora. Normally, I arrange to see her during the afternoons, but since time is of the essence, I have no choice but to go now."

"Sophie . . ." Ben's mind raced. What could he do or say to make her stay? He couldn't let her go to the tavern. He was responsible for her and would be held accountable. Unless he went with her . . . but that would never do.

"Good night, Mister Swain."

Ben reached out and pulled Sophie back, into his arms.

The yard crickets chirped in a noisy chorus, and an owl standing watch in the distance hooted at the rising moon. The sounds of nocturnal life signaled the change. Day slipped into night. Subtle changes marked the air—the coolness of the evening breeze, the smell of burning wood and smoke rising from the chimneys. In a not-so-subtle change, the gray sky darkened, becoming as black as the bottom of the sea, concealing lovers and others.

When Ben Swain's mouth came down on hers, Sophie Harrington tasted her first kiss. Initial surprise gave way to breathtaking excitement. A pleasant warmth whorled through Sophie's body like a simmering river of honey. She feared her heart might explode from her chest, it pounded so wildly.

Oh, sweet mercy, this was heavenly!

Sophie gave herself up to the most thrilling event of her life, thus far. The seaman's kiss. Enfolded within his towering form, she felt a strange, new excitement. Engulfed in Ben's lusty masculinity, Sophie came alive, newly and acutely aware of each scent and sensation. He smelled of soap and citrus and faintly of tobacco. Her knees felt as limp as seaweed. The wall of granite that was his chest took her breath away.

Lips that had crushed hers with bruising intensity grew soft, grew searching.

Oh, sweet, sweet mercy, she must have more! If only for her art.

Parting her lips, welcoming him with eager pleasure and curiosity, Sophie boldly returned Ben's kiss as best she knew how. Her deep-throated moan came unexpectedly, an instinct perhaps.

Oh, she had so much to learn. Sophie knew she must convince the lusty sailing instructor to teach her all that he knew about making love. The actual act of kissing proved far superior to listening to Flora's memories of a particular boatswain's kiss, or the blacksmith's embrace. Sophie understood now that much had been lost transcribing secondhand information about love. And her heroine deserved the real thing.

Too soon, Ben raised his lips from hers. Sophie could see the shock registered in his eyes, as if he didn't know how the toe-tingling kiss had happened.

His dark brows gathered in a deep, disturbed frown. "Forgive me. I—"

"Oh, no I enjoyed that so much! There is nothing to forgive," Sophie assured him rather breathlessly. She had yet to take a normal breath.

Ben rubbed his forehead in short agitated strokes. A series of scars marked the back of his large hand. The pale slices, visible reminders of forgotten pain, were conspicuously noticeable against his sun-darkened skin. She lowered her gaze. His right hand, splayed against his hip, was also scarred.

How had it happened? Had he been scarred in battle with men . . . or with the most dangerous mammals in the ocean? Did she dare ask? As it happened, the opportunity passed.

Swain spoke in a gruff, self-reproaching tone. "Your father placed his trust in me—"

"My father shall never know," she promised. "I am accomplished at keeping secrets from him."

"As I witnessed firsthand today. There are rules—"

"Meant to be broken," she finished for him.

He hiked a startled brow.

"Although I do not normally kiss men whom I hardly know in my garden," she added, giving him a saucy wink, "on this occasion I enjoyed the exception."

She would rather have the magnificent man, who had ignited the strange dance of bubbles deep in her belly, believe she was a woman of some experience.

"Miss Harrington, have you forgotten that you're an engaged woman?" Ben asked, glowering at Sophie, shattering her romantic notions and bursting all the little bubbles within her.

"Oh, but I'm not. Father engaged me. It's not of my doing nor to my liking!" Sophie declared. Seaman Swain possessed admirable integrity, but he protested too much and looked altogether too somber at the moment. Surely, one kiss could not be considered a sinful betrayal, however long it had lasted?

Ben didn't seem to hear her denial. Shaking his head, he ran a hand through his thick, coffee brown hair. "In any event it was wrong to take advantage of you."

Sophie began to feel uncomfortably like a bad accident that he regretted having with all of his heart.

"I certainly do not feel as if I was taken advantage of in any way," she said. "But if you insist."

He was scowling at her again.

"Let us not linger on the moment." Sophie had enjoyed his kiss and intended to keep on enjoying it as long as the warm glow she felt lasted. She refused to let Ben Swain's remorse ruin her memory. In the future there would be men who enjoyed her kiss, Sophie assured herself. Men who would beg for more, instead of frumping and frowning.

"No, you're right. We shouldn't linger on the moment," he agreed, far too quickly. "As a matter of fact, it would be best if we forget this . . . the moment ever happened."

"Of course."

Never!

Sophie would live it, feel it, taste Ben Swain's kiss forever. A woman never forgot her first kiss. There would never be another quite like it. And if Ben regretted his part, Sophie did not. While her lips still burned and her heart still raced, she needed to translate her feelings to paper. While it was yet fresh in her mind, she meant to describe his kiss in pulse-skipping detail. She would put the unforgettable experience to good use—as the thrilling climax to her novel.

He cocked his head, openly studying Sophie. His dark blue gaze narrowed on her with unsettling intensity. "Are you cold?" he asked.

"No."

"You shivered."

'Twas only a warming chill, an involuntary reaction when his eyes met hers. "I'm fine," she assured him.

Did she sound snippy? She hadn't meant to sound snippy. She was simply astounded at the lasting effects of Ben's kiss. . . . Now she understood how men enslaved women. A deep kiss and a warm embrace could dissolve even the strongest woman's will.

"Maybe you should go back inside where it's warm," he suggested.

Eager to return to her room and write, Sophie agreed. "Yes. I fear 'tis too late to visit Flora now. I'd rather not risk father coming home and finding me gone."

"I'll walk you to the door."

Ben appeared deep in thought as he walked her to the rear door. Sophie wondered if he were comparing her to the other women from whom he'd stolen kisses. And she felt certain there had been many. Ben Swain was even more dangerous than she first believed.

"Good night, Miss Harrington."

"Good night, Master Swain," she replied primly.

When his troubled eyes met hers, she beamed. The smile that had been building from the moment he kissed her could not be contained a moment longer. Unlike any others, this smile started from her toes, careened to her heart, spilled onto her lips, and radiated from her entire being.

His frown deepened. He appeared more alarmed than ever.

Without another word, Sophie turned on her heel and flew up the back stairs.

Once in her bedchamber, she wrote several pages devoted to the moment and described in frank and honest terms how it made her feel. She described the tingling, the curious ache, the smoldering sensation just beneath her skin. Sophie felt little need to exaggerate and only did so by the merest degree.

She wrote of the tall, former whaler as the hero who had come to save her heroine, Fifi LaDeux. Ben served as an excellent model. He was a man who was larger than life, a man whose magnetism could be felt across a continent, a man whose kiss could spoil a woman for any other.

Sophie imbued Fifi with her own feelings. And as she relived the emotions she'd felt while Ben held her in his arms, the words poured from Sophie faster than she could write. She did not disguise Ben by calling him by another name. She would change it later. All that mattered at present was describing how his kiss, how being crushed against his body, had physically stirred her to . . . what? Desire?

That was it! Sophie had at last discovered the meaning of desire.

When she finally finished writing, her fingers ached and the inkwell had gone dry. Weary but satisfied, she closed the black leather-bound journal she used to write her novel and returned it to its hiding place. As she tucked the journal behind her favorite black kid boots in the armoire, her hopes of earning her independence by becoming a novelist soared ever higher.

Long ago, Sophie had learned that the world she created eased the loneliness of the world she actually inhabited.

Five of Ben's friends gathered in his room in the first of the four brick row houses serving as officer and faculty quarters. Although superior to accommodation aboard a ship, the rooms were not much more comfortable than the midshipmen's quarters, but did boast the latest in gaslight and steam heat. The furnishings consisted of two chairs, a washbasin, looking glass, bed, desk, and dresser. When more than two people visited, Ben sat on the floor.

He considered the location of bachelor housing far from choice. The buildings sat squarely between Superintendent Stribling's elegant residence and the Commandant of Midshipmen, Admiral Harrington's home. Ben hadn't far to go after leaving Sophie earlier that evening.

The taste of her still lingered on his lips, her honeysuckle scent persisted, as if it had become imbedded in the fibers of his jacket. Ben had yet to drink enough ale to banish the admiral's indefatigable daughter from his mind. But he refused to give up trying.

"Here's to Mary Belle!" he shouted, raising his mug of ale in a toast.

"Aye! Aye!" His slightly inebriated colleagues cheered his toast as Ben hauled down a goodly amount of ale.

"And here's to sweet Jane!" He grinned, holding his mug high.

"Aye! Aye!"

"And join me now in a toast to the dark-eyed Cuban, Señorita Maria."

"Aye! Aye!"

Ben raised his mug again, but could not bring himself to publicly offer a toast to Sophie. If one of his comrades dared ridicule her, Ben would be forced to defend her honor. As much as she annoyed him, he could not hold the misguided beauty up to ridicule. And Ben was much too tired to defend her honor. Such a task might take all night.

Lowering his mug, he launched into his favorite sea chanty, immediately joined by his fellow instructors in a rowdy, off-key chorus of "The Lass That Loves a Sailor."

". . . The wind that blows, The ship that goes, And the lass that loves a sailor!"

After all the verses had been sung, the men collapsed in gales of laughter. They slapped Ben on the back in a show of affection and support that he appreciated, but he would have felt happier if word of his new assignment hadn't been discovered so quickly.

After refilling his mug, he dug into the bucket of freshly shucked oysters brought by the men to celebrate. With little to do in Annapolis, any occasion warranted a celebration.

"How will you serve the admiral?" Danny O'Toole asked.

"It's a secret assignment." Ben was too embarrassed to admit the truth. "Top secret."

Danny nodded sagely. "Yeah, well, good luck living under the same roof as the Harrington girl. She practices witchcraft, you know."

That was the first rumor he'd heard about Sophie that made sense to Ben. Ever since kissing her, he'd been under some sort of spell. He'd realized his mistake as soon as his lips touched hers. If he had any real backbone, he would have stopped her from leaving the house the old-fashioned way, at sword point.

"But she looks mighty fine," Zachariah conceded. "Spends all the admiral's money shopping."

Ben made a move to end the talk that grew increasingly disturbing to him. "One more round and one more little ditty, and we'll call it a night. We've got classes in the morning and I've a move to make."

But the slurring rendition of "Blow the Man Down" begun by Ben and his friends ended abruptly. The gunfire all but drowned them out.

Four

The morning gun had been fired at midnight.

Officers and faculty rushed out into the yard, Ben and his friends among them, only to discover they had been victims of a student prank.

Ben did not see Midshipman Baker in the crowd of innocent students that had gathered. Awakened from sleep, and half-dressed, the boys reported for morning roll call under the light of a full moon. They were none too happy.

Amused and curious, Ben took a casual stroll, pursuing the course he might have taken if he were the culprit. He rounded the corner just in time to see a dark figure jump over the fence and into the bushes of Admiral Harrington's garden.

If he wasn't mistaken, judging from the size and height of the interloper, Ben had found Joseph Baker. The boy showed gumption. Chuckling, he turned away. When there were not so many witnesses, he would reprimand the adventuresome midshipman. A light burned in a second-floor window of Dulany House. Ben looked up expecting to see the admiral. Instead, it was Sophie who looked down upon him and smiled. She was dressed in a high-collared white gown, her hair framing her face and falling in long silky waves past her shoulders. Caught in the moon glow, Sophie's shining mass gleamed like gold. She looked like an angel.

But Ben knew her too well now to mistake the spirited beauty for an angel. He thought of her more like a wildflower growing in the fields. A buttercup.

Light-headed, and feeling unusually amiable, most likely the result of too much ale, Ben signaled Sophie with a mock salute and a smile proven in the past to charm the ladies. She returned his salute with one of her own and a full, brilliant smile, a smile that outshone the moon.

As planned, his impulsive but not-well-thought-out kiss the evening before had served to distract Sophie. But Ben had been distracted as well by the touch of her innocent lips beneath his, soft and pliant, warm and willing. Kissing Sophie had been like discovering a new delicacy, one he could never savor again. The tangy, peppermint taste of her had been enough to create a craving, a craving that would go unfulfilled forever.

Sophie Harrington gave new meaning to the term *forbidden fruit*. She was the admiral's daughter, a woman promised to another, and a known mischief maker.

The following afternoon, sober as a ship's chaplain, but suffering from a minor headache and not feeling at his best, Ben moved into Admiral Harrington's house with his few possessions. Relegated to the attic room like some addled person, he indeed felt like a whaler out of water.

Whenever he bumped his head on the low-hanging eaves, he cursed Sophie Harrington. Ben's resentment knew no bounds. He tasted it with every breath he took. Sophie Harrington was responsible for this demeaning assignment. If not for her, he would be comfortably barracked in the faculty quarters where he belonged.

Hours after unpacking, he was told that Sophie was indisposed. Delighted to be free of her for however long, Ben did not question the reason she'd taken to her bedchamber. It was none of his business anyway. The less involved he was with the dimpled vixen, the better off he would be.

His attention would be much better served by straightening out Midshipman Joseph Baker than in coddling Sophie Harrington. He'd taken the boy to task for his prank of the night before and warned him that he would receive a year's worth of demerits if he should engage in any further mischief. The daring midshipmen who engaged in successful, but harmless, pranks were looked upon as possessing better-than-average leadership potential. A battle fought by the book might well be a battle lost if the officer in command did not use his head and think for himself.

Ben found Dulany House almost in as much turmoil as the academy grounds. Superintendent Stribling, charged with the growth of the Naval Academy, had rapidly acquired ever-increasing plots of land and launched a full-scale building program. Every day, except for the Sabbath, a horde of carpenters, craftsmen, and apprentices plied their trades within the school grounds. At least fifty civilians blended into the academy scenery, rarely noticed any longer by faculty and staff.

Rigorous spring cleaning caused the commotion within Dulany House. At every turn, Ben found the admiral's home in upheaval. Extra help, hired from town, fell over each other as they washed windows and beat carpets. The cleaners beat heavy drapes and carpets free from dust, scoured the cobwebs from nooks and crannies, and polished stacks of silver utensils and serving ware.

No matter where Ben stationed himself, he felt as if he were in the way of someone—and he usually was.

On the third day as he passed through the kitchen on his way to his quarters in the attic, the housekeeper accosted him. The narrow-lipped spinster shoved a tray at his chest.

"Would you mind takin' this up to the miss?"

A thin, wrinkled woman, Mildred Howser issued orders with the same authority as the admiral. If the Navy had allowed women to join, Mildred would have worn stripes.

Ben stared at the tray of oatmeal, dry toast, and tea. His slide to infamy had been swift and unforeseen. From the captain of a mighty whaler to common seaman to this, a male house servant. What further humiliation awaited him?

"Is Miss Harrington incapable of breakfasting in the dining room?" he asked dryly, attempting to hide his wounded pride.

Harriet was not cowed. "She's taken to her bed. Miss Sophie's come down with influenza."

"A pity," Ben replied. At least Miss Troublemaker would be in one place for a few days, he thought.

"Came from the dunking she took in the harbor," Mildred declared, shooting him a disparaging look, as if he were to blame for Sophie's plight.

He wasn't responsible and he could not feel sorry for Sophie. Even though he suspected his raw, scratchy throat might be the symptom of a shared illness. But he wasn't lily-livered enough to take to his bed. Besides, it was his own fault. If he hadn't kissed Sophie, he wouldn't have caught the influenza from her. Would he always be finding new reasons to rue the day he'd lost his head and kissed Sophie Harrington?

"Go ahead, you can do this," Mildred said, pushing the tray against his chest again. Thin wisps of snowy white hair escaped from the bun at the nape of her neck and tiny beads of perspiration had formed in the crevices of her high forehead.

Ben resisted. The less he saw of Sophie, the better. "Is there no one else?"

"I'm busier than a bee in a new hive. With Abigail gone, I need help. Got to watch these town people all the time or they'll be stealing the silver right from under us."

Though he doubted the silverware was in eminent danger from the good people of Annapolis, he took the tray from the insistent housekeeper.

A moment later he knocked on Sophie's door.

A faint voice responded. "Come in."

Ben, a man who prided himself on facing every kind of danger without flinching, took a deep breath before tentatively entering no-man's land. He discovered a lair appointed in delicious shades of lavender and cream, complete with yards and yards of ruffles and lace. There could be no mistaking this as a woman's chamber.

He felt as if he'd walked into a garden. Sunshine splashed through the windows and the sweet perfume of flowers scented the air. Roses blossomed in crystal vases and small silver bowls filled with lavender pot-pourri were scattered throughout the spacious room. During Ben's swift perusal he noticed that even the pillow slips were adorned with embroidered bouquets of deep purple and pale pink daisies.

And when his gaze finally came to rest on Sophie, his body jolted in shock. Dwarfed in the polished rosewood, four-poster bed, she appeared impossibly fragile. For a moment Ben thought the woman lying there might be an imposter. Someone had stolen Sophie Harrington!

Propped up against at least half a dozen lace-covered pillows, she had a complexion that very nearly matched the milky white bed coverings. In a startling transformation, once beautiful eyes appeared hollow, rimmed with plum-colored circles. She held a hanky to the previously delicate tip of her now swollen, fiery red nose. Her taffy-colored hair fanned limply against the pillow.

Ben's heart constricted as if it were being lashed to the mast.

"I brought you food," he said, lifting the tray in evidence.

The young woman who yearned for independence smiled weakly. Sniffling, she drew the down comforter up over her chest to her chin.

Too late. He'd already caught a tantalizing glimpse of one satiny shoulder. The right puffed sleeve of Sophie's lace-trimmed chemise had slipped to an enticing angle. He smiled in appreciation. She hitched up the wayward puff.

"I . . . I don't think I can eat," she said in a raspy, nasal voice. Sophie regarded the tray Ben carried as if it held poison apples.

"Have some tea then," Ben urged, setting the tray on the round lace-covered table at her bedside. He had not expected Sophie to look pitiful. It was damn disconcerting. Just because she possessed a stubborn streak and foolishly talked of independence, she did not deserve to die.

"I don't know . . ." Her voice trailed off and she lowered her eyes. "Just go. I'd rather no one see me . . . looking like this."

"You look fine," he lied. Years of experience had taught Ben there were times that you could never be truthful with a woman. This was one of those times.

"You're not going to go, are you?" she asked.

How could he when she needed him? Or someone. She definitely needed someone to nurse her.

"I'm not sure you should be alone," he said quite honestly. On the other hand, Ben wasn't certain how he could help Sophie. He possessed no known sickroom skills.

She sneezed. Feeling uncomfortably helpless, Ben watched as tears spilled from Sophie's sunken, watery eyes and slowly trickled down her pale cheek.

"Look," he said, "there's honey on the tray. I'll pour you a cup of tea and honey before I leave."

"If you must." She sniffled again.

He looked around. "Where are your cats?"

"Cats?"

"I understood that you had several cats as pets."

"No. Not one."

One rumor down. The other rumors he'd heard about Sophie were no doubt false as well.

She blew her nose, and not in a dainty fashion.

"Can't believe anything you hear," he mumbled heading toward the door.

"Where are you going?"

"You asked me to leave."

"I've changed my mind. It's been two long days since I've talked with anyone. Please stay. Talk with me."

He turned. Above sallow cheeks, her watery, red-rimmed eyes pleaded silently. His gaze fell to her lips, raw and chapped. Were these the lips that he longed to kiss again? Yes, they were the same lips that had triggered a slow burn in regions that he had not wished to have afire.

"Please, Ben."

He couldn't leave Sophie now, if only because he'd never seen a more pathetic-looking human being. She was sick. She needed him. "Well, maybe for a few minutes."

He sat uneasily on the edge of the lavender ruffled chaise fearing it might crumble beneath his weight. The feminine piece of furniture, positioned by the fireplace not far from her bed, had not been designed for use by men his size. Ben's knees came up to his chest.

She smiled then, a sweet, soft smile. On her sickbed, Sophie's disarming smile and beguiling dimple seemed all that remained of the beautiful, vibrant Miss Harrington. "Thank you."

"I'm not sure you should be taxing yourself with conversation."

"Boredom taxes me more. And I have not been able to write a word for days."

Ben expected that Sophie referred to her novel, Fifi LaDeux or something. "Don't fret, the world will wait for your novel."

"But time is of the essence."

"A few days cannot matter."

"But it may. Ben, I need your advice." As a result of her illness, Sophie's voice had taken on a whiskey quality that in any other circumstance Ben might have found provocative.

"My advice on what?" he asked warily, hiking an eyebrow.

"How to escape my father's punishment."

"I'm not sure what you mean," he hedged.

"I can't marry Andrew, you know."

Ben could understand her reluctance. Rigid in his beliefs, the pompous Captain Ferguson possessed the barest naval skills. Despite his lack of credentials, the captain had been regularly promoted during the Mexican War solely on the basis of his family's political connections. Throughout the conflict Andrew had remained at a desk in Washington.

"I don't know as you have a choice," Ben replied.

"Do you suppose that when I tell Andrew that I've taken a vow of celibacy, he might change his mind?"

Ben choked. His throat closed on a stream of air, trapping his last breath. Celibacy!

"Are you all right?"

No!

He rasped his answer. "Yes."

"Abstinence is the only way for a woman to—"

He shot up off the chaise. "Don't say another word—please." In the name of all propriety! Had she no modesty? No sense of decency?

Instead of lowering her eyes and apologizing for her brashness, Sophie sniffled loudly and then flashed a mischievous smile. "A woman must protect herself from the consequences of childbirth, Seaman Swain. Abstinence is —"

Ben backed toward the door. "Must you keep using that word?"

"'Tis the only certain method of avoiding a delicate condition. My mother died giving birth to me," Sophie told him, pulling at the hankie in her hands. Her voice reduced to a strained whisper. "My aunt and a great cousin also died in childbirth. In my family being with child is . . . is like being given a death sentence."

"This isn't a discussion we should be having." Ben ran a finger around the inside of his collar, loosening the fabric which tightened about his throat by the second.

"But it's 1853, for heaven's sake!" she squeaked.

"No matter how progressive you believe yourself to be, Miss Harrington, there are subjects that should never be discussed between a man and a woman," he snapped, feeling an unfamiliar heat suffuse his face.

"But—"

"Are you delirious?" The fever must be attacking her brain. "Don't say another word," he warned, backing toward the door.

"Do you have any brothers or sisters?"

Safer subject. His family. "Yes, there were five of us. Nantucket women prided themselves on having large families. They were, were—" He searched his mind for an inoffensive word. "Fruitful."

"Poor souls," she tsked.

She actually tsked!

"I can assure you, Ben, that I have no wish to populate a nation."

"I wasn't suggesting—"

"In all likelihood, Andrew Ferguson will wish to have a family. Men are born wanting to have sons so they may pass on their names and legacies. Don't you find that to be true? Do you not desire sons?"

Why hadn't her voice given out yet? Why was she still talking? She defied the odds.

"Yes," he admitted reluctantly. "But only because I am the last Swain."

At least he thought he was the last Swain. Ben hadn't heard from his youngest brother since Matt had left home for the California gold rush.

"Ah, being the last then, you must have at least a

dozen sons. You shall find a sweet wife who will gladly give you a passel of children." She sighed. Her voice had all but given out, yet she stubbornly continued. "A doting woman will one day care for you and all your young sons in a grand officer's mansion bound by a picket fence."

The picture Sophie created appealed to Ben. He did not doubt that he would enjoy returning from his adventures at sea to a warm hearth—and an equally warm woman waiting for him. If it wasn't for his lowly seaman's salary, Ben would have already started his family. With the loss of his family's fortune, he would have to wait until he received a promotion to lieutenant.

Nodding to humor Sophie, he grasped the doorknob. "That's exactly who I'm looking for, a sweet, doting woman. Now it's time for you to rest."

Celibacy. Abstinence. Fine talk! Ben suspected that Sophie had been cruelly influenced by the radical women's rights movement as much as by family history. In any event, it was plain to see that she was too ill to be sneaking out the back door and in no danger of dying. He was free. Sophie would not be causing trouble for several more days.

"I'll look in on you again soon." He paused, astonished by her crestfallen expression. "Rest well . . . Buttercup."

Buttercup. Sophie liked the name. The sobriquet sounded affectionate, though she doubted that the seaman could have meant it to be so.

Devoting herself to a speedy recovery, she felt well enough by week's end to attend the Saturday evening stag hop in the Recitation Hall. The weekly dances were held in the basement of the hall for the entertainment of the midshipmen. With the exception of the Masqueraders, the student theater group, it was the only recreation offered for the young men. And for Sophie. She found it difficult, if not impossible, to obtain her father's permission to attend many social events in Annapolis. Therefore, she never missed a dance in Recitation Hall. Tonight, unbridled enthusiasm for the dance, along with the need to be out and about, overcame Sophie's general peaked feeling.

The admiral escorted her into the hall and, astonishingly enough, right to Ben Swain, who appeared to be waiting for someone. He'd stationed himself among a row of midshipmen glued to their chairs along the wall.

After exchanging greetings, the admiral excused himself to have a word with the head of the mathematics department.

Sophie smiled.

Seaman Swain cleared his throat and stretched his neck as if his collar might be choking him.

"Are you not going to ask me to dance, Seaman Swain?"

"I believe the first dance is always with one's fiancé."

Kindly, he did not remind her that a woman was not supposed to ask a man to dance.

"Andrew is in Washington. And he is not my fiancé. He's my father's." Sophie could not prevent a small bubble of laughter at her own jest.

Ben frowned. When her laughter faded, he begged off. "I regret that I don't dance."

But Sophie was having none of it. "I find that difficult to believe. I suspect you are a man who does everything well."

"The last lady I danced with still walks with a limp."

Suppressing another chuckle, she put him to the test. "Follow me then. We shall sit in the shadows along with the poor, neglected Navy wives."

Ben's gaze followed hers to the gathering of matrons sitting to one side of the refreshment table. Dressed for the most part in modest black and purple silk, the women looked of a flock of crows awaiting their prey.

"Never mind," he said. "I shall attempt the impossible."

"Thank you. Look at my father over there with the other men. They've formed ranks about the refreshment table to relive the Mexican War. Soon, they'll be going outside to smoke their smelly cigars." Giving a small sigh of resignation, she shook her head. "'Tis always the same. They never enjoy themselves by dancing."

A clear look of longing passed over Ben's face. She knew he would give anything to be among them.

Once on the dance floor he held Sophie as if he feared contact with her, as if she might give him scurvy or possess the sting of a jellyfish.

With her hand resting on Ben's shoulder, a broad, rock-hard shoulder, Sophie wondered if she dare ask him about the crescent scar that nicked into his right eyebrow, leaving a small bare strip. She could not avoid noticing the scar. It marked the dark eyebrow that seemed forever raised in puzzlement, surprise— or perhaps shock—when he regarded her.

Although Ben moved stiffly, more like a man walking the plank than dancing a waltz, Sophie enjoyed the feeling of being in his arms. The solid length of him, even his calloused and scarred hands, made her feel sheltered and somehow shored her own strength.

Her heart skipped to a playful beat and her face felt flushed. Odd, but fascinating, pleasurable feelings.

"Why did you give up whaling to join the Navy?" she asked.

"Following the Mexican War, the Navy needed men."

"I read *Moby Dick* while I was sick."

Up went the eyebrow. "You did?"

Published last year, Herman Melville's whaling story was hardly considered women's reading. She'd found it in her father's study. "I wanted to know more about whaling."

He grunted, and looked away, toward the refreshment table. Sophie suspected he might be searching for an officer to dance the remainder of the waltz with Sophie. But no one looked his way.

"Whaling is very dangerous," she said quietly.

A single muscle constricted in his jaw but otherwise he remained expressionless as he continued to gaze over her shoulder. "Whaling killed my father and brothers."

"I'm so sorry." Sophie was having second thoughts. Perhaps she should not have pushed him to discuss his former life.

"During the early days, the whales were right there off Nantucket. We didn't have to go far to find them," he explained stonily. "But as the demand for whale oil and bone increased, the population soon dissipated. We were forced farther out into the Atlantic to find the big sperms. The hunt changed. Whaling took on new and different dangers. Worse for the women, we were gone for even longer periods of time, six months or more."

"Do you miss the whaling life?" she asked, wondering if she might cease wearing her whalebone corsets in protest.

"Sometimes," he confessed with a wry twist of his lips. One-two-three, one-two-three. Sophie closed her eyes and pretended to be her heroine, Fifi. The fictional French maiden had no fears of where intimacy between a man and woman could lead. She was French, after all. Fifi would dance all night with Ben Swain if it were possible.

As soon as the evening ended, Sophie would write it all down in her journal. She would describe in detail how she had felt in his arms, within the warming power of Ben's embrace. She would give her thoughts and emotions to Fifi LaDeux.

The small ensemble of midshipmen who played for the dance were not accomplished musicians. A pianist, two violinists, and a young man on the harmonica all missed notes with annoying frequency.

Ben held himself back, far enough away from Sophie, so that their bodies did not touch, even by accident. While he did not understand the jarring feeling of nerves on edge that her nearness aroused in him, he wasn't taking any chances. He was dancing with the most beautiful girl in the hall.

If a man did not know that the soul of a hellion lived within Sophie, he might easily be captivated by her loveliness. The sparkle had returned to her eyes, and the rosy blush once again stained her cheeks.

Sophie's lemon yellow silk gown boasted a voluminous skirt of three tiered flounces trimmed with bands of velvet ribbon. The off-the-shoulder neckline of her dress revealed creamy shoulders that seemed to beckon him. Ben felt as bedeviled as a man who hadn't had a drop to drink in days, suddenly finding

himself holding a cool, enticing glass of lemonade—
at arm's length.

He attempted to concentrate on his feet, notably
keeping them off Sophie's. And when he dared look
down at her, turquoise eyes as luminous and as mesmerizing as the tropical seas locked on his. For a
moment he neglected to breathe.

Before meeting the admiral's daughter, Ben had
believed that whaling was the most dangerous thing a
man could ever do. Now he knew differently. Looking
into Sophie Harrington's eyes, holding her in his
arms and dancing a waltz with her, were all infinitely
more dangerous.

Her questions about whaling had touched a raw
nerve and had taken him back to a time of a heart-
wrenching decision. Ben had been the first Swain to
leave the island in search of another way of life. Gen-
erations before him had lived and died on Nantucket.
The Swains had been fishermen, shipbuilders, and finally whalers. Whaling had made them wealthy but
cost them dearly. Ben had resolved to break the cycle.
And he still wondered if he had done the right thing.

By the time the music ended, Ben was ready to bolt.
He looked to the refreshment table, but the men had
adjourned to the yard to smoke cigars. He needed a
cigar. He deserved one. He'd just spent the longest
four minutes of his life holding Sophie at arm's
length, keeping temptation at bay.

"Ben, would you mind getting me some punch?"
Sophie asked, stepping back from his arms and flashing a dazzling smile.

Who could resist that smile? Damn. Yes, he'd fetch
punch.

"I'll just sit down over here while you're gone."

Prepared to swim though shark-infested waters for

Sophie if it was ever necessary, Ben turned toward the refreshment table and stopped. "Sophie, look over by the punch bowl."

She turned her head.

Andrew Ferguson.

Five

Andrew Ferguson reminded Sophie of a trout with facial hair. A full, mud brown beard, mustache, and coarse, curly side-whiskers could not conceal his enormous lips. Although pleasant, his full oval face would never be described as handsome. While Andrew was a tall man, he was not nearly as tall as Ben Swain. And unfortunately, Captain Ferguson possessed a rather formless, sloping-shoulder figure. This was the man her father had chosen for her.

He strode toward them grinning. 'Twas a nice smile, a friendly smile. Sophie only wished she was not the reason for it.

Beside her, she could feel the tension drain from Ben. The seaman's relief at no longer having to dance attendance upon her was quite tangible— and disturbing.

Andrew grasped her hand and brought it to his lips. "Sophie, my dearest."

Sophie forced a smile. He was not a cruel man, after all, just too old for her even if she were in the market for a husband. He was older than rock. And his bad breath did nothing to endear him to Sophie.

"Captain Ferguson, how nice to see you. I did not expect you would return in time for this evening's entertainment."

"Knowing you would undoubtedly be here, I made a special effort." His glance shifted to Ben. With a nod of his head in greeting, the captain shot Ben a cursory smile. "Seaman Swain, I believe?"

Ben offered his hand. "Aye, sir. We've not been formally introduced."

"An astonishing matter when you think of how few faculty members the academy claims. But then you have not been here long."

"No, sir."

Andrew gazed at Ben with cold intensity. "And while I instruct in the new steam enginery department, you are teaching the boys' basic sailing. Basic seamanship, I believe?"

The hint of a smile hovered at Ben's lips. "Yes, sir."

Sophie wondered at the reason for it.

"We move in decidedly different social circles as well," Andrew added.

"True enough." Ben's eyes never wavered beneath the captain's scrutiny.

Sophie tapped her toe as Andrew politely and methodically demeaned Ben. She would give up her best hat to know what Ben was thinking.

"I understand you're the man to beat at darts up at Reynolds Tavern," Andrew continued.

Unable to bear the captain's pettiness any longer, Sophie jumped into the conversation with information meant to stifle him. "Seaman Swain saved my life while you were away."

"Is that so?"

"Miss Harrington exaggerates. I happened to be at the right place at the right time."

"Were you in dreadful danger, Sophie?"

"Yes. I was sailing on the bay when a storm came out of nowhere."

Andrew's brows bunched together in clear disapproval. "You were sailing?"

"With a friend. I was merely a passenger."

"Speaking of friends," Ben said, "I see someone I must talk with before he leaves. If you'll excuse me?"

Ben was not a man to ask permission. He did what he pleased within the rules he was bound by. Sophie suspected he'd broken a few rules along the way with nary a guilty moment. She hated to see him go. She'd rather be left alone with a barracuda than Andrew Ferguson.

"You are excused." Andrew replied. "And my thanks to you for keeping my Sophie company, seaman."

"A pleasure, Captain."

With a dip of his head and after casting an enigmatic grin to Sophie, Ben strode toward the door as if he could not wait to make his escape. A compelling figure in his uniform, he turned heads as he made his way across the hall. Women young and old admired the handsome officer, and longing glances followed the larger-than-life hero who walked among ordinary men tonight.

"Sophie, dearest?"

But her hero had abandoned her to boring Andrew. Sophie turned to the large-lipped captain.

He shook his head as a father might in scolding his daughter. "Sophie, you really should not sail."

But she wasn't his daughter. "Everyone tells me so," she replied vaguely, her attention still on Ben. "Only I do not quite understand why men alone should enjoy the pleasure of sailing."

Ben had stopped to talk with Joseph Baker. She wondered if he had befriended the young midshipman after the . . . incident in the bay.

"We men have the strength for sailing and women

do not," Andrew responded a bit sharply. "Enough said. Would you like some punch, dearest?"

Tearing her gaze from Ben, Sophie looked to Andrew. Two so different men could not be found. "I . . . I don't think so."

"Shall we dance?" he asked.

She begged off. "I feel a bit fatigued."

The maze of crevices in the captain's forehead deepened. "Your father tells me you have been ill recently. I hope your health will not delay our wedding."

"I am still quite weak." It was only a small exaggeration.

In any event, Andrew was more intent on speaking his mind than listening to what was on Sophie's. "The admiral gave me the good news about our marriage this eve upon my return." He sighed, giving her a full blast of his sour breath. "Sophie, I cannot tell you how delighted I am that you have consented to be my wife."

"I did not think to be married so soon," she confessed softly, hoping he would offer to delay the nuptials.

"It's not soon enough for me, dearest. And be assured, I will endeavor to make you happy in all ways, Sophie."

Sophie could not think she would like to kiss a man with bad breath. She took a step back from him.

"Did your business go well in Washington?" she asked, eager to end the subject of marriage. Surreptitiously, she scanned the hall for Ben. He'd disappeared, left no doubt. She felt a vague sense of loss, of disappointment.

"Sophie, I will not fill your little head with Navy business now or ever."

"Andrew, I am quite capable of understanding Navy business."

"I'm sure you are, dearest, and I am pleased that you should take an interest. However, at the present I am eager to know how soon you can make the arrangements for our wedding."

"I . . . I'm not certain."

"We shall announce our engagement in church tomorrow."

"Oh, sweet mercy!" Did she say that aloud?

"Could we not wait until I am feeling more myself?" she hurriedly added in a softer, sweetly beseeching tone. "Perhaps next week?"

His furry brows bunched together once more, but after a moment of thought, he heaved a martyr's sigh. "Of course. How thoughtless of me. And if there should be anything I can do to help, let me know. Let me help you always, dearest."

Sophie suppressed a sigh of relief, but smiled. 'Twas a genuine smile. She'd won a reprieve of a week at least and decided to press her good fortune. "There is one small something you can do to help me."

"You have only to breathe the words."

"This is my first social engagement since having the ague and I'm quite exhausted. Would you mind escorting me to my father?"

"I'll go one better than that. I shall escort you home."

"Oh. Oh, how kind of you. But I cannot impose."

"Dearest, walking you to your door is hardly an imposition. It's my pleasure."

As Andrew escorted Sophie from Recitation Hall, she wondered if Ben had gone to Reynolds Tavern to play darts. Perhaps Flora was serving him a large mug of cold, foaming ale at this very moment.

Despite the cold breeze blowing in from Chesapeake Bay, and the light flavoring of damp salt in the air, the night boasted a blanket of sparkling stars. Although only the narrowest edge of the moon shone from above, the newly installed gas lamplights lit the paths of the academy grounds.

"Good night."

The soft, deep voice came out of nowhere, an unexpected sound that startled Sophie. But she recognized the voice. She turned her head. Ben leaned against the trunk of an ancient white oak tree smoking a cigar. She could smell the tobacco, see the last wispy traces of smoke rings rise in the air. And though she disliked that he smoked the cigar, she felt a curious warmth. Ben watched over her from the shadows. Was he prepared to come to her rescue? Did he think more of her than he let on? Somehow she felt much better knowing the tall, good-looking sailing instructor was close at hand.

Andrew nodded curtly. "Seaman Swain."

Though it couldn't be seen in the dim light, Sophie made certain Ben would know she smiled. Her smile resounded in the joy of her voice. "Good night!"

When they reached the door of Dulany House, Andrew Ferguson attempted to kiss Sophie with his large trout lips. Slipping her finger between her lips and his, she warned him he might catch whatever remained of her influenza.

Visibly disappointed, the captain kissed her hand instead. "Good night, my dearest. I hope you feel better in the morning."

"I hope so as well."

"I'll call upon you tomorrow."

"You are more kind than I deserve."

Sophie watched the captain turn down the path before she quietly let herself into the house. After making certain that her father was still out, she made a great show of being weary to the house servants.

Once in the privacy of her chamber, she immediately began to disrobe, trading her gown for a clean white linen chemise trimmed with lace and ribbon. Since Abigail had left, Sophie dressed and undressed herself. A chore she did not mind, but her father worried people would talk if a new maid was not hired soon. He feared they would believe he could not afford the finest for his daughter.

Sophie sank to her knees in front of the armoire. She knew the exact location of her black leather-bound journal. She kept it tucked behind her best riding boots.

But it wasn't there.

She searched anxiously, hands splayed, feeling, touching what she could not see.

As panic set in, Sophie tossed her shoes from the floor of the armoire. Blue kid leather, green pumps, white slippers, patent high shoes, and an old pair of pattens she'd thought she lost, sailed through the air. She sat back on her heels. The floor of the armoire was bare. Shoes of every color and kind were piled behind her.

Her novel had to be there. She hadn't moved it, hadn't looked at it since she'd written about Ben, shortly before she became ill.

In the end, Sophie removed everything from the armoire until it was empty. Near tears, she tore apart her chamber. She searched under the bed, the mattress, beneath the chaise. At one o'clock in the morning she gave up. *The Romantic Adventures of Fifi LaDeux* was missing.

Six

Dire consequences. Dire consequences. The words played over and over in Sophie's head. Sitting on the floor of her chamber in stunned disbelief, she could not even cry. Whether her journal had been unwittingly discarded or cunningly stolen, it was a devastating blow.

With Andrew Ferguson breathing down her neck, the key to freedom and independence was missing. Had the journal that she used to write *The Romantic Adventures of Fifi LaDeux* been discarded during spring cleaning? Or had it been stolen for some unknown and wicked purpose?

Sophie needed advice and she needed it now. Believing a solution could be found to every problem, she refused to give up. Why waste time speculating when a friend might help her come up with the answer to this particular catastrophe?

Springing into action, she donned a simple black dress and sturdy black button shoes. As she had done many times before, she stuffed her bed with pillows to make it appear as if she were sleeping. And then she tiptoed down the back steps, picked up a lantern, and slipped out the rear door.

Making a beeline for the shed, Sophie donned her heavily veiled bonnet and dark gloves. Miss Godey would never approve of Sophie's ensemble, but a disguise could hardly ever qualify as fashion-able. Driven by a stomach-churning sense of urgency, fashion was the last thing on her mind.

Sophie could not wait until the next day to speak with Flora. Her friend had a vast array of interesting experiences in her past and may have dealt with a similar circumstance. Short of running away, Sophie could not think what to do, with her mind so muddled.

Bolting past the guard at the gatehouse, she hurried through the streets lit only by gas lamplight. She was not alone. Lovers shared a bench at city dock, and several officers strolled along Main Street as Sophie, her head lowered, dashed up the hill to Reynolds Tavern.

Even before opening the door, she could hear the noise from the popular gathering spot. Once inside, she discovered the wooden floor of the narrow, mahogany paneled tavern vibrating. The loud, tinny piano music and boisterous laughter caused the walls of the wood and brick structure to tremble. Never having been in Reynolds on a Saturday night, the crowd, near suffocating din, and thick smoke overwhelmed Sophie. Her feet felt as if they were encased in a diver's lead boots as she viewed the mayhem.

Flora stood behind the polished bar flirting with the town's hog reeve. In a swift, furtive survey Sophie scanned the rest of the tavern, hoping not to find a familiar face. She canvassed every nook and cranny, clear back to where the dart board hung on the back wall. Although she recognized two other instructors from the academy playing darts, men she believed to be friends of Ben Swain, the seaman was nowhere in sight. This was one instance where she did not wish to feel his "protective" presence.

Elbowing her way through the cheerfully inebriated crowd, which included several ladies whom she suspected might be strumpets, Sophie made her way to the bar. The ten-foot, hand-carved bar with its gleaming brass rail was the sole furnishing of quality.

Waving a gloved hand at Flora, she sought the tavern maid's attention. Flora loved the lads, and often described the many ways in which she loved them to Sophie. Diverting the flaming-haired barmaid from a fisherman who resembled Blackbeard took longer than Sophie liked. She felt nervous being here tonight. The fear of being discovered caused her pulse to race at uncommon speed. A little advice from Flora and she would be on her way home.

"Sophie, it's Saturday night," Flora snapped. "You shouldn't be here."

With her forehead furrowed in an irritated frown and her green eyes narrowed, the tavern maid displayed more annoyance than seemed warranted in Sophie's opinion.

Lowering her voice and leaning over the bar, the words poured from Sophie in an urgent rush. "I had to see you. My novel is missing and Andrew Ferguson has asked me to set a wedding date."

Flora flicked her wrist in a dismissive fashion. "Nothing is lost under God's heaven. You'll find your novel."

"But I've looked everywhere!"

"And tell the captain that you'll marry him at Christmas."

"Impossible. My father has given me an ultimatum. I have no longer than six weeks before I must marry him."

The tavern maid rolled her eyes. "Flora would rather throw herself on a rusty spike."

Sophie was not prepared to die. "I must sell my novel as soon as possible. But first I have to find it."

"Are you certain your wanting to let the whole world read what Flora's been tellin' you?" Flora frequently spoke of herself in the third person.

" 'Tis not just your story," Sophie retorted, feeling a bit of indignation. "I have added my own feelings and experience, in the guise of Fifi LaDeux, of course."

"Hey, Flora, fill 'er up!"

Flora looked to the end of the bar, where a tall, lanky man held up his empty tankard. "Flora cannot be talkin' with ye now, Sophie. Can't you see?"

Feeling desperate, Sophie clutched Flora's white sleeve. "What should I do? What if my journal was thrown away during the spring cleaning?"

"Hold on to them horses, I'll be right with you," Flora bellowed to the thirsty customer. Sighing, she folded her elbows on the bar and leaned in to answer Sophie quietly. "Ye'll write your novel all over again, only this time you'll make it better, and then you'll take it to one of those publishing companies I heard about in New York and Boston."

Flora might not be the best source for information, but she was the safest. Sophie could trust Flora. "But that will take months. I'll be married by then."

Her fiery curls bounced on her exposed shoulders as Flora shook her head. The barmaid was a pretty girl who'd made her own life since being orphaned. Sophie had given Fifi, her fictitious heroine, Flora's pouty lips and titian-colored hair. She'd saved her friend's large ears for another character, another novel.

"Have you considered runnin' away?" Flora asked.

"No!"

"Flora! Another round over here!" An old man sitting alone at a side table held up his tankard. Soon every man in the tavern would be holding up their empty mugs.

Flora waved him off as if he were a pesky insect. "Flora's gotta go now. She'll meet you at the dock 'round noon tomorrow."

Disheartened beyond words, Sophie nodded. Her body felt heavy, as if it had tripled in weight with nary a drop to drink or morsel to eat. Moving with the speed of a tortoise toward the door, she pushed between and against male body after body. Most were too drunk to notice or care that a mysterious veiled woman moved among them. Everyone seemed so happy. Sophie's misery was lost among them.

A group gathered around the piano player in the far corner, near the windows, sang a boisterous, off-key rendition of "Buffalo Gals." Rowdy laughter from the dart section almost drowned out the sound of breaking glass that echoed from the back of the tavern. A chorus of ribald cheers and hoots punctuated with hearty applause followed.

Ben never expected to run into Sophie Harrington at Reynolds Tavern. Literally.

Assuming she'd retired for the night, he'd changed into civilian clothes and come out for a round of darts, ale, and a good flirt with the ladies. This evening he especially felt the need for one of the ladies who usually gathered at the tavern on Saturday night to offer comfort to a hardworking man.

"Drat!"

It was the sound of her voice as she pushed against him that alerted Ben. When he looked down, there could be no mistake. Who else would wear a black-veiled hat adorned with bright red cherries and the wings of a blackbird to a tavern?

While Ben knew how to move in a crowded saloon,

the admiral's daughter was obviously encountering some difficulty.

"Sophie."

Her head jerked up. The black feathers atop her hat quivered.

Clenching his jaw, he seized her elbow and strode toward the door, giving no man quarter. There would be no ale, no darts, no lady for Ben tonight. His gut sizzled with anger. Did Sophie Harrington live to thwart his plans and spoil his fun?

Honor bound to protect her from trouble, but not to linger with her, once out in the cool evening air, he hurried Sophie down the street and over the cobblestones.

"Let me go," she demanded, struggling to free herself from his grip.

"What did you think you were doing?"

"I had to see Flora."

"Ladies don't go to a tavern on a Saturday night."

"I wore my disguise."

"Sophie, this is not a disguise. It only serves to draw attention to you."

"No!" But her voice held a note of uncertainty.

"What if Captain Ferguson happened by after thinking he'd left you at home?" he asked. "Do you not think he'd see through your disguise?"

"No." She lifted her chin. "Andrew is not all that observant."

Ben heaved what sounded like a mixture of a sigh and a moan. To his recollection, it was a sound he'd never made before. "I hate to be the one to tell you this, but even green Midshipman Baker could see through your disguise."

"You are wrong and you are being unkind and ugly to me."

He was right and he was attempting to hold his temper and be civil. But his efforts were not succeeding with his obstinate charge. "What has happened that is so important that you had to see Flora right away?"

"My business is private."

She'd taken that snooty tone again.

"As the one who keeps rescuing you from trouble, I think your business is my business," he insisted.

"I do not require rescuing."

"I think you do."

"You sound just like my father!" she declared, all testy.

"Now you're trying to wound me."

"Why are you everywhere that I happen to be?" she demanded.

"If you were in your bed now like you were supposed to be, you wouldn't be seeing me. I can assure you," he said, picking up the pace of their downhill walk. "I do recall seeing Andrew Ferguson walk you home."

"Do you go to Reynolds Tavern often?"

"That is for me to know," he replied.

"Were you looking for a game of darts, or a woman?"

"Darts."

"I think you were looking for a woman," she said, a hint of accusation laced her tone. "You have a reputation."

"Every sailor has a reputation."

"Yours is more infamous than most."

"How would you know?"

"I . . . I overhear things."

She eavesdropped. Figured. He'd known right along Sophie had the makings of a meddling busybody.

"I'm trying to meet as many women as possible," he

explained. "I'm looking for just the right woman to bear my sons. Can't fault a man for that."

"And how will you know when you've met the right one?" she asked.

"I'll know."

Ben looked up to the sky. A silver canopy of stars twinkled above them, the moon shed a soft golden light, and a faint whiff of salt edged the evening breeze. It would be a splendid night for sailing.

He heaved another sigh. Main Street was almost deserted, so when he saw the figure of a man approaching, his nerves went on battle alert. Being accosted by a rogue would not make it easier for Ben to get Sophie home without her father knowing she'd snuck out. When the sturdy figure passed under a gas lamp, enough of the man's features were illuminated to give Ben a start.

"Whoa . . . there's Andrew Ferguson!"

Sweeping Sophie into his arms, he whirled her about, whipped off her telltale hat, and pressed her against a shop wall. Blocking her from view with his body, Ben lowered his head, making it appear as if he were whispering into his lover's ear. There would be little possibility of Ferguson determining the woman's identity. Sophie would be in a world of trouble if the pretentious captain thought Ben and Sophie were together.

As he nuzzled Sophie's neck, Ben breathed in her sweet honeysuckle scent. Her body trembled against him like a frightened hummingbird trapped against glass. Her cheek felt like warm silk. His anger slipped away. For a heartbeat in time, he forgot that this was a necessary ruse and enjoyed the moment.

Captain Ferguson stopped a foot away and chuckled. "Ben Swain, keeping up your reputation, I see."

Ben did not look around, just raised his head to reply, "Yes, sir!"

He heard Ferguson snort as he passed. "Carry on."

Sophie did not move and neither did Ben. He waited until the sound of Ferguson's boots had faded completely. With his body pressed against Sophie's lush, warm figure, he enjoyed the wait, dismissed the resentment he'd felt in the tavern. If sometimes her predilection for trouble interfered with his life, a moment like this more than made up for minor annoyances.

By shielding her tonight, at least he'd saved her from Ferguson and her father's wrath, and perhaps from more gossip. Although, Ben realized, most of the gossip he'd heard about her up to this point had proven false.

The warmth and softness of the honey-haired woman in his arms stirred a simmering ache deep inside him. If only he were nuzzling a woman who would wrap her arms around him and ask him for more. Ah, it had been much too long since he'd had a woman.

"Ha . . . has he gone?" Sophie whispered.

Ben looked up the street just in time to see Ferguson disappear inside Reynolds Tavern. "Yes." He let out his breath and stepped back from her. "That was a close call."

"Where do you suppose he was going?" she asked, lowering her eyes to smooth her skirt, as if Ben had wrinkled the silk folds with his closeness.

"I don't know." To have himself a woman and whiskey, Ben suspected. But such news wouldn't make Ferguson's reluctant fiancée feel any better about marrying him.

He offered Sophie his arm, but damn, it felt a whole lot better with her body crushed against his than with her hand tucked in the crook of his elbow.

The admiral's daughter came up with her own answer. "More than likely he's going to visit the senator," she said as they began walking again. "Andrew is good friends with Senator Johnson who lives up on Charles Street."

"That's it, of course," Ben replied, as if it were reasonable to go visiting at this time of night. He wasn't about to argue the truth with her. "Let's get you home before there are any more close calls. I'd hate for us to run into your father."

Her eyes danced with mischief when she looked up at him. "But Father likes you."

"Not as much as he likes Captain Ferguson. He wouldn't be pleased to see you out alone with me at this time of night."

"Because you're only a seaman?"

"Because you're an engaged woman." *And* because I'm only a seaman, he added to himself. He had no right to care anything about the admiral's only child.

He heard her soft, soft sigh. But Sophie didn't speak again until they approached the academy grounds. "When we get to the gatehouse, I'll go in alone," she said. "They'll stop you, but they never stop me."

"Why is that?"

She gave him a twinkling smile. "I'm the admiral's daughter. And known for my boldness. They don't dare ask me questions. They fear I may answer!"

Ben Swain escorted Sophie to her bedchamber door. He bid her a droll good night and left her with a nod of his head and wry twist of his lips. She wondered if he found her amusing. She wondered if the dark-eyed seaman thought of her at all when they were not together. With increasing frequency, Sophie found herself thinking of him, and longing for more moments like the one they had just shared.

When Ben had engulfed her body with his, against the shop on Main Street, Sophie felt a tingling rush of heat. Oh, such a glorious heat! She thought she might melt into him, through him and into him—like butter on warm bread, like sugar glaze over warm cake. Sweet mercy!

Within Ben's arms, she'd forgotten her predicament for a few precious moments. Against the steely wall of the whaler's body, she'd felt safe and small . . . like an acorn sheltered by a giant white oak. Light-headed, and yet more alive with anticipation than she could ever remember . . . Sophie likened herself to a shipwreck survivor discovering land ahead after days afloat on an empty sea.

Only a seaman? Oh, no! Ben Swain was more man than most.

Before withdrawing to her chamber, Sophie watched Ben climb the narrow steps at the end of the corridor that led to his attic room. She watched him until he was out of sight.

Ben listened again. Lifting his head from the pillow, he braced himself on his elbows. At first he'd mistaken the rap at his door for the sound of a rat in the rafters. But a two-legged someone was at the door. Someone who didn't want to be heard.

What now?

He threw back the covers and, after some fumbling, lit the lantern on the bedside table.

Two strides in the small attic chamber were all it

took to reach the door. Holding the lantern, Ben opened the door a crack.

"Hello, Ben."

Damn.

"Hello, Sophie."

"I know it's late but I have a . . . a pressing dilemma," she whispered.

"Of course, you do."

"May I come in?"

Seven

Ben considered Sophie's request for a fleeting moment. He could see just enough of her through the door opening to know such a move would be folly. She wore a dressing gown made of some flimsy fabric thrown over a chemise made of the same gauzy material. Both garments were white and adorned with embroidered pastel flowers that danced around plunging necklines. Hell, the woman was barely clothed!

No. Definitely not. She could not come into his chamber in the dead of night. In addition to all else, was she daft?

That's what Ben thought.

"Can this not wait until morning?" is what he said.

Sophie shook her head. Shining, tawny waves tumbled past her shoulders in a sun-kissed mass. "I shall not sleep a wink. Please let me in, if only for a moment. I don't know what to do."

"If your father finds you in my chamber, I'll be tarred and keelhauled."

"Keelhauled?"

"Dragged beneath a ship."

"My father would never do such a thing to you! And if I cannot have someone to talk with, I shall go mad before morning." Her remarkable eyes glistened with unshed tears. "Ben, please, I need your help."

He had not the will to resist the very real anguish reflected in her eyes, nor her soft pleading tone. Ben opened the door and Sophie darted into the small chamber.

"Watch your head," he cautioned. Ben was tall but the eaves on either side of the bed seemed inordinately low. During most of the time he spent in the room, Ben adopted a slightly hunched position.

"Do you not have a gas lamp?" Sophie asked.

"This is the attic. I have one window, a lantern, and a candle."

"Ouch!" she yelped.

"Shh!"

"I stubbed my toes," she explained, whispering again. "On the bed."

"Are you hurt?"

"Not badly."

"Don't move. And be very quiet."

"Do you mind if I sit?"

"On the bed?" he asked, thinking that a dangerous thing to do.

Sophie didn't wait for his answer. She perched near the foot of his bed, looking like Sleeping Beauty just awakened.

Sighing, Ben ran a hand through his hair. She'd have to sit where she was. He had no chair. The attic chamber was only large enough to hold a narrow bed and dresser with pitcher and bowl. Pegs on the wall held his clothing.

Her eyes briefly met his and then drifted downward. Ben became the object of intense scrutiny, from the top of his head—he knew his hair was mussed—

down the length of his knee-length nightshirt, to his calves and bare feet. And then she giggled.

"Is something funny?" he snapped. "I rarely find anything funny at two o'clock in the morning."

"No, no," she replied quickly, striking a serious pose. "It's just that I did not expect you to be wearing a nightshirt."

"As a guest in the admiral's home, I'm obligated to be clothed at all times."

"It's . . . it's a very nice nightshirt. Blue stripes, open collar. Flannel?"

He shifted from one foot to another. "My mother made this for me."

"She is obviously a fine seamstress."

Ben's mother had spent a lifetime sewing, cooking, and loving her family. But now she was sick and refused to leave the island, balking at leaving her friends and the place she was born. He worried over her constantly, wondering if the money he sent each month was enough. A brave woman who had endured much struggling and heartaches through the years, his mother would never ask him for anything. If the money ran short, she would not think of asking for more.

"You didn't come to admire my nightshirt," he grumbled.

Not only had she pricked the corners of his guilt concerning his mother, but Sophie's presence in Ben's chamber had triggered a burning sensation in his belly from the moment he let her in. He'd been a fool. He should have barred the door. Her seductive state of undress and his long-suppressed manly needs combined to make him jumpier than a sailor who's just spotted a pirate's flag.

"No, Ben. I didn't come to admire your nightshirt."

Her gaze settled on the paper atop the dresser. "Do you write as well?"

"No, I'm working on a design for a steam-powered battleship," he answered more tersely than he'd intended.

Couldn't she feel his tension?

Her eyes locked on his, her lips turned up in a faint smile. "You are a man of many talents."

"This is no time to talk about my talents." If Sophie stayed a minute longer, he might not be able to suppress one of his more pressing talents. He started to open the door.

"No!" Twisting the lace hanky she held in her lap, Sophie frowned as she gazed into the lantern light. "I . . . I don't know what to do. My novel is missing."

Closing his eyes, ever so briefly, Ben folded his arms over his chest. "I thought this was a dilemma that couldn't wait."

"It is! My novel will buy my freedom from Andrew. You know that I cannot marry Andrew Ferguson."

"I understand why you might not be eager to marry the captain, but Sophie, not everyone who writes a novel can sell it," Ben responded, with patience he did not know until this moment that he possessed. "If I were you, I would think of some other way to extricate yourself from the engagement."

Fire flashed within her sea green eyes. "My novel will sell."

There was no talking sense to this stubborn woman. "How can you be so certain?"

Sophie raised her chin to a clearly defiant angle. "I just am. But I can't sell *The Romantic Adventures of Fifi LaDeux, An Unmarried Woman* if my journal is missing."

"Most likely, you've simply misplaced it. Go back to bed and get some sleep. You've been ill, and you're exhausted. Chances are you'll find it in the morning when you're fresh."

His attempt to console her failed.

"I have kept my journal in only one place for the last six months," Sophie informed him in frosty tones.

Ben had attempted to ignore the fading fragrance of honeysuckle and the powerful, glorious scent of woman. He'd averted his gaze from rosy lips that glistened, and the enchanting indentation in her cheek. But he was just a man, a normal man with healthy desires.

He wasn't above taking surreptitious glances that provided him with the faintest outline of Sophie's curves. Enough of her slender figure was revealed to trigger his imagination. Beneath her robes there resided not only a bold heart, but round firm breasts, a flat belly, and full, luscious hips.

Most astonishing of all, in her innocence, Sophie appeared to be oblivious of her effect on him.

He slept with the window ajar because he normally found the cool night air bracing. But not with Sophie in the small attic chamber. Half-dressed, seated on his bed, and speaking in breathless tones, she warmed him, set latent fires flaring. To lie down with her would be—

Damn! Thoughts like that were more dangerous than facing a forty-ton whale without a harpoon.

Ben blew out a staggering sigh and turned his back on Sophie. He lightly pounded his fist three times against the eaves, drew a deep breath, and confronted her again.

"There's been a great deal of spring cleaning going on in this house. Perhaps while you were ill one of the maid's moved your journal."

"I've looked everywhere. It's not anywhere to be found in my chamber."

"Could it have been discarded during the cleaning?"

"Perhaps. But I don't think so. No one would dare remove something of mine without asking, even when I was ill."

"Are you asking me to help you find this journal?"

"Yes." She raised mournful eyes to his. "I must reclaim my novel before someone reads it. It could prove embarrassing for my father."

Ben groaned.

"Well, only if the reader believed what is written in the journal to be true rather than a work of fiction," she added hastily.

"You've written about the admiral?"

She lowered her eyes. "And you."

"Me?" His heart felt as if it had stopped. "Did you say, me?"

"Yes, but I mention you only briefly."

"Dear, dear God."

Ben sank to the bed, lowering his head into his hands.

And shot right up.

Tarring and keelhauling wouldn't be good enough if he was caught on the same bed with the admiral's virgin daughter. He'd be dangling from a mast before dawn.

"What did you write about me?" he demanded in a hoarse rasp. His throat had gone dry as bone.

"I made a . . . a vague reference to your appearance."

"My appearance?"

"Please don't glower, you're quite striking, you know. You possess the face and form of a true hero."

"A hero?" he repeated, astounded but flattered. Feeling a warning tightening in his gut, he quickly came to his senses. "And you used my God-given name?"

"I intended to change it."

"Intentions! Don't you know about intentions?" Ben growled through his teeth in an effort not to shout.

"They pave the road to—"

"Never mind!" He cut her off.

"Will you help me?" Sophie pleaded quietly. Her woeful expression caused his heart to squeeze tightly against his chest.

"I'll help you by giving you my best advice. Go to the admiral," he said, pausing to draw a deep breath. "Go to your father first thing in the morning and tell him what's happened."

"He'll send me to an asylum, or worse, Saint Louis!"

"If you try and hide this from him, Sophie, you'll find yourself in deeper trouble. What if your journal is found by some unscrupulous person and bandied about? Knowing your novel may be in the hands of strangers can help your father prepare . . . for any eventuality."

Sophie stood. Her pale coloring and forlorn demeanor reminded Ben of a whaler's widow upon hearing the news of her husband's death, bereft and inconsolable.

"I don't think I have the courage to go to my father," she said.

"But you do. I'm certain that you have stood up to the admiral countless times before."

"My father does not call that courage. He calls it defiance . . . and sometimes, insolence."

"From what I have observed, you have a brave heart, Sophie," Ben assured her truthfully. "In the morning, search your chamber again, and if you do not find your novel, or journal or whatever it is, speak with your father."

Her shoulders slumped as she moved toward the door. "Father will never understand why I have written a novel."

"You must tell him and *make* him understand if necessary. If the journal has actually been taken, confessing to the admiral is the only honorable thing to do. You can't keep this a secret from him."

With her hand on the doorknob, Sophie looked over her shoulder at Ben. "You will not help me find it then?"

"Speak to your father," Ben insisted. "He may understand and not be as harsh as you believe."

Dropping her hand from the doorknob, she turned and advanced toward Ben. "Father will never understand, and oh, it would be so much better if I could recover it without having to tell him," she said, pleading her case once more. "When I find my journal, and I will, he shall forbid me to take it to a publisher even if I promise that all of the names will be changed."

She never gave up. Despite himself, Ben felt a grudging admiration for Sophie's determination. And while he understood her reluctance to face her father with this sorry news, she had no choice.

"You must tell him, Sophie."

His patience was down to a thread. For a number of reasons he could hardly wait for her to be gone. She was like a siren of the sea, Lorelei personified, calling sailors to their doom. In this case, his.

Not only did she beg for him to join her in league against the admiral, but she teased him unmercifully, wearing the most enticing chemise and dressing gown he'd ever seen. The white flowing garments suggested that heaven-on-earth lay beneath their deceivingly innocent folds. Did Sophie believe Ben suddenly had gone blind and numb? What was wrong with her?

"I cannot go to my father. He will never understand. He's never understood anything at all about me."

"If the admiral is aware that the journal is missing, there's every chance he *will* help you find your novel, even if only for his own sake." Ben rubbed the stubble of beard on his jaw as he searched for the name. "The, ah . . . I don't seem to remember the title."

"*The Romantic Adventures of Fifi LaDeux, An Unmarried Woman.*"

He hiked a brow. "How could I have forgotten?"

"And it has been stolen from me," she insisted. "I could never misplace my novel."

"Stolen. Who would do such a thing?"

"Someone like me, who wants to be an author. One of the strangers who were in and out of my chamber while I was ill, like you." Sophie's eyes widened in alarm. "You!"

He held up his hands. "No. No, I wouldn't and I didn't."

But knowing what he knew now, Ben wished he had. It gave him cold chills to think of what she might have written about him.

If, indeed, the novel was stolen, it might be by someone seeking to hurt the admiral as well as make a name for themselves as an author without a lick of writing. Ben felt a headache coming on.

"Sophie, we'll sort this out tomorrow after a good night's sleep."

"You may sleep, but I have never been in as much trouble as this." Her forced, doleful smile tugged at his heart.

"Would it make you feel better about facing your father if I accompanied you?"

"Oh, yes!" Sophie's eyes brightened, then dimmed beneath gently furrowed brows.

"But make certain to look for it again as soon as it is daylight."

"You are a true friend, Ben."

He opened the door. "Good night, Sophie," he whispered.

She kissed him softly on the cheek. "Good night, Seaman Swain."

"You what?" The admiral appeared nonplussed.

Once again, Sophie stood beside Ben in her father's study. "I composed a novel," she replied quietly.

Her father peered at her over his spectacles as if she'd taken in another wounded animal as she used to do as a child.

"Why?" he asked. One word, filled with suspicion.

Sophie could hear the thud of her fearful heart, the sounds of midshipmen drilling in the distance, and the buzz of a fly as it winged through the open window. But all else was still inside the austere study. She tightly clutched the balled hanky within her fist.

"Because I wish to do something with my life other than play the piano and host tea parties."

The admiral rolled his eyes. "Foolishness!"

"My journal containing the novel is missing."

"Write another—if you must. I cannot be bothered with this foolishness."

"Father, it took me six months to write those two hundred pages."

Beside her, Ben shot an impatient glance from the corner of his eye and cleared his throat.

She knew it was his way of nudging her toward the truly difficult part of this confession. Sophie ignored him. She could hardly breathe as it was. "I would like to recover my novel. 'Tis written in a journal."

"If you want to waste your time, I'll not stop you, but don't allow your search to delay making marriage arrangements."

"Thank you, Father."

Ben cleared his throat again, deeper and stronger.

While she'd wanted Swain's support, Sophie began to think she'd made a mistake. He wasn't going to let her leave the room without telling her father the complete story. She drew a deep breath, straightened her shoulders, and steeled herself as she poured out the words in a breathless rush.

"Father, the novel was stolen before I had a chance to change the names, and as chance would have it, your name is mentioned several times."

"*What?*" In a matter of seconds, the admiral's round face reddened to a dangerous shade of scarlet. His hands trembled and his eyes bulged. "You mentioned my name? In what manner?"

"I patterned Fifi LaDeux's father after you," she said softly.

"Who is Fifi La—Who?" As his fierce-some frown deepened, his voice trailed off into sputtering sounds.

Knowing whatever she said next could not make it any worse, Sophie attempted to explain. "Fifi is the heroine of my novel, *The Romantic Adventures of Fifi LaDeux, An Unmarried Woman.*"

Raising his anguished gaze to the ceiling, her horrified father placed a hand to his throat as if the life were being choked from him. "I'll be ruined. I'll be laughed out of the Navy."

"I did not write my novel to ruin you," Sophie assured him quickly. "I wrote the tale to gain my independence. You see, I do not wish to marry Andrew

Ferguson, or any man for that matter. I would support myself by writing novels."

"Before you came along, there was no history of madness in the family," the admiral declared in decidedly icy tones.

She lowered her eyes, unable to look upon his distress any longer. Although she should be accustomed to it by now, her father's disapproval cut as sharply and deeply as the blade of a dagger.

He addressed Ben. "Find my daughter's journal and you will be assigned to a ship within thirty days. Furthermore, I shall see to it whatever ship designs you have shall be reviewed by the proper parties."

"Yes, sir."

"Spare no expense. Return my daughter's journal before it proves to be an embarrassment I cannot overcome. Find it before Captain Ferguson turns and runs from her as if she were Medea."

"My students—"

The crimson-faced admiral interrupted brusquely. "Captain Ferguson will be assigned to teach your classes temporarily."

In less time than it took to write her name, Sophie had been removed from her own predicament. Her father and Ben Swain proposed to solve the matter as if she no longer existed. Furious, she clenched her fists. Frustration emboldened her.

"If Seaman Swain retrieves my novel," Sophie inquired in cool, clear tones, "what will happen to me, Father?"

"You will marry Andrew Ferguson."

"No!" Unable to stifle a furious outburst, Sophie stomped her foot and lashed out at her father. "Why will you not bargain with me as you did with Ben?"

The admiral retreated behind a martyred air. "What is it that you want, Sophie?"

If she did not stand her ground now, all would be lost. "If I retrieve the novel, I may offer it to a publisher under an assumed name like George Sand—"

"George Sand?"

"George is a *she*, Father. A woman author. Like her, I would take another name, perhaps a man's name."

The admiral's eyes narrowed on her. Although his coloring had returned to normal, his jaw was clenched. "There's more, isn't there?"

"Yes. If I sell my novel, I shall be able to retain my independence. You will not force me to marry Captain Ferguson."

"Do you honestly believe that you can recover your journal before an intelligent, skilled seaman like Swain?"

"Yes."

Her father laughed. It had been a long time since Sophie had heard any sound of mirth from him, even if it rang hollow.

"All right, my incorrigible daughter. If you recover the missing novel first, you will retain your—"

"Independence, Father."

"Independence," he repeated, as if it were a strange, foreign word.

After requesting that Ben stay for further discussion, the admiral coolly dismissed Sophie from his study. He obviously expected her to fail. She had failed him the day that she was born a female.

Sophie's determination to prove her worth to him had never been stronger as she sailed from the room.

* * *

The unbiddable admiral's daughter ambushed Ben.

After receiving his extraordinary orders and teaching his morning sailing class, Ben set out for town. He strode up Main Street toward Reynolds Tavern, meaning to have a heart-to-heart talk with Flora. A nagging feeling deep in his gut told him that the tavern maid, as Sophie's confidant, held the key to recovering the notorious journal.

Even his palms broke out in a cold sweat whenever Ben dared speculate on what Sophie might have written about him. The admiral's daughter was as unpredictable as the weather.

Why, then, was he surprised when she stepped from the doorway of the Sugarplum Sweet Shop and into his path just as he passed?

"Ben Swain, imagine running into you like this." With fringed parasol a-twirl, and bonnet bedecked with feathers and bright orange and yellow flowers, she smiled broadly.

But Ben didn't believe in accidents where Sophie was concerned. He tensed, eyeing her warily. "Imagine."

"It's called serendipity, I believe. As it happens, I wished to speak with you away from Dulany House."

There it was, the trap. Ben sidestepped. "You did the honorable thing this morning."

"If I were a midshipman, I would take solace in that," she said.

"I'm sorry your father gave you such a rough time."

"He always does." She gave a little shrug. "I am accustomed to his ways."

Sophie hadn't stopped smiling, purposefully beguiling him with her dimple. Her constant smile made Ben nervous. Something wasn't right here. The instincts of a survivor urged him to be on his way.

"I'm afraid I'm in a hurry," he said, sounding as apologetic as possible. "Can't stop to talk right now."

The quicker he recovered Sophie's journal, the faster he'd be out at sea, back where he felt as if he belonged. Although when teaching what might prove to be his last classes this morning, he'd felt an odd twinge. He'd miss the boys. Their eager young faces never failed to take him back in time. Only once in a young man's life did the mystery of the sea and the excitement of adventure ahead blind him to all else. Ben relived those moments with the boys. He especially regretted missing the opportunity to work with Joseph Baker. Joseph had the makings of a fine officer.

"Please, please speak with me for just a minute," Sophie pleaded, laying a hand on his arm.

Damn those eyes. Big, extraordinary, mesmerizing eyes, misty and imploring. Could eyes like those ever be denied?

"Five minutes."

She tugged at his arm. "Come into the shop with me. I shall buy you an apple cider."

"Cider?"

"Or ginger beer, if you prefer."

Ginger beer? Grog and ale were his drinks!

A tinkling overhead bell rang out as Ben opened the door. Removing his hat, he followed Sophie into the shop, which was heavily scented with cinnamon and sugar.

Ben had not been inside the Sugarplum Sweet Shop before. In front of the store, by windows overlooking the street, sat several small circular tables with delicate chairs.

Sophie headed for a table in the corner away from the window. Averting his eyes from the provocative sway of her skirts, he fixed his gaze on the counter.

Except for the wooden stools and a shorter length, it resembled the Reynolds Tavern bar. Ben had never been inside an establishment that featured a bar but no ale or whiskey. Barrels of hard candy and licorice abounded, along with trays of fat cinnamon muffins and macaroons still steaming from the oven.

He held a chair for Sophie and eyed the one opposite her skeptically. Fearing it might give way beneath his weight, he gingerly lowered himself into the ladies chair.

"Good morning!"

Satisfied, the chair would hold him, Ben loosed a sigh of relief and looked up to see a petite young woman hurriedly approaching them. Rosy-cheeked and plump with a nest of tight blond ringlets piled high on her head, she wiped her hands on the large calico apron that covered most of her compact figure.

"Sorry to keep ye waiting, I was in the back stirring a fresh batch of fudge."

"We haven't been waiting," Sophie insisted, with a wide smile of assurance. "I have brought my friend Ben to sample your cinnamon muffins, Lulu."

"And one for ye, I know."

"I am especially fond of Lulu's cinnamon muffins," Sophie told Ben with a sheepish smile.

"Would ye like some tea or cocoa to go along with yer muffins?"

"Nothing for me," Ben said.

Sophie ordered tea, and as soon as the young woman bustled away, she leaned toward Ben and whispered. "Lulu is a widow with a young son. Her dream is for her boy to attend the academy one day."

Ben nodded. He wasn't having any of this social

chitchat. "Why do I have the strangest feeling that we're engaging in a clandestine meeting?"

"I don't wish for my father to think we are in league. 'Twas wicked, the way he set us against each other this morning."

If she only knew.

"Sophie, we aren't in league."

She reached across the table and clutched his hand. "Ben, you have to help me. We must work together."

"Did you hear what the admiral said?" he asked, taking forbidden but excessive pleasure in the warmth and softness of her hand. Exercising an equal combination of good judgment and willpower, Ben withdrew his hand. "If I recover your Fifi novel, I'll be rewarded with a ship assignment."

"And that's what you desire more than anything?"

"Yes." Ben experienced an uncomfortable feeling, rather like a fox being led into a trap. "Unless the Navy would like to build one of the steamships that I've designed. Though I fear it will never happen, I should like that even more."

Sophie's gently arched brows dove together in a wounded frown. "More than doing the noble thing and saving an innocent young woman from marriage with an old sea ogre?"

"Sea ogre? Are we talking about Andrew?"

"Yes."

"And you would be the innocent young woman?"

"He will rule me just as my father does."

"But I expect you can save yourself in this instance," Ben said. "You're an intelligent young woman who I have no doubt will come up with a brilliant scheme to avoid marrying Captain Ferguson."

"Your confidence in me is not shared by many."

He took a deep breath. "Sophie, you did the right thing by telling your father."

"Then why don't I feel exhilarated? Are you not supposed to feel exhilarated after doing the right thing? I have unburdened my soul and feel nothing but misery, thanks to you."

"Thanks to me?"

"I shouldn't have confessed if it hadn't been for you."

"I see. Well, quite often, it takes time for the, uh, thrill to set in after unburdening one's soul."

Lulu interrupted the conversation by returning with a tray of steaming muffins and tea. But as soon as the cheerful proprietress left them, Sophie started again.

Leaning across the table and lowering her voice, she pleaded with him. "Please help me, Ben. You know that eventually you will return to sea. But if I'm forced to marry Andrew Ferguson, what will happen to me?"

She had a point. But he couldn't interfere in something that wasn't his business. His business was to get away from Annapolis as soon as possible to a place where he felt at home, aboard a ship. If he meddled in Sophie's life as she wished him to do, he'd end up back on Nantucket without so much as a net.

He attempted to explain. "Returning to sea eventually isn't what I'm after, Sophie. I have responsibilities. A mother who is ill, and a woman who is waiting somewhere in this world for me to find her and start a family. I need to get back in the action or sell one of my steam engine designs as soon as possible. I need to earn stripes and more pay."

Tears welled in her eyes. "I did not realize you were selfish as well."

"What?" She was testing his patience now. "Sophie, a woman with your intelligence and charm will find her way in life. You don't need me."

As he regarded Sophie's crestfallen expression, Ben knew that what he'd said to placate her was all true. Although a bit headstrong, she possessed all she needed to lead a happy, successful life. Her beauty alone would see her through. A man would come along who would change her misguided interest in women's rights and her absurd vow of celibacy.

"Then you won't help me," she stated flatly.

"I can't, Sophie. I'm sorry."

"You think of me as a silly, frivolous woman."

Not entirely. In recent days Ben had learned first-hand what a tight reign the admiral held on his daughter. Sophie could do little else that met with her father's approval but shop.

Was it guilt nipping at the edges of his conscience? Whatever it was that he felt, Ben softened his stance. "No. I think of you as headstrong maybe, but not silly, never silly."

"I must be stubborn about gaining my independence. Someday all women will be independent of men, just like Lulu Malone. We will be with husbands if we chose to be, not because we must be."

There she went, talking crazy again. "I'm not going to live that long," he replied.

Glaring at him, Sophie stood. Her mouth opened and closed as if she wanted to say something but changed her mind. Whirling on her heel, she marched over to the counter and ordered.

"A pound of fudge, Lulu!"

Ben stared at the cold muffin. He'd like to pocket it but had lost his appetite. He unfolded his frame slowly from the delicate chair and ambled over to where Sophie waited for her bag of fudge.

"I'm sorry, Sophie."

"You shall indeed be sorry when I best you, Ben Swain."

Eight

Ben hadn't seen Sophie in the drawing room when he asked the butler for Mildred. Curiosity spurred her to follow, quietly and at a discrete distance, as he headed toward the indoor kitchen. She stopped in the adjoining serving pantry. Flattening one ear against the dividing wall, Sophie held her breath for fear of making a telltale sound. A sneeze would spell trouble.

Sophie had no compunction about eavesdropping for her art. However, she wasn't listening to Ben's conversation with Mildred for information that she might include in her next novel. No, this was more in the form of self-preservation. Tamping down niggling guilt, she pressed a hand over her heart in an effort to ease its nervous fluttering.

The admiral had successfully put Sophie and Ben at odds with one another. In order to save herself in the life-and-death situation in which she'd become embroiled—death being marriage to Andrew Ferguson—Sophie felt it necessary to possess the same knowledge as Seaman Swain. Born to rationalize, Sophie justified her position by believing that any information that Ben gleaned would prove more important to her than to him. She'd been forced to eavesdrop.

"Well now, I hire the same people year after year," Mildred told him. "Emma Dirkins was the only new help and she's the daughter of Reverend Dirkins. She wouldn't take a thimble belonging to Miss Sophie."

Aha! Just as Sophie suspected! Ben intended to question all of the servants.

"What about Miss Harrington's maid? Didn't she leave just before I moved into Dulany House?"

Rather than reply, Mildred asked a question of her own in a decidedly piqued tone. "Just what is it that's missing, young man?"

"I'm not at liberty to say."

"Miss Sophie has not said a word to me about anything of a personal nature being missing from her chamber."

"Reluctant to alarm you, most likely. Now, Mildred—may I call you Mildred?"

Uh-oh. Ben had turned on his charm. Sophie could hear his dazzling smile in the flirtatious timbre of his voice. She could see the teasing sparkle in his dark blue eyes as clearly as if he were standing beside her. Mildred hadn't a prayer.

"Well . . . I guess that would be all right."

The housekeeper would tell him anything he wanted to know.

"Thank you. Now, do you think Miss Harrington's personal maid might have had any need to steal?"

"Abigail? Oh, no. The girl comes from a poor family, of course, but she was no thief." The white-haired housekeeper lowered her voice. "Are any of Miss Sophie's jewels missing?"

"No." Ben assured her. "Not that I am aware. The admiral has asked me to make general inquiries."

Which meant he acted on orders from the top and Mildred shouldn't ask any more questions.

"I see," the housekeeper replied primly.

Sophie could almost see the spinster's lips tighten. "Can you tell me why Abigail left, Mildred?"

Although Sophie strained, she couldn't hear Mildred's reply. The housekeeper had lowered her voice to the point of being barely audible. "Family" was the only word Sophie could make out. Why the housekeeper whispered was beyond Sophie. Abigail had made no secret of the fact that her family needed her at home.

"I see. Do you know where she went?" Ben asked.

"She has family living just outside of Washington, in Falls Church, I believe."

"And does Abigail have a last name?"

"Certainly," Mildred responded indignantly. "Abigail Grant."

Mildred had made Ben work for his information. Though her appearance gave one the impression of a brittle twig that might easily break, she possessed a staunch will. The housekeeper's loyalty reassured Sophie.

"One more question. During the spring cleaning, were many items discarded from Ms. Harrington's chamber?"

"No, nothing. 'Tis up to Mistress Harrington to decide what to keep and what to discard and she was ill at the time."

"You've been very helpful, Mildred."

Extremely helpful. Sophie now knew that her journal hadn't been carelessly thrown out. Ben knew it too.

"Thank you. You couldn't tell me what this is all about?"

"Sorry."

Uh-oh. The interview had ended. Fearing she

might be caught eavesdropping, Sophie scurried away without waiting to discover if there would be further conversation.

Abigail had been her maid for the past three years. Sophie had dreaded losing her, and now she missed the shy, quiet girl. Never would she have considered Abigail the culprit. She simply wasn't capable of stealing a hairpin from Sophie let alone her journal. But in all life-and-death matters, every avenue must be explored. Abigail had had access.

Sophie resolved to come up with a plan.

Within the hour she stood in her father's academy office. He had not looked up since Sophie had been ushered into the small space. His pen scratched against paper as he sat behind his desk, finishing whatever edict he penned. Determined to be patient, she stood waiting.

While Sophie could not imagine dear Abigail stealing her novel, she meant to make certain. And on the off possibility that her former maid was the culprit, Sophie meant to reach the girl before Ben Swain.

"What is it now, Sophie?"

Smiling as if she hadn't noticed the admiral's weary sigh, she handed her father the pouch of tobacco she'd purchased for him before waylaying Ben earlier in the day. "I have been shopping this morning and bought you some new tobacco. Mr. Peavey says it is new and excellent."

Her father's granite gray eyes narrowed on her as he tugged at the point of his beard. "What do you want, Sophie?"

Wounded. Again. She'd purchased the tobacco because she was thinking of him; it wasn't meant to be a bribe. But it did give her the excuse to see him in the middle of his workday. "What makes you think—?"

"Out with it. I am a busy man and you are interfering with my work."

"I shall not keep you then. Rosalind Montrose has invited me to visit her in Washington. You might remember me mentioning her from boarding school. I spent a Christmas holiday with Rosalind and her family."

"You wish to visit a school chum?"

"Rosalind would be the perfect companion to help me select a new wardrobe . . . for the benefit of my future husband."

To Sophie's vast relief, her father leaned back in his chair, adopting a more relaxed posture. "You've reconsidered marriage to Andrew?"

"I have given the idea much consideration."

"Hmm." He continued to stroke his beard as his gaze met hers. "It might indeed be good for you to have another young woman's opinion."

"Indeed! Thank you, Father. I shall take the stage tomorrow."

If luck were with her, she would be at Abigail's home before Ben Swain even realized that Sophie had left Annapolis.

One hour later, Ben stood in Admiral Harrington's office. He'd been summoned just as he was about to seek out Joseph Baker. Worried that Captain Ferguson's instruction might fall short, Ben wished to discover how the young midshipman fared before he became too deeply embroiled in the recovery of Sophie Harrington's infamous journal.

The admiral's academy office appeared even more austere than his home study. The intimidating chamber consisted of only two windows, two upright chairs, a desk, and a bookcase. A single portrait of

George Washington hung on the wall behind Harrington's desk.

"Have you discovered anything of import yet?" the admiral asked.

"I suspect Sophie's maid Abigail might have taken your daughter's journal, sir."

The admiral gazed out of his window, appearing to watch the workers at the landfill. He shook his head. "You cannot trust anyone these days."

"Apparently not," Ben agreed. After a day of interviewing servants and acquaintances of Sophie, he'd discovered teaching youngsters basic sailing to be a joy in comparison. "Has Sophie ever mentioned a problem with her maid?"

"No. Poor little thing seems an unlikely thief."

"She had the opportunity."

"But why? And surely we would have heard by now if she were holding the journal for ransom?"

"Not necessarily. I think I should pay the lady a visit."

"It's always the ones you never suspect. Quiet child, she was." The admiral turned away from the window, crossing toward his desk. "You'll be relieved to know that Sophie has decided to let you recover the journal."

"Really?" A knot the size of a frigate anchor formed in the pit of Ben's stomach. Instinct warned him that the daughter of the devil was up to no good.

"Yes, my daughter may have come to her senses. She's received an invitation to visit an old school chum and is leaving first thing in the morning."

Ben's suspicion deepened. "Is this school chum a close friend?"

"Yes, I believe so. Seems that I recall the name. Rose . . . or was it Rosaline?" Frowning, he removed his spectacles and wiped them on the corner of his jacket. "Whatever her name, she's going to help Sophie shop for a new wardrobe. Women must have a new wardrobe when they wed."

Sophie giving up on her dream to go shopping? Sophie agreeing to marry Ferguson? Ben couldn't fathom such an abrupt change of heart. Indeed, her father did not know his daughter well. She was up to something scandalous. But Ben thought better of voicing his suspicions to the admiral. "A shopping expedition?"

"Yes and I would like you to escort Sophie to her friend's home."

"I beg your pardon?"

"Travel can be dangerous these days and you appear to have won my daughter's trust."

"Sir, Sophie is quite intelligent. If I accompany her, she might realize I am—"

"Her watchdog?"

"You."

"Once she is safely at her destination, you may leave Sophie and attend to this Abigail business until it is time for the journey home."

"When do we leave?" Ben asked.

"Early afternoon."

His jaw set in grim resignation, Ben saluted the admiral. Just when he thought things had to get better, or at least less complicated, they got worse.

"Swain."

"Yes, sir."

"Find that damn journal. If you save me from embarrassment, I'll see that you get aboard the best ship in the fleet."

"Yes, sir."

Offering another firm salute and a rigid about-face, Ben strode from the admiral's office.

* * *

Back at Dulany House, he took the stairs two at a time, stopping on the second floor at the door to Sophie's chamber.

He rapped softly. "Sophie, I must speak with you."

"I'm exceedingly busy, Seaman Swain."

"I'll bet you are. Packing, perhaps?"

She did not reply.

"Come out into the corridor and speak with me for just a moment. Surely you have a moment."

"No. Actually, I do not, and if you will not leave, I shall have to send for my father."

Ben took two steps toward the stairs to his attic chamber, and then turned back. "You're not going to get away with this."

He heard no sound from the other side.

"Sophie?"

No answer.

"I'm going with you to Washington tomorrow."

The silence deepened.

Women did not ignore Ben. He was not accustomed to being met with silence. Rejecting the urge to pound on her door once more, he changed course and stormed down the stairs. Giving in to his anger wouldn't serve his purpose. A game of darts and a couple of tankards of ale would settle him down.

"Seaman Swain!"

He turned. Sophie stood at the top of the staircase, pale and beautiful.

"I believe I have time for a short stroll before supper. Would you accompany me to Graveyard Creek and back?"

Once outside, Ben let Sophie take the lead. In

frosty silence she walked at his side with her chin defiantly angled. She did not even glance at the Mexican Monument as they passed. Erected five years before in tribute to the Navy men who had died during the Mexican War, a rectangular base of four upright cannons supported its marble shaft. Ben found the design most impressive but noticed women nearly always averted their eyes.

Although she twirled her parasol in an agitated fashion, Sophie did not speak until the creek was in sight.

"Why are you coming with me to Washington?"

"Because your father fears for your safety."

She continued her march, staring straight ahead. "I am quite capable of taking care of myself."

"While I am convinced of it, your father does not agree." For the first time in memory, Ben found himself on the receiving end of a cold shoulder. He did not care for the feeling.

"Will you leave me once we arrive at my destination?"

"Yes. But I will return for you in four days' time."

"Four days?"

"The admiral's orders," he announced.

They walked in silence, allowing Ben to appreciate the idyllic countryside. As they neared the creek, he wondered if the mellow feeling flowing through him in languid waves had anything to do with the abundance of honeysuckle fragrance he breathed, Sophie's honeysuckle, or the tranquil setting. Nothing stirred in this corner of the academy grounds but the breeze rustling through the sturdy oak trees and the fish jumping in the creek. Perhaps he simply felt at peace, but on guard. One had to be on guard in the company of Sophie.

"I cannot possibly do . . . purchase what I shall require for my marriage in four days."

"I suggest you do your best."

Sophie stopped in her tracks, turned and lashed out at him. "Do you enjoy acting as nanny to a grown woman?"

Ben's mellow mood evaporated in less time than it took to scrape a barnacle from his boot. "You know I do not."

"Why then do I see a whaler, a big, strong, fearless man, reduced to acting as companion to the admiral's daughter, relegated to a lady's escort?"

"Protector. I prefer to think of my assignment as protecting you." From yourself, Ben added silently. He refused to say more, and give Sophie the satisfaction of knowing how her outburst angered him.

"Have you no pride?" she sniffed.

"Have you no compassion?" he countered, watching as she stormed to an enormous oak tree. With her pale lavender silk skirt billowing around her, she sank to the ground, facing the creek.

"Sophie, I know what you're trying to do," Ben said, leaning against the oak's broad trunk, calming himself. "Riling me won't accomplish anything. Don't you understand? I follow orders whether I like them or not. If I don't accompany you to Washington, another officer will."

"I would rather travel with someone who is not working to deprive me of what I have worked so long and hard to attain."

Meaning anyone but him. He folded his arms across his chest. "I do not wish to be your enemy."

"'Tis too late for that. You made your choice this morning in the sweet shop."

Damn. Ben hated talking to the back of Sophie's bonnet. Purple silk, the hat boasted three sweeping peacock feathers amid a nest of lavender lace and bows. But he had no choice—she refused to look at him. She continued to pretend fascination with the fish jumping in the creek.

"The admiral told me that you've decided not to attempt retrieving the journal. Is that true?"

"If I stumble across my novel, I will most certainly recover it."

"Stumble?" If she weren't already so angry with him, Ben would have laughed. "What are you planning, Sophie?"

"A visit to my friend Rosalind."

"A sudden trip, is it not?"

"Rosalind has been after me to visit for an age."

"You know, if you had made friends with Lulu at the sweet shop instead of Flora, your novel most likely would not have disappeared."

"Lulu is my friend, but she is too much like me. She leads a boring life like mine, not the stuff of novels at all. Flora, on the other hand, has experienced many . . . adventures."

"Not the sort of adventures you should be writing about."

"Pish! You are cut from the same tyrant cloth as my father."

"I am not a tyrant!"

"Arrogant and domineering."

"You are way off the mark." Ben bit back his anger. Ever since he'd met Sophie, he'd been biting back his anger.

"My father fears how I've portrayed him in my novel. Are you not the teeniest bit worried about what I might have written about you?"

"No," Ben lied. The straight hairs on the back of his neck curled whenever he thought about it. "But it would have been clever of you to change the names, Buttercup."

She angled her chin a notch higher. "I had intended to do so before I submitted the story for publication."

Ben could no longer bear talking with Sophie's back. Striding swiftly to the creek bank, he sat on his heels directly in front of her. Her brows gathered in a disconcerted frown. Scorn darkened her eyes and settled on her lips.

"Have you thought there might be another way to lead the independent, celibate life you wish?" he asked. "One that does not require publishing a scandalous novel?"

"No. Women are not allowed choices, in case you hadn't noticed." Without so much as a glance at Ben, Sophie stood up and brushed her skirts. "I cannot stop you from coming to Washington with me. 'Tis a most innocent journey yet my father allows me no freedom at all."

Unable to hold his temper any longer, Ben snapped, "The admiral just might have good reason to keep a tight rein on you."

"Sweet mercy!" she exclaimed.

And before he realized what Sophie was about, she pushed him. Ben rocked back on his heels and fell into the creek.

Grinning, the mischievous admiral's daughter waved her lace hanky and sashayed away.

Abigail waited for Fletcher Thurman in the one-room shack behind her mother's house in Falls Church, Virginia. By trade a washerwoman, Abigail's mother kept a large vat in the shack for those days when rain forbid washing outside. Overhead lines of slender rope crisscrossed the room in a weblike fashion for drying. With little room for a bed, Abigail slept on a pallet. Her living conditions were a far cry from the cozy attic room she'd called her own in the Dulany House. The most difficult thing she'd ever had to do was leave Sophie and Admiral Harrington's employ.

At last Abigail heard the sound she'd been waiting for, a bird call signaling Fletcher's arrival. She opened the door.

"Where have you been, Fletcher? I've been waiting for days."

Fletcher frowned and wiped his nose with the back of his hand. She knew he didn't like being questioned, but Abigail had never been so frightened.

"Had to see a man about some horses in Williamsburg," he said.

Abigail had fallen in love with the tall, strapping lad the instant she'd set eyes on him. What some viewed as a scruffy appearance, Abigail thought of as virile.

Fletcher earned his way farming. He'd worked at several of the finest tobacco plantations in Virginia, but he was not without ambition. The brown-eyed boy dreamed of having his own farm one day.

He kissed Abigail on the lips, a bruising buss without the emotion he'd showed the night he took her virginity. "Did you get it?" he asked.

"Yes. But . . . this is wrong. Sophie was good to me. She trusted me."

"And I trust ye too."

"We're having a child. Stealing isn't the way to start our life together."

"If you want me to marry you, Abby, you'll give me the girl's journal and leave the rest up to me."

"I . . . I thought we'd be married as soon as I brought it home to ye."

"Nah, did I say that?"

"Yes."

"When we have the money in hand, we'll see the preacher."

Tears sprang to Abigail's eyes. She was seven months with child, although thankfully, she looked no bigger than most women at four months.

Her mother had cast her out and now Fletcher was putting off making her an honest woman. She gave him the thick, black journal. "This is Sophie's novel. But 'tis more like her diary, or a journal."

"Did you read it? Does she say naughty things?"

Fletcher couldn't read but Abigail could both read and write. She'd gone to school for four years.

"She speaks about the first time she made love but doesn't mention the man's name. But from the description of his body, I think he is the new sailing instructor, Seaman Ben Swain. Sophie devoted the last pages to him. She repeats how good looking he is and how tall and how she would like to touch his . . ." Abigail broke off. "'Tis too private for me to repeat."

Grinning, Fletcher rubbed his hands together. "Good. We ain't gonna get any money for a book with no secrets. And if we don't get money, I can't afford to be marrying you. You'll have the little bastard on yer hands."

His verbal blow hurt so badly that Abigail laid a protective hand over her stomach, which constricted painfully. Tears streamed down her cheeks, making Fletcher become a blur. This wasn't the same man who'd wooed her with sweet words when she'd come home on one of her visits to her mother months ago.

Abigail could not even take much satisfaction in the fact that she'd held back on Fletcher. She hadn't told him how Sophie portrayed her father in her novel. Fletcher would probably make her pay more if he knew about the admiral.

"Fletcher, I never thought ye'd be so cruel."

"And I never thought ye'd be cryin' all the time. Do you think you can stop long enough to write a message to Miss Sophie?"

"I . . . I . . . think so." Fletcher had to marry her. What would she do if he refused to marry her? Abigail sniffled loudly and stifled her tears. "What do you want me to say?"

"I have yer book. If you want it back, you'll leave six hundred dollars in a sack at the Graveyard Creek Bridge in 4 days' time."

"That's too much!"

"Not if the admiral's daughter wants her journal back."

Abigail's hand trembled as she printed the message. After a few minutes, she handed the dirty, smudged paper to him.

Fletcher couldn't read but he stared at the paper as if he could. "Add a warning."

A cold shiver ripped down Abigail's spine. "What sort of warning?"

"I want Sophie Harrington to know that if she gives us trouble, I'll kill her."

Nine

Damn. Sophie was wearing bloomers.

Not only did Ben have to serve as an escort, but to a woman wearing bloomers! This was enough to make a man seriously consider resigning his commission. Within a week, Ben could be back in Nantucket, where he'd been respected, hell . . . he'd been revered. His mother might have refused to leave the island, but she would welcome him back to the whaling community with open arms.

Ben greeted Sophie formally. He hadn't as yet forgiven her for pushing him into the creek. "Good morning, Miss Harrington."

"Good morning, Seaman Swain. It appears to be a lovely day for sailing."

Ben averted his eyes from the billowing pink pantaloons she wore beneath her knee-length balloon-shaped skirt and brocade tunic. "The weather is equally as good for land travel."

"It shall take us tedious hours to reach Georgetown."

"I'll be riding alongside the coach enjoying the scenery all the way," he assured her.

Sophie's obvious attempts to dissuade him from making the journey were expected. In other circumstances he might find them amusing.

Ben lowered his voice. "Does the admiral know what you're wearing, Sophie?"

"My father left for his office before I came down to breakfast this morning."

More than likely she had waited until the admiral left. Still, Ben thought it a shame her father had not made the effort to wish her a safe journey. More than that, Ben wished he had the power to insist she change to a more suitable traveling costume.

"May I help you into the coach?" he asked.

"I'm waiting for my maid."

"I didn't know you had hired another."

"Fortunately, I found help quickly, since my father stipulated I could not make the trip without a companion."

"If nothing, you are resourceful."

She scowled.

"That's a compliment."

"I find it interesting that my father is sending you with me," she said, her tone rife with suspicion.

"Why is that?"

"You have moved into Dulany House to work more closely with him. It's a steam enginery project, I believe?"

"Yes. Your father is considering one of my steam ship designs." Would that it were true. Ben had submitted his designs to the admiral but he held little hope Harrington had actually looked at them.

"If the project is so important, why is he letting you go?"

He hiked an eyebrow as if he could not believe she had reason to ask. "Because your safety is more important to the admiral than any naval project, of course." Again, Ben wished what he said were the entire truth, but sadly, he feared Sophie would always be second to the Navy in her father's regard.

"I have not noticed such concern on my father's part in the past."

"Women don't always recognize the signs of a man's concern."

She shook her head. "And what of your search for my journal? That would not have anything to do with your taking this journey with me, would it?"

"In fact, this trip may assist me in making a hasty recovery." Ben grinned. He was beginning to enjoy the sparring.

"Humph!" Sophie obviously was not. With a disdainful toss of her head, she set in motion the profusion of pink rosebuds, ribbons, and silk sweetmeats atop her bonnet. The gay adornments bounced with abandon.

Ben followed Sophie's gaze to the steps of the house.

"Ah, here is my maid."

Flora, looking astonishingly unlike herself, skipped down the steps carrying three hat boxes. Dressed in a high-collared, buttoned-up black silk dress, the tavern maid's fiery red locks were hidden beneath a somber black bonnet.

Ben knew a minute of horror.

"Does your father know that Flora is acting as your maid?" he asked, after collecting himself.

"Father did not have time for an interview."

"The admiral would not approve."

Flora undulated to his side. "Good morning, Ben. Did you ever expect to see Flora serving as a lady's maid?"

"No. I am quite astonished."

"I needed to slip out of town for a few days, and my

friend, here, needed me," she informed him beneath her breath.

"Perfect."

"Will you delay the journey all day?" Sophie asked, obviously impatient to be on her way.

Ben helped her into the coach, and then Flora, who gave him a saucy wink and sly smile. The wench had a reputation for loving the lads, and she'd attempted to seduce Ben on more than one occasion. Cold shivers skipped down his spine. An excursion, which would normally take but half a day, promised to be a long, long journey. Damn. But he should have known. He'd had nothing but trouble since meeting Sophie Harrington.

With the crack of a whip and a cry from the driver, the coach lurched forward, causing Ben to jump back out of the way. Swinging onto the big black gelding provided to him by the admiral, he followed, shaking his head.

The rain storm began late in the afternoon. Heavy sheets of rain fell in a cold, steady stream. Before he knew it, Ben was soaked to the skin. Thunder rumbled in the distance and lightning flickered in the far sky. When he heard Sophie scream, he shouted up to the driver to turn in at the next inn. Although they had only an hour more to travel, Ben knew how lightning frightened Sophie.

Ben helped her from the coach and dashed with her through the cool, driving rain. He hired rooms immediately, as continuing on seemed impossible in the torrential storm. Flora and Sophie would share a chamber, but Ben paid for his own rather than share a room with the coach driver. Graham possessed an eye tic and displayed an annoying need to clear his throat every few minutes. Next, Ben ordered a small

repast of sausage, bread, cheese, and berries to be delivered to their rooms.

The raging storm had served to subdue Sophie.
She took no issue with Ben's orders. But while he con-
ducted business, he noticed that Flora received a
more welcome, dare he think, eager, response to her
flirtation from the coach driver than she had from
Ben.

The rooms at the Oriole Inn were small but clean,
fragrant with a mixture of lemon polish and cinnamon potpourri. A small fire burned in the fireplace
of the room shared by Sophie and Flora. But the noisy
crackling and popping of the blaze could not drown
out the fury of the storm.

Hours later, although she lay still, Sophie could
not sleep. She had overheard Flora make plans to
join Graham and was not surprised when the feisty
tavern maid slipped out of the bed not long after
extinguishing the lantern and bidding Sophie good
night.

Because Ben had insisted on having his own room,
Graham also had a chamber to himself across the
hall. Ben had been ushered into the room next to
Sophie's.

Rain pelted against the windowpane in a steady
stream, and the wind swirled and howled with fury
against the inn. Lying on her back, dressed only in
her chemise, Sophie stared up at the beamed ceiling. Her clothes, along with Flora's, were spread to
dry before the fireplace. The fire gave off a soft orange glow and took the edge off the cold damp night.
Alone in the large four poster-bed, Sophie cringed at
each sharp retort that flashed across the sky, shedding
its deathly, bright white light in her chamber.

Lightning killed and maimed. Lightning ignited

fires that burned houses and barns down to the ground. Sophie hated lightning, feared it, and could not bear to be alone during a storm such as this. She should have stopped Flora from leaving her.

After lighting the lantern on the bedside table, she wrapped herself in a blanket and, twisting her linen and lace hanky in her hands, paced before the fire in her stockinged feet. But the nervous activity proved useless. No matter what she did, she could not feel weary or ignore the storm raging outside. She started, she jumped, her heart skipped at each bolt of lightning; a series of shudders swept through her at each deep, bone-rattling roll of thunder.

Unable to stand being alone anymore, Sophie gave in to her fear, swallowed her pride, and rapped on the wall dividing her chamber from Ben's. She heard no response. She rapped again, louder. The thick silence prevailed.

Leaning against the wall, Sophie pressed her ear to the thin partition. The hearty seaman must be in a deep sleep. Apparently, he did not snore. Picking up one of her boots, she used the heel to rap once, twice . . . six times.

And then, at last, there came a knock at her door.

Hugging the blanket closer to her body, Sophie hurried across the cold floor to let him in.

She attempted to act surprised. "Ben!"

Shocks of his dark hair stood on end. Thin-lipped and narrow-eyed, he appeared to be on the brink of an explosion of some sort.

"What do you want, Sophie?" he growled.

"Want?" Sophie repeated as innocently as possible. In his sleepy, disheveled state, she found the sailing instructor even more appealing. He had the vulnerable air of a small boy about him.

His shirt hung outside his trousers. Obviously dressing in haste, the handsome seaman had not bothered closing the top buttons of his shirt, thus revealing an enticing glimpse of dark chest curls. Sophie's mouth felt a bit dry as she stared, wondering if she dared touch.

With effort, she raised her gaze from Ben's broad chest to the stubble of beard that shadowed his jaw. She longed to reach up and stroke his cheek, to feel the sharp growth against the soft palm of her hand. Unwilling to risk his wrath, or make a cake of herself, she looked away, into his eyes. Ben's fierce frown reached new depths as he ran a hand through the dark waves of his hair.

Ice glazed his indigo eyes. He regarded Sophie as if she had sunk his prized sloop. "You didn't just rap against the wall six times?"

She gave a little shrug. "I might have."

"Why?"

Sophie took a deep breath. "Flora is gone and I'm frightened," she admitted in a small voice. "Please, come in."

"No."

A crack of lightning and roll of thunder shook the walls.

Quaking, she pleaded. "Please, just talk with me until I am so tired I will fall asleep despite the lightning."

Heaving a sigh, Ben closed his eyes and stepped in, quickly closing the door.

"Are you still angry with me for pushing you into the creek?" she asked.

Ben towered over her, glowering. "I'm tired. I was sleeping. And if I'm discovered in the room of the admiral's daughter, I'll be drummed out of the Navy.

More 'n likely, I'll be hanged," he added, in a deep, disgruntled tone.

A bolt of zigzag lightning crackled close by, bathing the room in an eerie silver glow. Thunder boomed directly above, roaring like the explosion of a hundred canons.

Without thinking, Sophie covered her eyes and rushed into Ben. She trembled against him, against the solid steel wall of him.

Slowly his arms went around her, stiffly at first and then strong and sheltering. In the warm, safe harbor of Ben's arms, Sophie felt protected. The lusty essence of him filled her senses and soothed her. And when her body stilled, he guided Sophie back to the bed.

"Why are you so afraid of lightning?" he asked softly.

"My friend Mary was struck and killed by lightning. We shared a room at boarding school for over two years. She was like a sister to me."

Tears Sophie could no longer contain slowly trickled down her cheeks. Oh! She hated to be such a weak sister. Struggling for composure, she attempted to explain.

"Mary was just twelve years old, a year older than I. And in a flash she was gone. I saw her fall from the oak tree where we used to meet." A shudder rocked Sophie's body.

"I'm sorry." Ben's arm circled her shoulder and he squeezed her closer to him, to his warmth and strength. "Losing Mary must have been difficult for you, but it was a freak accident. A terrible freak accident."

"Don't you fear lightning at all?" she asked, hoping that he would stay with her through the night. Sitting side by side with him on the feather bed talking softly, voicing her fears, proved comforting. Ben listened; he soothed.

"No, but I realize its dangers and exercise caution."

Drawing in a ragged breath, Sophie dabbed at her wet cheeks with her lace hanky. "What do you fear, Ben?"

He stared straight ahead, into the darkness. "I . . . I don't know."

"Did you not fear the big whales? I have read that the whales are ten times larger than the whaling boats, sometimes as big as the ships."

Ben nodded. "Yes, I've seen them as big as the ship."

"Tell me about the last time you went out," she urged.

"Why?" he asked with an irritated scowl. "It's not all that interesting."

"A story will help me forget the storm."

"I don't know . . ."

"Please, Ben."

He looked down into her eyes, and sighed.

"I hired out aboard the *Trina,* a whaling ship I'd just sold to help pay off my brother Matt's gambling debts. We were out at sea for almost five months before we came across a large family group of whales. There were at least a dozen."

"You must have been far out in the Atlantic."

"We were. It was bitter cold when we lowered the whale boats from the ship. We lowered two boats that day. I led the first crew. We were after a male, a male the size of the White House—"

Sophie inclined her head. "Now who exaggerates?"

"Not by much," Ben insisted. "He weighed at least thirty tons."

"Go on."

"In the first attack, the whale swept close to the boat and knocked Billy back. Billy manned the harpoon. When he fell back, he cracked his head and passed out, so I took his place."

Ben became silent. Sophie expected he relived that cold afternoon in his mind.

"What happened then?" she prodded softly.

"The sperm circled us. As the men rowed toward where his head would next appear, I positioned myself up front on the bow." Ben paused, feeling the cold salt spray sting his cheeks all over again. "I held the harpoon out ready to plunge the blade between his eyes. But then he stalled. He flipped his tail with such force it catapulted our boat out of the water. The seas were high, and when the whaler fell, it broke up."

"Your boat fell apart?" she asked in a breathless voice.

He nodded. "There were ten men in the whaler. Four started swimming toward the ship in waves so high they would have reached the roof of the washer-woman's shed."

"Sweet mercy."

"The damned beast came at me as I grabbed Billy. But he did a strange thing. I don't know why, and I can't explain it to this day, but that whale stopped dead in the water. He looked straight at me, as if he could see me in the same way I saw him and was taking my measure. I prepared to die."

"Oh, no! What happened?"

"I swam away. What did I have to lose? I turned my back and swam away, hauling half-dead Billy along with me to the ship. The whale submerged. He let me go for whatever reasons, but he'd marked me. If I'd ever came across him again, he would have killed me."

"Oh, Ben!"

Ben squinted into the darkness. He spoke softly, to himself. "I'd never looked one of those beasts in the eye before. And when I did, I lost courage."

"No, you did not lose courage. You chose the wise course and saved your harpoon man," Sophie soothed. "Your courage was tested and you survived."

"The farther out in the Atlantic we went in search of the whales, the more our chances of getting killed increased. If I died, my mother would have no one to support her. And there would be no one to carry on the Swain line."

"All of your brothers are . . . gone?"

"The youngest, Matthew, may still be alive. He left home a year before I did. We'd become . . . well off, thanks to whaling, but Matt liked to gamble. Unbeknownst to me, my little brother continued to gamble even when he lost. It took a good deal of family money to pay Matt's gambling debts."

"Is he still gambling?"

"That's my guess. He left Nantucket and set out for California, promising to strike gold and repay what he'd lost. I think I have a better chance to command the fleet than Matt has of striking gold," he said with a droll twist of his lips.

Ben's lopsided smile sent Sophie's heart into a spin. The corners of his eyes crinkled as his smile spread to twinkling orbs. A stream of heat more powerful than a thousand suns flooded through her.

The fire hissed and popped.

"Is that why you joined the Navy, to become an admiral?"

"The pay is steady. My mother lives in the house she

loves, surrounded by lifelong friends. She has all the food and money she needs. She asks only one thing of me now."

"And what is that?" Sophie asked, resisting the urge to trace his eyebrow with her fingertip, the one with the crescent slash.

"She wants grandchildren."

"Oh." Ben required a wife who did not fear childbirth. He deserved such a wife. He deserved a family.

"And believe it or not, I want to give her grandchildren. It's time. I come from a large family and I'd like to have a large one of my own someday soon."

"Have . . . have you a girl back on Nantucket?" Sophie asked quietly. She didn't really want to know. Even if she threw off her vow of celibacy and could give Ben a family, her father would never permit her to marry a lowly seaman.

"No. The girl back home married someone else."

"Oh." Her brows lifted in surprise. How could any woman in her right mind leave Ben for another? No other man could compare. If she could only take his hands in hers and tell him how wonderful he was . . . could be, on occasions like this. But Swain already thought her a forward woman, influenced by mad women bent on improving a woman's lot in life. So instead, Sophie simply said, "I'm sorry."

"I was gone too long, too much of the time chasing whale oil, whale bone, and ambergris," he explained. "Martha couldn't wait."

"The right girl will come along, Ben." But selfishly, Sophie hoped the woman would not come along too soon.

The thought saddened her somewhat, the thought that Ben would spend his life with someone she did not know. She stared into the fire.

Silence gripped the room, and an odd tension flowed between Sophie and Ben that she did not understand. Sophie no longer heard the lightning nor the low rumble of thunder.

Her flesh prickled with excitement as Ben's gaze locked on hers. Fire burned deep within his dark sapphire eyes, transfixing her. Sophie's heart danced in a strong, uneven rhythm. She could not drag her gaze away from his, even when she heard the chamber door open.

"Oh! Forgive the intrusion. Flora will leave if you need more time. There's nothing like a good cuddle on a stormy night."

"There's a difference between cuddling and offering comfort," Ben snapped, leaping to his feet. "And a maid is not supposed to leave her lady," he added.

Flora ignored Ben's set down with a knowing grin. "Cuddling is the nicest way of offering comfort."

"Good night, ladies."

Hell, what was the matter with him any way? Why had he told Sophie his life story? Because she kept asking questions, that's why. The woman pried relentlessly, got beneath his skin, stuck in his craw, floated into his thoughts when he least expected.

But Ben hadn't been entirely truthful with Sophie. He did harbor fears. He feared failure, and he had failed.

He had failed at whaling. At the last, he had feared the whales and the sea. He'd saved two lives when that fifty-foot sperm rammed and upended their boat. But he'd never gone back out. What good was a man without courage?

His second failure had been to his people, the people of Nantucket. He'd failed them dismally. The notion plagued Ben that if he had stayed on the island rather than joining the Navy, he might have been able to do something to improve life for the islanders. They had looked up to him and expected great things from Ben. But he hadn't been able to stop the disastrous fire on the wharfs and he could not bring back the whales to Nantucket. Unable to earn the living that he had when the island reigned as the whaling capital of the world, he left. And he knew that in the leaving, he'd proved a disappointment to many old-timers.

Sinking to his bed, Ben pressed his fingertips against his temples. His head throbbed, his manhood throbbed. Hot all over, he floundered like a fish on a hook.

It had been better to tell Sophie his story than take her right there and then on the feather bed of the Oriole Inn. And damned if he hadn't been tempted. The aching of his need for her persisted, reminding him of yet another fear that grew stronger each day. It frightened Ben to the marrow to realize how much he wanted Sophie Harrington.

The following morning, after traveling beneath a gloomy gray sky, Sophie's small entourage arrived at Rosalind Montrose's grand Georgetown estate. Rosalind received Sophie in the music room of her spacious brick Georgian home.

"Sophie!" The tall, slender girl rose from the piano and rushed to greet her. "How good to see you!"

"I beg your forgiveness for this sudden intrusion, Rosalind. But my future independence is at stake."

"When I received your message, I thought a visit from you too good to be true," Rosalind exclaimed, twirling one fat midnight curl around her finger.

In school Rosalind had always been delighted to join Sophie in any sort of rebellious or mischievous behavior. She only needed the slightest inspiration. With her doe brown eyes wide with anticipation, she grasped Sophie's hands. "What do you plan to do while you are here in Washington?"

"Find my former maid, Abigail, I hope. I shall slip out with Flora early tomorrow in my search. Abigail's mother lives in Falls Church and that is where I expect to find her."

"How long will you be away?"

"No more than two days. But I must elude Seaman Swain."

"Who is he?"

"The watchdog my father has sicced upon me."

A conspiratorial smile turned up the corners of Rosalind's full mouth. "Would you like me to keep the seaman occupied?"

"Oh, yes."

"It shall be my pleasure to assist you."

And she did. During and after dinner that evening, Rosalind engaged Ben in nonstop conversation. She touched him, batted her eyes at him, played the piano and sang for him.

Sophie began to worry about leaving Ben alone with Rosalind in case she should devour him. But then perhaps her former schoolmate would enjoy giving the sailing instructor as many children as he could count. But not Sophie. In the unlikely event her father would allow her to marry Ben Swain, she could not give her handsome champion the family he wanted.

The thought weighed heavily on her heart. But she had no time to agonize. Sophie meant to find Abigail on the morrow, and if all went well . . . her journal.

Ten

Early the next morning, Sophie set off in search of Abigail. The journey would take her across the Potomac to the small village of Falls Church. Rosalind Montrose provided a gentle spotted mare, and a shy groomsman to be her guide. Her gracious hostess twittered with delight, savoring her role as conspirator in Sophie's daring pursuit of independence. Much too timid to attempt such a life personally, Rosalind concerned herself mainly with caring for her frail mother and ensnaring a husband.

If her wide-eyed, sausage-curled friend entertained thoughts of making Ben Swain her husband, the poor girl was doomed to a broken heart. As a friend it was Sophie's duty to set the girl straight. While she could not blame Rosalind for being attracted to the tall, dark-eyed seaman, Ben would always love the sea more than any female, no matter how beautiful and intelligent she might be. Further, he was an ambitious man, and although he spoke of his desire for a wife and children, Sophie feared his naval career would always take precedence over his family. On the other hand, Rosalind needed a man who would devote himself to her and her mother. Even though Sophie had no intention to take a mate, she possessed enough sense to know that lifelong happiness with a man depended on more than a set of squared shoulders and lusty good looks.

As soon as Sophie found Abigail and retrieved her novel, she planned to speak frankly with Rosalind. Of course, the silly goose might believe her warning to be merely the spiteful ranting from a jealous woman. But Sophie could not be jealous. Even when she freed herself from the entanglement with Captain Ferguson—and she would—she had no wish to marry a man already wed to the Navy. A man much like her father.

It made no matter that her heart beat a bit faster when in the company of Seaman Swain. All Sophie truly desired was her independence. She chose to be free, to fly like the butterfly.

Admittedly, it was disturbing to realize that most of her thoughts on the uneventful journey to Falls Church centered about Ben.

Sophie reached Abigail's small home at midday. No one responded to her knock at the cottage door, but she could see steam rising from behind the shabby dwelling. Her pulse pounded in nervous anticipation as Sophie hurried to the rear of the cottage. Rounding the corner, she came upon a dirt yard with two large iron vats supported on bricks above open fires. Positioned over the nearest vat, Abigail stirred the boiling clothes with a wooden paddle. An older, much worn woman who could only be her mother stirred the other.

"Abigail!" Sophie greeted her with pleasure, elated at having found Abigail so easily and quickly. In her heart, Sophie knew her former maid could help recover the journal with her novel.

Abigail appeared immobilized. Her mother shot Sophie a sharp, forbidding frown.

In the space of a few short weeks, Abigail had grown gaunt—except for the slight bulge of her belly. The truth became clear to Sophie. Abigail was with child!

Sweet mercy!

Slightly aghast, Sophie studied her maid as if she'd never seen the young girl before. Abigail's bright hazel eyes had become sunken hollows and her dark brown hair clung in lank wet strands against her face. She was about to become a mother and had taken up the trade of her own mother. She'd become a weary, overworked washerwoman.

Sorrow nicked at Sophie's heart.

Abigail dropped her paddle. "Miss Harrington?"

"Yes, 'tis I," Sophie declared, striding to where Abigail stood in a daze. "I was passing through Falls Church and so decided to pay an impromptu call. I have missed you," she said, taking up the girl's hands, red and roughened from the work.

Abigail continued to stare at Sophie as if she were an apparition.

Sophie turned to the girl's mother. "And you must be Mrs. Grant. We have never met but I must tell you how much I enjoyed having your lovely daughter with me. I miss Abigail terribly."

Abigail's mother nodded, and still frowning, dipped her head curtly. "Pleased to meet you, ma'am."

"May I have a private word with you, Abigail?" Sophie asked.

The girl nodded and turned to the shed behind them, motioning for Sophie to follow her inside. The small one-room shed held a vat for washing clothes when it rained. Abigail's dresses, hand-me-downs from Sophie, hung on pegs along one wall. A pallet that evidently served as a bed lay on the hard wood floor. There were no rugs or paintings, only a small mirror strung from a ribbon nailed into the rough plank wall.

"Are you living here?" Sophie asked as gently as possible.

"Yes." A great sadness permeated Abigail's entire being.

Regarding her maid's downcast eyes and sloping shoulders, Sophie made her decision instantly. "I would like you to come back to Dulany House."

Abigail's faint brows squiggled into a frown of disbelief. "You have come all this way to ask me to return?"

"I have indeed."

"Thank you for your kindness but I cannot. Look at me. I am with child."

"A babe is just what is needed to cheer Dulany House," Sophie replied in all sincerity. Babies charmed her as much as any woman. She simply feared birthing them herself.

"But I am to be married." The sad girl forced a smile, and lay a hand over her stomach.

"Oh, I see." Sophie's gaze fell with Abigail's hand to her belly, more rounded than usual. "Then you are only helping your mother until you wed."

"No, I shall always be a washerwoman, I expect."

"But why? Will not your husband care for you?"

"He is not a well-educated man, but I love Fletcher with all my heart." Abigail's misty-eyed gaze pled for Sophie's understanding. "I will do what I must to be with him."

"When is the wedding?"

"In a few weeks. We have not set a date."

Sophie nodded as if she understood, which she did not. "Why did I not see that you were with child?"

"Fortunately, I remained quite small until recently. I was able to conceal my condition beneath my skirts."

Again, Sophie nodded, still a bit dazed by this un-expected circumstance. "I don't remember you telling me you were in love. Although I don't know why you should," she added quickly. "It's just that we shared so much."

"I met Fletcher on a visit to my mother. It was love at first sight, it was."

"He got into her and got her with child," a flat voice stated from the doorway.

Abigail colored. "Mother!"

"It's the truth," she grunted. "I came to ask if I can get the *lady* a cup of tea."

"That would be lovely," Sophie said, ignoring the elder Grant's caustic tone. "Thank you."

When the sour woman trudged away, Sophie crossed to Abigail's side. "Do not be disheartened. If things do not turn out as they should, there will always be a home for you with me," she said, wrapping an arm around the girl's shoulder.

Abigail lowered her head. "You are too kind. I do not deserve your kindness."

"Please don't cry, Abigail. All will be fine."

"'Tis a love child I'm having," she explained in a soft quavering voice. "You understand now why I could not stay with you."

"Yes, of course. I only wish you would let me help you."

"There is nothing you can do. Nature will take its course."

"Are, are you afraid?" Sophie asked in a hushed, hesitant tone.

Abigail regarded her curiously. "Afraid of what?"

"Afraid of giving birth."

"Why should I be? It's the way of a woman. Babies are born every day." For the first time, Abigail smiled, a tender, happy smile. "And to have a babe that is a part of me and a part of Fletcher is a wondrous thing. The babe will be a living symbol of our love."

Obviously Abigail was besotted to the point where she would risk her life for Fletcher. Sophie hoped the man was worthy of Abigail's sacrifice. "When will Fletcher marry you?"

"We have not the money to pay the preacher as yet."

Sophie dug into her reticule. "I shall be delighted to pay the preacher."

"Oh, no, Miss Harrington," the bedraggled mother-to-be cried, with a horrified expression. "Fletcher will marry me soon. Do . . . do not fret."

"I cannot help but worry."

"There is no need to worry." A dreamy expression fell across Abigail's plain face. "Someday you will feel this way too, the way I do."

"Oh, no." No, Sophie was certain she would not.

"You will meet a man and love him and want to bear his child. You will know complete joy as you feel the life growing within you."

Feel life growing within her? A stunning idea. Sophie doubted she would feel joy if she found herself in the life-threatening condition. As she searched for a proper comment, Mrs. Grant returned and handed her a chipped cup half-filled with pale amber liquid.

"Here's yer tea. Do not tarry, Abigail. There is wash to be done today."

Abigail's mother did not bring tea for her daughter.

Sophie sipped at the tea feeling guilty. "I will not keep you long. But there is another matter I need to discuss with you."

Wariness shadowed Abigail's eyes. "And what would that be?"

"My novel. I . . . I kept a black leather-bound journal in my armoire and now it seems to have been misplaced," she said. "Nothing is the same since you've been gone. I no longer know where anything is to be found. Would you know what might have happened to my journal?"

Abigail's eyes were flat and dull. She lowered her gaze to the floor as she slowly shook her head.

Sophie set the teacup down on the edge of the vat. "Do you remember the leather-bound book I speak of?"

"Yes," she replied in the faintest of whispers.

"I must find it. It is my only hope of establishing a life of my own. My father wishes me to marry Captain Ferguson. But if I find the book and sell it to a publisher, I can lead life the way I wish."

Her former maid continued to stare at the uneven floor boards. "I . . . I wish that I could help you."

"Are you certain—?"

"Forgive me, but I must return to work before my mother becomes angry." Abigail started toward the door.

Sophie stepped in front of her, blocking her path. "Do you have any idea who would take such an item?"

"No."

"My father fears blackmail. Before I had an opportunity to change the names of my characters, the journal disappeared. It says some unflattering things about the admiral." She did not mention her own fantasies concerning Seaman Swain; fantasies were all they were.

"I . . . I cannot help you, but I hope you find your journal."

Sophie pressed several gold dollars in the girl's palm. "If you think of anything, anywhere it might be, please send word."

Tears glistened again in Abigail's eyes. "You are too generous, Miss Harrington. I cannot accept—"

"You must, and if you think of where I might look for my journal—"

"I shall send word," Abigail said, repeating Sophie's instruction.

Needles of frustration swirled through Sophie to the point where she wished to stomp her foot. Although Abigail behaved strangely, still, she could not imagine her former maid stealing from her.

"Might I meet Fletcher before I leave Falls Church?" she asked on a hunch.

"He's away . . . on business."

"Oh. Well," Sophie shrugged, attempting not to let her disappointment show. "Perhaps I shall meet him yet before you are wed. And how will I be addressing you, Mrs. Fletcher—?" she raised her eyebrows and the lilt of her voice in question.

"Mrs. Thurman." Abigail's voice held a note of pride. "Mrs. Fletcher Thurman."

Sophie smiled. "If there's anything you need, anything I can do for you. Send word."

"Thank you, Miss Harrington. You have a kind heart."

But a suspicious mind. Sophie knew Abigail well enough to know she hadn't been entirely truthful. The hesitancy in her voice, her refusal to make eye contact, indicated she might be holding back information.

Sophie trailed Abigail from the shed. As a result of her interview, she had more to do before returning to Georgetown. With luck she meant to find Fletcher Thurman. Sophie sorely wanted a word with that young man.

Another worry niggled in the recesses of her mind. She wondered how Ben fared with the fawning

Rosalind. As it happened, she did not have long to wonder.

Sophie stopped in her tracks. Drat.

Ben Swain, larger than life, as splendid as Poseidon in uniform, stood in the yard talking with Mrs. Grant. Rosalind had allowed her handsome prey to slip away.

A brilliant blue sky and a breeze laced with the wild-flower scent of spring provided a perfect day for riding—but even better for sailing. If Ben were in Annapolis now, he would be sailing. As it was, he'd been up at the crack of dawn. He'd had a bad feeling in his bones and meant to make certain that Sophie didn't get away from him. Sure enough, from his back window he caught sight of her with Rosalind heading for the barn. As he hastily dressed, she rode out of the barn astride a bay mare and accompanied by a Montrose groomsman.

Ben raced to the barn and swiftly saddled his gelding. Within minutes he rode out, shadowing Sophie at a safe distance. He guessed she was heading to Falls Church in search of her former maid. He'd been right.

"What are you doing here?" she blurted.

"Keeping you safe and sound."

She rolled her eyes before turning to Abigail's mother with what appeared to Ben to be a forced smile. "Good day, Mrs. Grant."

"Mrs. Grant, my pleasure to meet you." Giving a slight bow, Ben winked at the washerwoman, who responded by giggling.

Sophie rolled her eyes once more and heaved a sigh before sailing on to the front of the house, where her mare waited.

She looked around, plainly puzzled. "Where is the groomsman?"

"I sent him home. You have me to protect you now."

"Protect me from what?"

"Yourself."

"I neither need you nor want you."

Chuckling, Ben snatched the reins from her. She was the first woman who had ever said she didn't want him. "You'll just have to put up with me for a time, anyway."

She raised her chin. "There is no choice, I suppose."

"No." Sophie was a beautiful martyr, but much too spunky to play the role convincingly. Ben led the horses and she walked beside him on the path toward town without further objection.

It was a day made for walking. Black-eyed Susans sprinkled the meadows on either side of the dirt road, along with a colorful landscape of daisies and periwinkles amid the long green grass. He recognized the big white oak trees and a smattering of cherry trees in blossom.

"Did Abigail return your novel?" he asked.

Sophie shook her head. "Abigail does not have my novel."

"Does she have a lover?"

His companion came to an abrupt halt. "How did you know?"

He shrugged. "Just a reckless guess."

With her brows gathered in a minor scowl, Sophie ambled on. "Abigail is to wed soon," she said. "Which is why she left my employ. She did not leave because she stole from me."

"Did you confront her outright?"

"Yes."

"Did you expect her to tell you the truth?"

"Certainly."

But Sophie didn't sound convinced. Ben had spent enough time with her to recognize the difference between her attitude and her feelings. He knew when she felt confused, angry, or vulnerable. He knew when she felt happy. And, he realized with sudden insight, that he'd never known another woman as well. The knowledge jarred him.

"I fear you are easily misled and not quite ready for an independent life," he said with matter-of-fact honesty.

"Your opinion matters little to me," she snipped. "I am quite capable of taking care of myself."

She deluded herself. Sophie needed him—or someone like him—and Ben knew it even if she did not. But there was little point in rising her ire, so he changed the subject. "If I'm not mistaken, you were off to find Abigail's future husband when I so rudely appeared."

"She told me he is away on business."

"You don't believe her?"

"Of course I do," Sophie declared. Steadfastly loyal, her expression clearly accused Ben of being brutish. "'Tis only that Fletcher might have returned without Abigail knowing."

"Did you say his name was Fletcher?"

"Fletcher Thurman."

"I have a proposition for you."

"What?" Sophie again came to a halt in the middle of the road.

Ben thought how perfectly Sophie's pink-ribboned bonnet framed her heart-shaped face. Her eyes, her lips, her nose were in sweet, enchanting symmetry.

"A proposition?" she repeated.

Realizing how what he said had been interpreted, he rushed to apologize. "Sophie, you didn't think I meant . . ."

Glaring at him, she planted balled fists on her hips.

"Do you truly believe that I would proposition the admiral's daughter in *that* way?"

"I believe you are capable of almost anything," she bristled, and stomped away.

Laughing, Ben caught up with her. "This is what I propose: that instead of riding into town and asking about Thurman, which will certainly call attention to you, we should wait and follow Abigail. If she did steal your novel and turn it over to her lover, and if indeed he is in Falls Church, she will certainly warn him."

Again, Sophie came to a halt. "You wish to work with me? Have you changed your mind about forming a pact?"

"No. But I shall wait with you. I am here to protect you. If anything were to happen to you on this journey, your father would retract his offer of sea duty for me and put me on a rock pile with a pick instead."

"You are here to recover the journal before I do. You pretend to be my friend, but you prepare to betray me."

"Have it your way."

Sophie slowed her gait and shot him a sidelong glance. "How long do you expect the wait to be?"

"As long as it takes for the girl to get free. That might be in two hours or twelve. Her mother appeared to be a stern taskmaster."

"She treats Abigail abominably!"

"That's evident."

"But Abigail is in love. She is with child."

"A maiden with a child and without either money or a husband is a woman in desperate straits," he pointed out.

"I asked her to return with me, but she is too much in love to listen. If Fletcher truly loved Abigail, he would have married her at once."

"I agree," Ben said, although he'd not known many men who had rushed to the altar, no matter what the circumstances. To the contrary, more of his friends had fled at the mere mention of the word "marriage."

Sophie heaved a long sigh. "Poor Abigail. I fear she may have an unhappy life."

"Life is a gamble. We all make our own choices."

"I should love to have a choice!" she retorted.

Ben had no ready answer for a lamentable truth. His heart felt as if it were being squeezed by a giant squid. Grimacing, he led the horses off the road toward the meadow. "I'm going to wait over there behind those bushes, but you are perfectly free to go into town and search for Fletcher," he told her.

"You know very well that I am not free at all. But someday I shall be."

If Sophie had been born a man, she could have commanded a fleet of whaling ships. "I should not be surprised," he responded.

"And then no man shall ever tell me what to do again."

"Yes, but in the meantime may I suggest that instead of searching for Fletcher Thurman, you might look for an inn in Falls Church. The hour grows too late for us to return to Georgetown today."

He gambled that Sophie would stay with him rather than set off on her own. If he didn't miss his guess, she would allow Ben to recover the journal and then attempt to wheedle him out of it.

"If Fletcher Thurman has my novel and Abigail leads you to him, I shall be none the wiser if I am resting in a comfortable inn," she objected. "Worse, I shall be married to Andrew Ferguson. No, I shall wait in the bushes with you."

Sinking to the ground, Sophie spread her skirts,

and smoothed the folds. After tethering the horses in a copse behind them, Ben lowered himself down beside the distressed authoress. He plucked a long weed to chew on and drew his knees up to lean on. An array of bushes, vines, and trees shared the spot in the meadow he'd chosen to wait. Well concealed, Ben and Sophie could see the road clearly but no one passing would notice their hiding place.

An hour passed. Sophie shifted positions and sighed frequently. During the second hour she spoke. "The daisies are lovely."

"Would you like me to gather a bouquet?" he asked.

"If I could eat flowers," she sighed. "I'm feeling hungry. Are you hungry?"

"No, and I have nothing but a cigar and spruce gum."

"We can't eat a cigar."

"There are blackberries on the bushes behind us."

"Perhaps some are ripe," she said, pushing to her feet.

Sophie removed her bonnet, and with it the pins holding her hair. The taffy mass fell to her shoulders and Ben knew a sudden desire to slip his fingers through the silken strands.

"I shall use my bonnet to collect the berries," she announced. Her startling aquamarine eyes shone with the pride of innovation.

"There could be no better use for it," Ben said.

She inclined her head and shot him a look that would weaken a lesser man.

"It's a charming hat," he added hastily.

With a toss of her head, Sophie turned. Hunkering down, she stayed low as she made her way to the berry patch.

Ben removed his jacket and rolled up his sleeves.

The day was too warm to undertake surveillance in full uniform. For one unguarded moment he lay on his back in the grass and weeds. Spread-eagle, he basked in the sun. Like a man with no obligations or concerns, he allowed himself to enjoy the soothing rays as he had when he was a boy.

But too soon the moment passed. With a small groan he raised himself up to lie on his side in the sweet-smelling grass. Braced on one elbow, he propped his head up with his hand. In this casual manner he managed to watch both the road and Sophie for the next hour.

It was clear by the delighted expression on her face that she enjoyed her task. He noted that she popped every other berry she picked into her mouth. Ben smiled as he watched her, aware of a warmth stirring within him, a warmth far different from that given off by the spring sun. He could not deny that in her way Sophie Harrington was endearing—for a woman who wore bloomers.

Before long she returned with a bonnet full of berries, most not quite ripe. With a beaming smile that displayed her disarming dimple to its fullest, she sank down beside him. Ben declined her offer to share the berries but watched with unduly keen interest as she devoured the ripest. Her relish made itself known in the low moans of pleasure and the sensuous motion of the tip of her tongue as Sophie guilelessly licked the juice from her lips and fingers.

Purple berry juice nestled in one corner of her mouth.

If she were anyone else but Harrington's daughter, Ben might have given in to the rather insistent desire he felt to sip the juice from her lips, to roll with her in the warm grass.

"It's rather like having a picnic," she said cheerfully.

"Quite," he replied absent-mindedly. His gaze remained on the berry juice that clung to the corner of her mouth and stained her lips. His palms itched to skim over her curves, to feel her lush breasts and the waist he could span with the slightest spread of his fingers. Sophie had done nothing to excite him, and yet Ben spiraled out of control, hot and uncommonly bothered.

She puffed an exasperated sigh. "It doesn't appear Abigail is going to leave. We've waited over four hours."

"Maybe she's waiting until dark," Ben said, turning his gaze up to the road.

"Or maybe she has nothing to do with my journal being missing."

"If you're getting restless, go on ahead to Falls Church and hire a room at the nearest inn," he said, sitting upright. "I'll find you. There can't be many inns in such a small town."

"No. I shall stay with you. If I leave you, you may go off searching for Fletcher by yourself."

She always seemed one step ahead of him. "We'll wait another hour," he said. "Make yourself comfortable."

"Easier said than done," she replied, closing her eyes and raising her face to the sun.

Ben stared in fascination, wondering if he had fully appreciated Sophie's natural beauty before. She belonged in this field of flowers and green, green grass. From the elegant contours of her cheekbones to her rose-and-cream complexion, she required no powders or rouge to enhance her appearance. If he were an artist, he should like to paint her as she was in this moment, a radiant loving spirit born of the spring and sun. If he were a poet, he would write of her as a rare flower that must forever be allowed to bloom and grow.

But he was neither, and damn, he itched. Ben was bedeviled by more than the ordinary male itch for Sophie—he truly itched. He scratched his arm without taking his eyes from her. And then he scratched the other. Something in the grass must have bitten him. Irritated, he looked down . . . and saw the rash.

"Uh-oh. Poison ivy," Sophie said, brushing against him to get a closer look. "You must have exceedingly sensitive skin."

"Sensitive skin?"

"It itches, doesn't it?" she asked. Her cheerful tone was not what he would have liked.

Ben glowered at the offending rash. "Yes, it itches."

"You mustn't scratch," she advised.

Sophie leaned even closer to him, filling his senses with sweet honeysuckle and the provocative scent of pure woman. He was beset with a needles-and-pins tingling beneath his skin and a fierce need to scratch the fiery patches of itching on the surface. A man could lose his mind like this.

"Poison ivy is common in fields like this," Sophie told him. "You must have brushed against it mistaking it for an ordinary weed."

He frowned at the rash as if he could scowl it away. "How do you know about poison ivy?"

"I've read *Family Nurse,* a very necessary book for every household. Mrs. Lydia Childs is the author. Yet another example of a woman who makes her own way by writing."

"Is there anything to make the itching stop?"

"I believe Mrs. Childs recommends soaking in a cool bath of salt."

"Soaking?" he repeated. "I'm not soaking in a bath like some foolish dandy. I'm in and I'm out of a bath."

"You're more stubborn than I am!"

"It's safer on the sea than on land," he grumbled, rising to his feet. "There's no poison ivy."

"No, only scurvy."

"Perhaps we should find that inn now." Ben extended a hand to help her up.

She eyed his large palm warily. "Have you touched your hand to your arm?"

"I don't remember." He looked from her to his reddening hands.

Sophie took advantage of his momentary distraction to rise on her own.

"You're willing to give up the watch?" he asked, shoving his hands in his pockets as they started toward the horses.

"Yes," she announced firmly. "I have decided that Abigail is not involved in any way. I should like to return to Annapolis and question everyone who worked in the house while I was ill."

"Such a course will cause talk," he warned, rubbing one arm with the other—which didn't seem to help.

"I am talked about as it is. Don't rub."

"I'm not," he shot back.

"When you scratch or rub, the rash gets worse. If I recall correctly, Mrs. Childs warns poison ivy easily spreads to any and *all* body parts."

A lock of hair fell over his forehead. He blew it back. Sophie's implication was clear. She had no shame. She'd spoken aloud of abstinence and celibacy and now, quite brazenly and matter of factly, made clear reference to his private parts.

"Do you believe everything you read? Never mind," he said before she could answer. "Let's get you to an inn before dark."

Eleven

Sophie was tired and hungry and unable to go any farther when she and Ben rode up to the Shady Lane Inn. Even though the establishment housed a saloon as well, Sophie followed Ben through the swinging doors, thankful to have come upon a resting place.

Although obviously plagued with poison ivy itch, Ben strode into the saloon with an air of unassailable authority. Sophie stayed close on his heels.

She'd always worn her disguise into the Reynolds Tavern and felt a bit disconcerted without the heavily veiled hat. Her berry-stained bonnet served no purpose any longer. Straightening her shoulders and holding her head high, Sophie ignored the rude stares of the male customers.

If her father ever discovered Sophie had been in such a place, he would disown her for certain. Still, the experience might be valuable for her future literary endeavors.

A peaceful atmosphere existed within the rough plank walls of the Shady Lane Inn and Saloon. A dozen or so men played cards. Several tables appeared to be occupied by tradesmen softly swapping stories over tall mugs of ale. In contrast to the Reynolds Tavern in Annapolis, the Shady Lane Inn was so quiet that Sophie could hear the sawdust swish beneath her feet as she followed Ben to the bar.

"What can I do for ya?" the paunchy, mustachioed bartender asked. "Lookin' for a room?"

"Two," Sophie corrected.

"One," Ben said firmly.

"Don't got but one. There's political doins' goin on in town, don't ja know?"

"We'll take it," Ben said before Sophie could protest.

"Is this the missus?"

"Sure enough," Ben drawled.

The barkeeper chuckled.

Sophie scowled on the inside while smiling on the outside. A strained smile, perhaps, but it was the best she could do. Just when she hoped they were on the brink of making peace, or at least a truce, Ben had slipped into his arrogant, high-handed ways.

"My name's Hank. If you need anything, let me know." The burly fellow tossed a key upon the bar. "Take room two."

"Thanks."

Turning away from the bar, Sophie came to a sudden stop, rearing back from the frightening yowl of a young man who had staggered through the swinging doors. He sounded like a coyote and looked as if he'd lived in the same clothes for several weeks.

"I came back for one more," he bellowed. Wearing a sloppy grin, he held up an index finger.

Hank, the barkeeper, shook his head. "You ain't havin' one more, Cade. You're done."

Cade, blond, blue-eyed, and disheveled in a blue denim work shirt, lurched forward in the direction of Sophie and Ben. She sidestepped behind Ben. His towering, broad-shouldered form offered protection from the offensive young man, who had apparently had too much to drink.

"The boy's the minister's son," Hank informed Sophie and Ben, sotto voce.

Cade took a step forward, straining to get a better look at Sophie. He grinned at her as if she were playing some game with him. Despite his grin, Sophie felt afraid of the inebriated young man. Her heart beat a quick tattoo and she felt, as much as saw, Ben stiffen.

Seemingly oblivious to Ben's presence, Cade began to coax Sophie, "Hey, pretty lady, come out and play with me."

"Son," Ben said, "walk on out of here. You're only asking for trouble."

The boy swayed. "Who would you be?"

"Her husband," Hank said, quickly interceding.

"Maybe she's tired of him. Are you, honey? Would you like to try something new?"

"If you don't leave by the time I count to three, I'm going to have to thrash you," Ben warned in deep, ominous tones.

"Says who?" the belligerent boy demanded, stalking forward.

"Says me." Ben planted his feet and folded his arms across his chest.

The poison ivy would surely spread, Sophie thought, unable to accept the fact that at any moment she might be in the midst of a barroom brawl. The admiral's daughter. Oh, drat!

"One."

"My husband is a decorated war hero, known for his great strength and courage," Sophie proclaimed in hopes the boy would back down.

Swain stood as tall and unyielding as a mountain. He continued his count coolly. "Two."

"No stranger tells me what to do," Cade snickered defiantly.

"Three."

No one moved in the Shady Lane Inn and Saloon. Sophie did not even breathe. The buzz of a circling fly seemed inordinately loud.

Ben gave a doleful shake of his head "Son, I gave you fair warning."

"Ha!" The young man put up his fists.

Ben pressed the room key into Sophie's hand. "You go ahead. I won't be but a minute."

Giving him a wide berth, Sophie swiftly made her way around Cade, but as quick as a cat, he reached out and snatched her, pulling her back against him. The minister's son smelled of stale whiskey and ale, which caused her stomach to somersault. Struggling to free herself, Sophie felt Cade's lips on her neck, wet and repulsive. Just as she was about to scream, she was suddenly free of his grasp. Sophie stumbled as Cade was lifted up and away from her.

By Ben. He flung the amorous young man to the ground.

"Get up," the sailing instructor growled, standing over the crumpled boy.

Sophie watched over her shoulder as she made her way to the staircase. Breathing heavily, Cade pushed himself to his feet. He swayed a moment before swinging at Ben and connecting. The blow glanced off Ben's jaw, below his eye.

Cade wobbled as Ben lashed out with a fist that knocked the blond boy back into an empty table. Gasping in horror, Sophie came to a dead stop midway up the stairs. A mixture of fear and morbid curiosity held her riveted to the battle below.

In her most fanciful daydreams she would never

have imagined Ben Swain fighting for her honor. If something happened to him while she cowered behind a locked door, she would never be able to forgive herself. If something happened to him while she watched, she would never forgive herself.

Sophie started back down the stairs. Bristling indignation overcame fear. Determined to help Ben rather than see him hurt, she picked up a spindly old chair and watched, waiting for her opportunity. If only the brawling men would stop long enough for her to take aim, she'd crash the chair down over Cade's head.

Her heart seemed to stop as Cade rushed at Ben head-down like a mad bull. The drunken boy's head slammed directly into Ben's midsection. A piercing pain flared deep within Sophie's own belly as if it were she who had received the crushing head blow.

The gallant seaman grunted, rocking on his heels as Cade brought both fists up and landed a single blow to Ben's jaw.

Afraid for the man who was both friend and nemesis, Sophie felt her breath get stuck in her throat. She clenched the chair with so much force that her knuckles turned white. But the smelly, blond boy had expended his last ounce of energy. His glazed eyes appeared not to focus as Ben drew himself up. In seconds the powerful sailing instructor had delivered a mighty blow first to Cade's jaw and then to his stomach. The minister's son folded like a Chinese fan.

As Cade fell, Sophie dropped the chair and dashed up the stairs and into room two. Ben didn't need her anymore. He'd successfully saved her honor.

For a long moment, no one moved. The barkeeper poured a shot glass and slid it to where Ben rested against the bar, catching his breath. A clinking of glasses and a smattering of applause broke the silence.

Acknowledging his audience with a dismissive wave, Ben ordered a bath, two bowls of stew, and plenty of salt for room two. Bruised, battered, itchy, and aching, he dragged his body up the stairs.

The door was locked.

"Sophie, it's Ben. Open the door."

She opened the door slightly and peaked out the crack. In no frame of mind for games, he pushed the door back and strode into the thimble-sized chamber.

"Thank you, Ben. Thank you for what you did down there."

"Don't mention it."

He sank to the edge of the bed and examined the rash on his arms. Damn, it itched.

He rubbed his jaw. Damn, it ached so badly he thought it might be broken. And his eye, that was a whole different matter. Who'd ever guessed a drunken boy could do so much damage?

"Your eye is swollen," Sophie said softly as she sank to her knees and gazed up at him.

"Must be why you look all blurry. Guess it will probably be black and blue in the morning," he said, doing a quick survey of the room.

An old lantern burned on a rickety table. He recognized the smell—whale oil. The dimly lit room offered one window, framed with faded and limp calico curtains.

The meager furnishings included a bed large enough for one average-sized body, a wash stand, and a straight-back Shaker chair. The rough plank floor was bare. The crude chamber was not exactly what the admiral's daughter was accustomed to in the way of accommodations.

"Are you in pain?" she asked in the same hushed and reverent tone she'd used since Ben had entered the room. This new Sophie, oddly unlike the woman he knew, confused him, made him wary.

"I've been hurt worse."

She reached up and touched his jaw. "You're bruised."

The touch of her hand on his aching jaw somehow lessened the pain. She ran her fingertips gently over the spot. Ben's heart beat madly, out of rhythm, out of control. Drawing a deep, steadying breath, he closed his eyes, allowing himself to enjoy the warmth of her touch.

Dear God, he'd lost his mind!

Grasping her hand in his, he moved it away. Her simplest gesture had aroused him to a state where he felt he could no longer trust himself. How had it come to this? Sophie Harrington, the daughter of his commanding officer, a woman engaged to another, a hellion in bloomers.

"Did I hurt you?" she whispered.

"I'm sore," he said.

Her troubled gaze met his, pools of ever-changing light and color took him back to balmy days in the Caribbean and filled him with a new warmth that spread through him like a sweet syrup and smoothed the sharp edges of his soul.

Shifting his gaze, Ben ran a hand through his hair. It startled him to think not only that this impertinent female had gotten under his skin, but that she might truly care for him. It could not be. He placed the blame for such mad thoughts on his physical misery.

"I'm sore, I'm itchy all over, but I'm fine."

"You should lie down," she said.

Ben shook his head more vigorously than necessary. "I've ordered a bath and salt."

"I shall bathe you."

"No you won't!"

His outburst obviously startled Sophie. She jumped and her remarkable eyes widened to an extraordinary size. Nevertheless, she bestowed the smile of a saint upon him. "I'll lay cold salt compresses over your rash and—"

"I don't need a nurse!" Ben stood up and strode to the opposite side of the room, which took only four steps. "I am perfectly capable of bathing myself, but I ordered the bath for you. The salt is for me."

Sophie rose. She gazed at him as if he had just slain a dragon for her. "You have defended my honor and ordered me a bath all in the same day? How can I repay you?"

"You could renounce your vow of celibacy."

Damn! Why had he said that?

She colored. Before his eyes, Sophie's complexion changed from cream to crimson. Her eyes blazed. "Just when I think you might be a remarkable man, you reveal yourself to be a rogue!"

With a toss of her head, Sophie turned on her heel and marched to the washbowl stand. "There's water in the basin. I shall bathe your arms now and add salt when it arrives."

The thought of her touching him again made Ben nervous. His needs had been denied too long and were growing stronger by the minute. He wanted Sophie. He wanted her now. And she was the last woman in the world that he could have.

"I'll take care of it myself," he said. Frustration sharpened the edge of his tone "I've always taken care of myself."

"Do you carry a knife?" she asked.

"Yes." He was leery.

"I'd like to borrow it," she said, moving to the rickety table by the bed.

A weapon in the hands of a bloomer girl gave Ben pause. "What for?"

"I wish to shorten my petticoat."

"Now?"

She sighed. "Yes."

Reluctantly, he withdrew the knife from his boot and handed it to her.

"Thank you. Now sit down."

He hiked an eyebrow. "That sounds like an order."

"It is."

Ben sat on the edge of the bed and watched with increasing apprehension. Sophie raised the skirt she wore over her bloomers and proceeded to cut two pieces of her petticoat away, creating bandages of sorts. After submerging the fabric in the water, she brought the bowl and wet bandages to the bedside table.

Tensing his body as if he were preparing for a fight, Ben braced for her touch. But he could do nothing about the hammering of his heart once again.

Sophie rinsed and squeezed the soft linen cloth out and laid it over his right arm. "Does it feel better?"

It itched like hell, but at least now it was a cool itch. "Maybe we should wait until the salt comes."

Ben found it more than a little disconcerting to have Sophie nursing him. But his protest fell on deaf ears.

"No, we have no time to waste. This is the worst case of poison ivy that I have ever seen."

His groan was cut short by a knock on the door.

The barkeeper and customers from the Shady Lane

Inn and Saloon had arrived with a tub and buckets of water. A woman who looked quite as burly as Hank followed with a covered tray. Sophie pulled the basin away to accommodate their dinner.

With thanks for putting Cade in his place, the men filled the copper tub and left.

Ben removed the cover from the tray. Two bowls of steaming thick stew, two mugs of ale, and a sack of salt. He could just imagine the conversation downstairs as to what he and Sophie were going to do with the salt.

Sophie contemplated the tub. "Either our meal or the tub will grow cold."

"Get into the tub while it's still warm. I'll go downstairs."

"If we eat first, then the tub will cool and you can soak in it after I pour the salt."

He did *not* understand women—this one in particular. "I thought you wanted a bath."

"You need it more," she said.

"I beg your pardon?"

She flashed a disarming grin. "For your rash."

In truth, the results of his encounter with the poison ivy gave him more grief than either his aching jaw or swollen eye. At this point Ben would give almost anything for the itching to stop, but not his pride. "I can wait. Let's eat."

"You are the most obstinate man."

This from the most willful of women.

She perched on the edge of the bed, and he pulled up the only chair, one leg being at least two inches shorter than the rest.

Sophie peered inside the mug. "Did you order ale?"

"Have you ever drunk ale before?" Of course she hadn't. He'd ordered without thinking.

"No. I drink milk or tea."

"Then perhaps you shouldn't start with ale now."

Smiling, she held up the mug. "But this is an opportunity to experience something new which I may use in a future novel."

Ben watched with mounting concern as Sophie sipped at the ale.

"I like it," she announced.

He was afraid of that. A small line of foam danced on Sophie's upper lip. First the berries and now the ale had come to rest enticingly on her mouth. If he could only lick away the tiny white bubbles.

"Most women talk of babies, not books," Ben said, lowering his gaze to the stew, a much safer area. He wondered if he should worry that she seemed to be drinking a good deal of ale.

"I am different from most women."

"I'll say." He took the sting out of his comment with an afterthought wink. "It would be a shame if you lived your life only for what you might write about someday."

Sophie cast him a sidelong frown. "I would never do such a thing," she countered coolly before dipping into her stew with the gusto of a boatswain.

After several minutes during which the only sound was that of their spoons scraping the bowls, Sophie paused for another sip of ale . . . and conversation.

Her sea siren eyes locked on his. "Why did you ask for one room?"

Ben put his spoon down. Several silky wisps of Sophie's hair had escaped from the knot at her nape to frame her face. He regarded these wayward strands with undo fascination as he answered her question. "If we were in separate chambers, I couldn't be certain that you'd stay put. I'd hate to wake up in the morning and find you gone."

"You don't trust me," she said flatly.

"No." Ben gave her a rueful half-smile as he reached over and tucked a strand of taffy-colored hair behind her ear.

Inclining her head, she folded her arms and made an astute accusation. "Your Nantucket lady broke your heart and you've never been able to trust a woman since."

"Martha wounded my pride, more than my heart. If I'd really loved her, I would have made her my wife sooner, wouldn't have kept her waiting." Ben would never admit to a broken heart, nor to his seeming inability to trust a woman again.

"Then why won't you trust me?"

"We're after the same thing, you and I, and you're too willing to take crazy risks. If anything happens to you, the admiral will have me bailing bilge water."

"While recovering my journal means everything to me, it means nothing to my father but saving his reputation. And I have not written meanly of him. I have cleverly disguised the admiral within another character."

An overwhelming desire to end her argument took hold of Ben. If he took Sophie into his arms, crushed her against him, lowered his mouth down on hers, and kissed her fiercely . . . she might cease her chatter. She might stop attempting to win his help. She might even stop thinking of her journal for one glorious moment.

Ben warmed to this unique solution. His body warmed. His groin warmed. But to take her would be to lose her. He would lose everything he'd been working toward.

Standing abruptly, he pushed his chair back. "I'm going downstairs to play cards. You'll have plenty of time to take a bath."

"But what about your rash?"

"Playing cards will take my mind off it." He fervently hoped. For a while there, while contemplating showering the beauteous Sophie with his kisses, the constant itch had been forgotten.

He strode to the door.

"Whatever you do, don't scratch," she warned.

"Don't wait up, Buttercup."

Ben had more than a rash to scratch. The pain he experienced had nothing to do with poison ivy and everything to do with self-control.

Damn. Doing the honorable thing sometimes stank.

Moments after Ben left the room, Sophie peeled off her grass-stained bloomers, tossed her tunic aside, and slipped into the tepid tub. Despite her disappointment, a bath had never felt as wonderful as it did in this small room by the light of a flickering lantern. She had hoped Ben would kiss her. She'd been secretly waiting for him to kiss her again—and her desire had nothing to do with her writing. She'd not even thought of describing such a personal sensation in a novel.

But she wondered ever so briefly if Ben was right. Had she fallen in the habit of simply living for what she might write about someday? Sweet mercy!

Slinking deeper into the water, she forced her thoughts to Abigail. Even this poor chamber was better than the shed in which her former maid had been consigned. Sophie worried for her safety. At the same time, a feeling that Abigail had not been completely honest with her niggled at the back of her mind.

She admired the girl's apparent devotion to Fletcher Thurman and her bravery for choosing to have a child, but Sophie suspected that one had everything to do with the other. Perhaps Thurman, the father of her child, had persuaded Abigail to steal Sophie's journal.

What an unlikely plot! Sophie was grasping at straws now.

She'd drunk too much ale, traveled too far and too long over the past two days.

How could she not be exhausted when her emotions seesawed from day to day? If only she could convince Ben to work with her in recovering her novel. Sophie truly disliked being at cross-purposes with a man who took her breath away whenever he entered a room. Such a condition put her at a dreadful disadvantage. She must outwit him, and yet her body conspired against her, coming alive in a most exciting way whenever he came near. Her heart swelled and fluttered like an innocent schoolgirl whenever he slanted his enigmatic grin her way, whenever she met his twinkling deep blue eyes.

Utterly against her will, Ben Swain roused feelings within Sophie that she'd only heard whispered about by Flora. The brazen barmaid had hinted of a woman's need to be filled by a man, just as an empty vessel must be filled with potent ale.

Flora had advised Sophie to beware of a mysterious yearning, a honeyed heat, to heed the insistent need to touch a man, or to be held close to his heart. Sophie had laughed, not believing those feelings possible. Until the arrogant seaman had melted her heart with a rakish wink and a crooked smile.

But if she did not find her journal quickly, she would be married to Captain Ferguson, seeming more than ever a terrible fate.

* * *

Abigail folded laundry with her mother by lantern light. She felt so weary she feared her bones might break. But her mind was not on her monotonous work; her thoughts were elsewhere, with Fletcher. In all probability he had reached Annapolis by now. Soon Admiral Harrington would receive the message she had written demanding payment for the return of Sophie's journal. Instead of feeling excitement or relief that her ordeal was about to end, Abigail felt sad and burdened.

Miss Harrington had been all kindness to her. Even today, despite the obvious fact that Abigail had conceived a child out of wedlock, Sophie had offered to take her back to Dulany House. Certainly the admiral's daughter would forgive her if she knew Abigail had no choice. Fletcher had refused to marry Abigail unless she agreed to his scheme. Her mistake had been in telling him about the journal in the first place. She'd found it one day in the midst of cleaning Sophie's armoire. Although Abigail had only read a few pages of *The Romantic Adventures of Fifi LaDeux, An Unmarried Woman*, she had been both shocked and amused. Weeks later, after an evening of drinking forbidden whiskey with Fletcher, Abigail had confided Sophie's secret. In a bout of giggles, she'd described the contents.

"Where's yer boyfriend?" her mother asked.

Abigail put her regrets aside to answer. "Fletcher is out of town doing business."

"Some no good business, likely."

Her mother never made an effort to conceal her dislike of Fletcher.

"You'll see," Abigail told her. "When he comes back, we'll be getting married."

"How many poor girls have heard that story when their man runs out on them?"

"Fletcher has not run out on me," Abigail insisted. "He's coming back with the money to buy us a little house."

Her mother snorted. "Mark my words, if Fletcher Thurman gets a hold of any money, he ain't comin' back, dearie."

Abigail regarded her mother. Aged and worn before her time, the older woman's leathered face and flat eyes reflected ingrained stoicism. Never smiling, she exuded a weariness beyond this world and a cynicism too bitter to swallow. But she was wrong about Fletcher. He'd never take the money and run off, leaving Abigail behind. No. Never.

Just the same, Abigail knew a moment of doubt and, with it, the truth. She could not completely trust Fletcher.

Twelve

Ben played cards for as long as he could keep his eyes open. He asked questions and got some answers during a lengthy but friendly game of poker. When no one was looking, he rubbed his arms, which was not the same thing as scratching. In case Sophie asked later.

By midnight, he expected Sophie to be asleep and he could get some rest as well. He said good night, pocketed his winnings, and climbed the stairs.

A dim, wavering light shone from the crack beneath the door.

Damn it. Hoping that Sophie had fallen asleep with the lantern lit for him, he quietly entered the room. After closing the door behind him, he looked up.

She sat on the bed. Writing!

"Ben!" She cast a dazzling smile his way. He couldn't be certain if it was a smile of relief or happiness. He only knew in the light of her smile that the edge of his annoyance evaporated.

"What's that?" he asked, pointing to the brown leather-bound journal resting on her lap.

"I was worried about you," she answered, ignoring his question.

"Is that what I think it is?"

"'Tis a journal," Sophie replied blithely.

"What are you doing?"

"I am writing, of course. I always carry a pencil and journal with me."

Ben threw up his hands. "Haven't you learned anything?"

"Yes. Yes, I have." Sophie straightened, sitting as prim and proper as a Sunday school teacher. "And I'm certain you will find peace of mind knowing that I am changing the names as I write and disguising my characters very well. None resemble anyone I know."

As long as none resembled him. But how could he be sure?

Gleaming waves of sun-streaked hair fell to her shoulders. Her skin glowed pink and white in the lantern light; her lips glistened moist and rosy. In contrast to the hellion he knew her to be, Sophie appeared all propriety, a sweet, demure innocent.

She'd dressed following her bath and once again wore her lace-trimmed bloomers. But apparently with a nod to comfort over modesty, she'd left the pearl buttons of her brocade tunic undone. Ben caught a glimpse of her ivory linen chemise beneath the narrow opening. He wondered if Sophie knew what an alluring picture she presented. He wondered if she had purposefully set out to distract him. If so, she had succeeded. After he'd finally cooled down.

"I believe my second novel will be even better than the first," she said with the confidence of Charlotte Brontë.

Her tendency to exaggerate could turn Walden Pond into the Pacific Ocean. "Let me see that."

"No!" Jumping up from the bed, Sophie held the journal behind her back. Her eyes gleamed defiantly.

Did she believe for one minute that she could keep

the journal from him? Ben could wrest it from her before the minx could blink an eye.

"Hand it over."

"It is not yet in a state for others to read."

"Sophie, it's been a long day. I have a swollen eye, a bruised jaw, and arms that itch like the devil. I've run out of patience. Just give me the damn journal."

"No."

The witch! A smile played at the corner of her lips.

As Ben started toward her with every intention of seizing the journal, Sophie dashed to the other side of the room.

"Do you think you can escape from me in this small room?" he demanded.

She inclined her head as if she were thinking about his question. And then she gave him a saucy smile. "Perhaps."

No midshipman had ever tried his patience more than Sophie Harrington. Ben's muscles tightened. His stomach, his arms, his shoulders grew taut as his trained body prepared for battle. He extended his hand once more. "Sophie. Give me the journal."

Her eyes sparkled mischievously as she shook her head.

Clamping his jaw and narrowing his eyes, Ben took a step toward her.

With hummingbird swiftness, Sophie sidestepped, eluding his grasp.

To Ben's horror, she then dove under the bed.

He got down on his knees.

"Sophie, come out." He ground the words between his teeth.

"Come and get me."

She knew very well that he was too big to crawl beneath the bed after her.

"I am not in the habit of playing these games."

"You have missed great fun while you have been busy sailing and whaling."

Sophie's idea of great fun did not come close to his. "Come out."

She sneezed. "It's dusty."

Ben could see the shape of her in the dark. He reached an arm toward her. She wiggled out of his reach. Cursing beneath his breath, he stood and pushed the bed against the wall to ensure that Sophie had only one way to escape.

"No fair," she called.

"What do you know about fair?" he muttered. Ben fell to the floor again and flattened himself as much as possible. He then wedged himself underneath the bed as far as he could. Grasping what he believed, what he hoped, to be her arm, Ben dragged a laughing Sophie out from under the bed to his side.

Laughing!

She did not fight him even when half of his considerable weight lay atop half of her. She laughed softly, a sound like a low sweet bell echoing in a meadow.

Ben raised himself up and looked down upon Sophie. Her tunic had fallen open, revealing the delicate rise of creamy breasts beneath her fine linen chemise. His breath caught in his throat.

Sophie looked up into his eyes and his soul fell into the beckoning depths of aquamarine. Like a beautiful mirage, she lured his heart to rocky shores.

Ben doubted he could save himself. He was overpowered by the intense heat that curled through him, immobilized by a deep, demanding desire unlike any he had ever known. His aching manhood insisted on relief.

But this was Sophie, for God's sake! Off limits.

Sophie Harrington stirred these fiery feelings within him. Feelings he could not act upon—unless he was ready to die. The admiral would kill him. Ben would be returning to Nantucket in a wooden box, buck naked. No uniform, no naval burial at sea.

A slow smile spread across his temptress's lips to deepen the dimple he could not resist. Ben wanted her. He wanted to taste her lips, savor the exquisite hollow of her throat. He longed to dip his tongue into the exquisite valley of her cleavage. He drew a ragged breath.

"Have I managed to make you forget your poison ivy?" she asked with the softest of smiles.

Poison ivy?

"Has the itching subsided?"

Itching? Nothing itched. Everything ached.

"Perhaps if you take a bath, you'll feel better. I left the water and added a heaping measure of salt."

Only an ice bath would make Ben feel better. "Take a bath with you in the room?"

"I shall close my eyes and go to sleep."

He rolled over and pushed to his feet. In the future he would keep his distance from Sophie. If he touched her, he burned. He'd learned that lesson more than once tonight. For the present, she could keep her journal.

"No, no bath." Sharing the same room put them in a compromising position. Ben refused to make matters worse no matter how much he itched or ached. "Your father would have me sent to the Arctic in a rowboat if he ever found out."

"You will find a bath soothing and my father will never know," she said while buttoning her tunic, too late reclaiming her modesty.

The admiral will never know? If only Ben could be certain.

He helped Sophie up from the floor. She immediately crawled into the bed, her journal held snugly against her breast.

"Turn down the lantern."

She did as he requested.

The tub stood in a dark corner.

Ben took pride in his body; nature had blessed him. Compared to most men, he possessed an admirable physique. But Sophie had no business being in the same room with a naked man.

With a glance to make certain her eyes were shut, Ben quickly undressed and hopped into the tub. Even the cool used water felt good. Too large for the old tin tub, he folded his knees before him and the water barely covered his waist. But just as Sophie had predicted, the water proved a soothing balm to his arms. After a half-day riding on horseback, hiding in poison ivy, fighting a drunken boy, and playing too many hands of poker, he needed a bath.

"What were you doing while you were away?" Sophie asked.

The whisper in the darkness jarred Ben. He stiffened and issued a warning. "Sophie, you promised to sleep."

"I feared something had happened to you. That you might have gotten yourself into another barroom brawl."

"I don't brawl."

"Were you playing darts?" she asked.

"I played poker."

The lantern flickered on.

Ben scrunched down as far as he could in the water. "Did you win?"

"A few dollars," he grumbled. "Are your eyes closed?"

"No, but I can hardly see you at all. You're bathing in the dark. I never would have guessed you to be so shy."

"I'm thinking of you."

"Protecting me again?"

"Yes."

Ben lowered his gaze to the scented soap he rubbed to a lather against his chest and belly. Damn. He was going to smell just like a rose. Just like a woman. "I learned a few things while I was playing cards."

"Like what?"

He caught a movement from the corner of his eye. Sophie had sat up in the bed. "Don't move," he warned.

"Like what?" she repeated.

"Abigail's boyfriend Fletcher Thurman is a no-good. Seems he doesn't take to work and he's earned a reputation for shady dealings."

"Do you think he forced Abigail to take my journal?"

"He might have."

Sophie threw the light blanket back and slipped out of bed.

Ben stiffened in the water. "Where are you going?"

"It's difficult to hold a conversation from the far side of the room," she said, approaching the tub. "I'm just coming closer."

"You're close enough."

She stopped. A smile hovered on her lips.

That smile worried him. Confused him. If he didn't know better, he'd think she teased him. But a woman who intended to remain as chaste and pure as new-fallen snow didn't play with a man's needs. Ben shored up his resolve. If he didn't want to be drummed out of the Navy, he sure as hell better protect Sophie's virginity.

Seemed a damned shame though. She was made for love. He'd seen actresses on the stage that Sophie would put to shame. Constructed with the sleek lines of a swift sailing ship, her willowy curves, tiny waist, and full, proud breasts promised a man pleasure. But could she ever treasure a mere mortal man more than her independence? Ben doubted it.

"Are we going to see Fletcher Thurman tomorrow before we return to Rosalind's?" she asked.

"I have no idea what you're going to do. I only know what *I'm* going to do." The soap slid out of his hand. As he began a search for it in the dim light, he felt the slippery bar lodge by his butt. He managed to grasp it, but when he looked up again, Sophie stood a foot away from the tub.

"What are you doing?" he growled.

She inclined her head. "You have a beautiful body."

He locked his knees together. "Get back to bed."

"Do you know how many portraits there are of naked women, and how few of naked men?" she asked in a trance-like tone.

"What does that have to do with me?"

"A girl must educate herself where and when she can."

"Your curiosity will get you killed one day, Sophie. I swear if you do not go back—"

"What will you do, jump from the tub and drag me away?" She burst out into peals of laughter, infectious laughter that caught Ben up and forced him to smile.

He gave in to the laughter and the merry light shining in her eyes. How did a man defend himself from the likes of Sophie Harrington? He would suggest her as the next secret weapon of the United States Navy.

"Please return to the bed and I'll get out of here." Before it was too late. He wouldn't put it past her to jump in the tub with him.

But her gaze fixed on his chest. Her tone softened to a somber note. "Where did you . . . how did you get those scars?"

He lowered his eyes. Although Ben seldom gave it a thought, he knew to someone seeing his bare chest for the first time, the raised, jagged scar tissue presented an ugly sight.

"Got in the way of a harpoon," he replied shortly, dismissing the disfiguring scar that ran diagonally across his chest.

"From the looks of it, you are fortunate to be alive."

He reached for the towel. "I was in the wrong place at the wrong time with a new kid holding the harpoon." Ben had little doubt that he'd repulsed Sophie. She shouldn't have come to inspect him as if he were a side of beef at the market.

"I'm glad you were not killed," she said softly.

"Thanks, so am I."

"And I'm glad you joined the Navy instead of remaining a whaler. I'm happy that you were assigned to the Naval Academy."

"It's good that one of us is happy about that," he said, refusing to look at her, fearing he might see pity reflected in her eyes.

"If not, I would not have met you nor known you. And I am very glad to know you, Seaman Swain."

Ben could not help respond to Sophie's serious tone. He looked across the small space that separated them. She stood in the shadows regarding him with an unwavering gaze of admiration. All at once he felt at a loss, confused. He grabbed the towel, and with his gaze locked on hers, he rose out of the water.

"And I am glad to know you, Sophie Harrington . . . novelist."

The room dipped into a silence so profound, Ben could hear his heart beat. Unable to move, he stood dripping in the tub like some daft old man. Only a towel covered him from midchest to barely below his privates.

Sophie whirled on her bare feet and padded back to the bed. Without another word, she lowered the lantern, throwing the room into darkness. "I shall say my prayers now."

And Ben would say his. He would pray that, after spending this day and night with Sophie Harrington, he would not be thrown to the sharks by Admiral Harrington. He'd bathed in the same room with her, washed in the same water. Tonight he would be sharing the same chamber with her, a chamber above a saloon.

He'd be lucky to get off with fifty lashes.

Once dressed, Ben spread his bedroll on the floor beside the tub. He'd said he was glad to know her. And it was true. As infuriating as she might be, Sophie kept Ben alert. He never knew what she might do next. Dreaded what she might do next, and was curious about what she might do next.

In Sophie's company he felt like the lookout on a great frigate, always searching for the rocks and shoals that could mean disaster. Ben wondered how Andrew Ferguson intended to tame her spirit. The captain wasn't the type to be seen with a wife wearing bloomers and spouting the outrageous beliefs of Margaret Fuller, Lucretia Mott, and their ilk.

Ben had no doubt that the admiral's cohort meant to mold Sophie into a less formidable force. A docile woman. Unless by some miracle the dimpled hussy found her novel before Ben did and actually sold *The Romantic Adventures of Fifi LaDeux*. It was the only way Ben figured that Sophie could remain the free, unpredictable spirit—that enjoyed taunting him.

Andrew Ferguson would then lose his politically important bride.

"I don't think we should mention to my father how we spent this night," Sophie whispered in the dark.

Not mention that they slept in the same chamber, Ben thought, not mention that he lay in the dark wanting Sophie with the searing desire of a starving man craving a scrap of bread.

"I think you're right," he said.

On the theory that out of sight might indeed be out of mind, Ben rolled over. He would spend the night pretending she wasn't there.

Early the following morning Sophie rode with Ben back to Abigail Grant's for another visit. When Ben had pulled her from beneath the bed the night before, when his heart was inches from hers, the roaring in her blood caught her by surprise. She'd only meant to have fun with him. Yet his closeness created an anticipation, an excitement, she could not fathom. Her pulse raced, as if she had run to the top of the highest mountain. Her body felt flushed, as if she crossed a desert on a hot summer day. Sensations she had never experienced before ricocheted through her.

When she'd seen him bare-chested in the tub, his male magnificence weakened her knees. Ben's scarred chest, broad and muscular, was the most beautiful sight she'd seen outside illustrations of sculpted forms created by the masters. Her heart fluttered so that she had barely been able to catch her breath.

Sophie did not know what to think, only that she must be wary.

Ever since Ben brought her cocoa at dawn this morning, Sophie had moved carefully about the seaman.

"Sophie, you'll stay outside. This time I'm questioning Abigail by myself," he said as they approached the Grants' humble dwelling.

"Do you think you shall learn something I did not?"

"Yes."

His confidence maddened her. "Why may I not be present when you question Abigail? Give me one good reason."

"Was I present yesterday, when you quizzed her?"

"No," she acknowledged. "Still, I think we will learn more by working together."

A knock on the door brought no response. Ben strode to the back, followed closely by Sophie.

Mrs. Grant worked at the giant vat, washing clothes on the scrub board. Her knuckles were scraped and raw.

Ben approached her with his disarming grin at full force. "Good morning, Mrs. Grant."

She eyed him skeptically. "Mornin'."

"I've come to see your daughter."

"Abigail ain't here."

"Do you know where I might find her?"

"Nope. Ran away. Gone after that no-good Fletcher Thurman, I expect."

Sophie came up to Ben's side. "Do you know where Fletcher has gone?"

Abigail's mother scowled, creating a rather disagreeable expression. "No, and I don't care neither. Promised he'd bring her money. Promised he'd buy her a house and marry my girl. Blowin' smoke in the wind and Abigail so stupid she believed him."

"Abigail's not stupid," Sophie shot back.

"And what kind of lady are you?" the worn and bloodied woman demanded. "Where's your chaperon?"

"I do not require a chaperon," Sophie replied, angling her chin. "I am an independent woman."

"Ha!" Abigail's mother threw her head back, matted tendrils of stone gray hair falling across her eyes. She did not brush the strands away as she narrowed her gaze on Sophie. "No, Miss Harrington, you ain't. Take a look at me and you'll see an independent woman. Look at me real close like. Ain't had no man to support me nor my babe, never. He died before Abigail was born."

The knot in Sophie's throat felt as big as a boot. She did not dream of the type of independence the washerwoman knew, had never considered such a life.

"Admiral Harrington has assigned me to protect Miss Harrington on this visit," Ben informed Mrs. Grant. "In effect, I'm her chaperon."

Abigail's mother brushed the damp, stringy hair out of her eyes with the back of her hand. "And who will protect the young lady from you?"

Ben reacted with a frown and a prolonged clearing of his throat—unnecessary, Sophie suspected. "You may be assured that Sophie Harrington is safe with me."

The independent Mrs. Grant did not appear impressed with Ben's assurance.

"Do you have no idea where Fletcher or your daughter might be?" Sophie inquired once more.

"No, and good riddance to them."

Ben's expression remained pleasant as he took leave of Abigail's bitter mother. "Thank you for your help, Mrs. Grant. Good day."

Giving the washerwoman a small salute, he turned and left the yard.

Sophie hurried to catch up with him. "What are we going to do now?"

"Why do you keep using the term 'we'?" he asked without stopping. "You and I are not in league together."

"We are both after the same item."

"For different reasons. I am buying my freedom, not yours. Try to remember that."

"Which is an extremely selfish stand to take," she snipped. Would she never convince him to help her?

"It's for your own good, Sophie. With a wealthy husband, you will lead a secure life. You can shop until your armoire overflows."

"Do you think me so shallow that I care only to shop? I'd hoped you were different than the rest. I'd thought you were more farsighted, more sensitive."

"Now you know the truth. I'm just a man."

"What are you going to do?" she repeated as he unhitched their horses.

"I am preparing to leave Falls Church," he said.

"Then I shall ride with you and return to Georgetown," Sophie said as if she had a choice. "Rosalind will help me think what to do next. She is a true friend."

Ben helped her into the saddle. His crooked smile mocked her determination, made her heart sing.

In that moment, Sophie realized that she needed Ben Swain. She needed him far more than he needed her.

Thirteen

"Where have you been?" demanded a plainly beleaguered Rosalind. "I have been utterly distraught!"

Sophie's hostess ran to greet her as she entered the vast marble foyer of the Montrose estate. Weary and a trifle irritable, Sophie had no wish to explain her prolonged absence. Her heart's desire at the moment included a hot bath and a long nap on a thick, downy featherbed.

"I do apologize, Rosalind. I did not mean to cause you concern."

"It is no wonder your father insists that Seaman Swain stand guard over you!"

"Please forgive me," Sophie implored, grasping her friend's hands. Rosalind's hands felt uncomfortably cold and bony. "My intentions were to return yesterday but I encountered an unavoidable delay. You know I would never purposefully do anything to alarm you."

"You never have before." Rosalind lowered her eyes and withdrew her hands from Sophie's grasp. "But I failed you."

"Whatever do you mean?"

"Although I did my best to make him stay, the seaman set off after you immediately."

"He found me."

"Will you forgive me? I so wanted him to stay."

Sophie smiled at her friend. "Of course you are forgiven."

"He did not harm you in any way, did he?"

"Don't be silly. Ben would never hurt me."

Rosalind's heavy brows turned down in a frown. "Ben?"

"Seaman Swain," Sophie quickly corrected herself.

"I thought you were attempting to escape from him."

"As it happened, he proved helpful."

He had fought off the minister's son at the Shady Lane Inn, and gleaned enough information to draw certain conclusions concerning the whereabouts of her novel. Sophie might not have made the same deductions, but recognized the value of his. Ben possessed a keen intelligence.

Nevertheless, on the ride from Falls Church to Georgetown, he had been exceedingly quiet. As had Sophie. They'd reached an impasse and the tension rose between them like a mile-high wall of ice. She had no doubt Ben's thoughts were on finding Fletcher Thurman, just as hers were.

"I am relieved to hear Seaman Swain's company did not interfere with your search." Rosalind smiled faintly as she added with a palm's-up shrug, "All's well that ends well."

"I've heard that said."

"Did you find your maid?" Rosalind stepped closer, lowering her voice to a barely audible degree. "Did Abigail have your journal? Was she indeed the thief?"

Sophie had told Rosalind her journal was missing, but not that it contained a novel. In her present state she could not risk being ridiculed by her friend. She'd told Rosalind that the journal contained her very private thoughts, and knowing they would be read by another would give her much distress.

"Abigail denied knowing anything about the disappearance of my journal," Sophie replied. Which was true enough.

"Then you were off on a wild-goose chase!"

"No, I eliminated Abigail as a suspect."

Rosalind stepped back. Inclining her head, she folded her hands and launched into a scold of sorts. "Well, if you had missed the masquerade, I would have never forgiven you, Sophie."

"Masquerade?"

"Yes, tonight," she affirmed with a wide grin. Rosalind appeared quite delighted with herself. The twin raven sausage curls swept to the side of her head bounced with what seemed their own enthusiasm. "Masquerades have become all the rage again in Georgetown."

"Truly?" Nonplussed, Sophie could think of nothing else to say. She would rather wash clothes for Mrs. Grant than attend a party this evening.

"It's a hasty gathering I planned as soon as I knew you were coming," Rosalind explained. "I extended invitations to all of my acquaintances, but as I am certain you will understand, with such short notice, not everyone could come."

The promise of sleep in a soft bed had been all that had kept Sophie upright in the saddle on the return trip from Falls Church. The idea of getting a good night's rest and returning to Annapolis at dawn tomorrow had been uppermost in her mind. Continuing the search for her novel was all that mattered. She was running out of time. If she did not find Fletcher Thurman and Abigail before Ben, and recover her novel, her dream would end.

"Rosalind, you are so dear and thoughtful, but I have no costume. I fear I shall be unable to attend."

Rosalind beamed, baring the slight gap between her two front teeth. "I have the perfect costume for you. It is one that I wore to a gala several months ago. You'll find it awaiting in your chamber."

Sophie's first instinct was to burst into tears. Instead, she forced a smile. "You have thought of everything. I do not know what to say."

"You do not need to say anything, but I would like you to see to it that Seaman Swain attends the masquerade as well. I have provided him with a costume."

"Do not worry yourself on that account," Sophie sighed. "Anywhere I go, the seaman goes. In Benjamin Swain, my father has provided a watchdog for me to make certain I do nothing to mortify him."

"If I were you, I would not complain to have such a handsome watchdog."

"Ben Swain is an arrogant man."

"Broad-shouldered and tall," Rosalind countered.

Flicking her wrist, Sophie gave a puff of impatience. "He believes himself to be the cleverest of men."

"Are his eyes blue or black?"

Ben's eyes were blue. Sapphire blue eyes that twinkled and teased and seduced all in one glance. How could any woman not notice, not know, or ever forget that Ben's eyes were blue?

"Rosalind, all you need do to ensure his presence is tell the seaman that I shall be attending your masquerade."

"I shall." Her gray eyes sparkled as Rosalind clapped her hands together in obvious delight. "I cannot wait. We shall have such fun this eve."

Sophie dragged herself to her bedchamber, where Flora waited to help her bathe and dress.

"Did ye find Abigail?" she asked.

"Yes, but she denied taking my journal. And when we went back to question her, she'd disappeared."

"'We' must mean that Ben Swain caught up with you. Flora thought as much. You're the only woman who could sound upset for having that good-lookin' sailor serve as her escort," Flora chided.

"I wasn't upset all of the time," Sophie admitted softly.

She finished her bath somewhat refreshed, but too soon, she stood in front of the looking glass while Flora draped and redraped the toga-style costume bestowed by Rosalind. At last, the tavern maid stepped back to assess her work.

"The gown becomes ye," she pronounced.

"I suppose," Sophie agreed, glancing briefly at the looking glass. "But I truly am not looking forward to a masquerade."

"When you hear the music, you'll forget your problem . . . which in Flora's humble opinion ye need to do. You've become much too wretched."

"You'd be wretched too if your novel were missing and Ben Swain raced you to recover it."

Flora threw her head back and laughed. "What did ye write about him?"

"Never you mind. Only a paragraph or two."

"Wicked paragraphs?" Flora teased. Her green eyes twinkled with amusement.

"How can you laugh when a whole lifetime is at stake?" Sophie demanded. "My lifetime. Instead of dancing, I should rest and think and plan."

"Be careful," Flora warned, wagging a finger. "For what you're plannin'. I'll tell you quite frankly, bein' an independent woman myself, 'tis not always a happy life."

"I shall make my life happy," Sophie vowed stubbornly.

"Starting tomorrow. Tonight Flora's thinking you'll be the belle of the masquerade. Rosalind has lent you a dress that will turn all eyes your way."

Sophie shook her head, but slowly, careful not to dislodge even one curl of Flora's handiwork. "I do not care to be a belle. I had not counted on being entertained on a grand scale."

"Rosalind told her maid, who told me, that she expected an invitation to Dulany House soon. There's a lot of gossip goin' on in the kitchen," she added in a disapproving aside. "Your school chum is under the impression that you'll reciprocate in every way for her hospitality. Once in Annapolis, Rosalind Montrose plans to find a handsome naval officer like Ben Swain to marry her."

"But Ben is not an officer."

"Miss Montrose is eager to start a family according to Mary Jane—her maid."

"Of course I shall invite Rosalind to Annapolis, but I do not believe Ben is attracted to her, do you?"

"No. Ben Swain needs a woman, not a girl. A simpering miss will not keep the seaman's interest for long."

Sophie had to bite her tongue in order not to ask Flora what she knew about Ben's women. Strumpets regularly frequented Reynolds Tavern, and she'd seen the longing glances Ben received from the town girls as he strode down the street.

Did he favor tall girls or petite young women? Did he seem partial to any woman in particular? If anyone knew, it would be Flora. But Sophie couldn't ask her without appearing personally interested in Ben's affairs.

"I wish you could attend the masquerade," she said, taking one last glance in the looking glass. Could she be mistaken for a simpering miss? Not likely!

"Flora needs her sleep."

"Did you pass a sleepless night?" Sophie asked. "Were you that worried about me?"

"Indeed, Flora was worried about you, but Graham and me spent the night in the gazebo down by the lake."

"What were you doing in the gazebo?" Sophie asked offhandedly.

"What do ye think?"

"Are you not afraid that . . . that you might find yourself in a delicate condition?"

"Flora has told you there are measures to prevent such problems."

The measures Flora spoke of must work or else the tavern maid would have begot a dozen or more children by now.

"But I wouldn't mind havin' Graham's child."

"You wouldn't?"

With a sly, almost shy smile, Flora shook her head.

The tavern maid wished to have a babe! Abigail would soon give birth and Rosalind had expressed the desire to conceive children, preferably by Ben. It seemed the women Sophie knew most intimately were not afraid to make love with a man. Neither did they fear bearing children. But then, they did not share her family history.

Reluctantly, Sophie made her way down the corridor toward the music and laughter. At least Ben would also be in attendance. He would not be in his chamber laying plans to capture Fletcher Thurman. She might even be able to play a bit of fun with the heart-melting seaman.

"Do not forget your domino!" Flora called. The red-haired tavern maid dashed after Sophie waving a sizable plumed and beaded mask.

"Oh, thank you!" Sophie could not hope for a successful hoax without her mask.

"Now then, you are properly disguised. Not a soul will know you."

"There will only be two present who might. Rosalind and . . . Ben Swain?"

"He will never guess."

"Rosalind shall recognize her gown."

Flora grinned. "But she never looked so beautiful in it."

After bidding her friend good night, Sophie positioned her domino and made her way down the stairs. Tangled with her desire to make the evening memorable, she felt a down-deep restlessness, a need for something she couldn't define. And she felt a bit reckless as well.

The spacious music room overlooking the gardens had become a sparkling ballroom. Sophie glided toward a long lace-covered table laden with punch and small cakes. Behind the table she could observe from the shadows.

Musicians dressed in bright crimson and peacock blue livery played from a raised platform at the far end of the room. A glittering combination of gas lighting and wax tapers shed a golden glow on the costumed dancers as they whirled about the floor in spirited three-quarter time.

Ben hovered on the rear edge of the crowd, hoping to go unnoticed. He felt like a fool in the costume provided for him, a monk's robe. The occupation and nature of a monk were in stark contrast to Ben's life. He would not be surprised to learn he committed blasphemy simply by wearing the garment. But the loose-fitting robe proved comfortable. In the dark, mud brown hooded robe and mask, he presented a rather ominous figure—which suited him just fine.

If he had not been forced to attend to keep watch over Sophie, he would be in his chamber asleep. But Ben could not trust Sophie. Impulsive as she was, it would be just like her to leave in the dark of night to get a head start in the search for Fletcher and Abigail. And that would be dangerous.

Rosalind, dressed as Marie Antoinette in a low-cut brocade gown that revealed most of her ample breasts, fluttered about him like a wounded butterfly. She'd brought Ben one crystal goblet of champagne after another. He feared he might be three sheets to the wind by the time Sophie made her appearance. Finding himself in an inebriated state might make recognizing the admiral's daring daughter difficult no matter what costume their hostess had provided for her.

Ben danced with Rosalind while keeping an eye out for Sophie. Their dark-haired hostess chatted incessantly, mostly about her own attributes. But while dancing with Sophie's schoolmate, another beauty caught his eye. A woman dressed as a French maid flirted openly with him from across the hall.

He began to feel the carefree spirit of the affair. Emboldened by champagne, he was seized by the brash liberated feeling of being in port after a long stretch at sea. Ben had enjoyed many a lark in those whaling and early naval days, amusing himself with easy women, alcohol, and rowdy games of darts. A rollicking life of laughter and revelry had been his.

After returning Rosalind to her mother's side, he prepared to ask the French maid to dance. He needed a woman. Especially after he'd been confined last night in the same room with Sophie, listening to her soft breathing, suppressing his manly needs.

Removing a goblet of champagne from the tray of a passing servant, Ben stepped to the refreshment table to grab a sweet before approaching the alluring French maid. As he contemplated an almond cake, a flash of light caught his eye. He looked up.

Diana, the goddess of love, sipped champagne in what might be the only dark corner in the room. She offered him the smallest of smiles, a slight parting of moist lips.

His gaze drifted from the goddess's inviting mouth to the long, graceful column of her neck. This, too, Ben found inviting. He imagined his lips settling in the sensitive hollow at its base for a lingering caress. He moved closer to the goddess.

"Good evening," he said, startled to hear an unfamiliar huskiness in his voice.

She dipped her head in demure acknowledgment. But there was nothing demure about her appearance.

She wore the toga fashion favored by Greek legendary figures in all the paintings Ben had ever seen. The clinging, snowy white fabric was draped over one shoulder, leaving the other exposed. His gaze lingered on the bare, silky shoulder inviting his kiss. Lowering his focus ever so slightly brought the creamy swell of the goddess's breasts into view. Narrow ribbons of faint blue veins made tantalizing paths beneath her silky, translucent flesh.

Ben's gaze swept the length of her in rapt admiration. His palms ached to skim her soft rounded hips, press her trim sensual body against his. His perusal drifted farther down to the teasing slit in her toga. A slight movement exposed long legs and shapely calves. Ben trembled like a boy about to hoist sail for the first time.

Not a man at the masquerade could resist this heavenly goddess. Not a man in the room would hesitate to give his wealth away to know her identity.

"May I have this dance?" he asked. He hated to dance but it seemed the swiftest way to get her into his arms.

She dipped her head in acquiescence.

Her silk-beaded domino with pearly egret plumes covered most of the goddess's face, except for her lips. Those lips. No, it couldn't be. He prayed it was not . . . Sophie.

He would know in a moment. Ben gathered her into his arms, holding her closer than he should. But she did not protest or step back. She floated in his arms like an ethereal creature as they danced in the dark corner.

"May I ask your name?" he asked.

"Diana," she whispered.

A whisper! If Ben could see her eyes, he would know for certain if the goddess was Sophie. He stepped back. She lowered her head.

"Diana, the goddess of love." He murmured the words, taking her to his heart again, lost in the warmth of her and the smoldering fire burning deep within him.

He'd been aching for a woman. And the woman in his arms could not be more desirable unless the genuine goddess of love had descended in the flesh.

"Have you been to the gazebo, Brother?"

Was she asking him to leave the dance floor? Ben could not believe his good fortune. "No, no I haven't. Would you show me the way?"

"Come." The goddess turned away. Her hips swayed softly as she led the way into the garden.

Without a moment's hesitation, Ben followed the

enchantress out into the garden. Did honeysuckle grow in the Montrose garden? Or did the perfume cling to the lovely leading him into temptation?

Dear God, Sophie!

No, she could not be Sophie. He knew honeysuckle to be a common fragrance. If only he could see her eyes, see her full smile, then he would know for certain. Ben could not bear it if this lithesome temptress turned out to be Sophie and therefore untouchable to him. On the other hand, if it was she, he must know what game she played. Did she mean to seduce him? Was she again using him for the sake of her writing, in the name of research?

He bristled at the idea. Such an escapade would be in keeping with her tricks. The goddess of love? The goddess of mischief was more like it!

Sophie would learn a valuable lesson tonight. Ben would allow her to believe that he thought her to be a beautiful stranger. He would make love to her, take her to the edge of bliss and then come to a halt. And then he would leave her to contemplate the dangerous game she played.

Not many masqueraders dallied in the crisp evening air. A scattering of torches set along the garden paths and a bright crescent moon provided the only light. The Goddess Diana pulled him through an opening in the hedges. She led him from a stylish garden into a field of wildflowers and long grass.

Seducing a woman was like matching wits with the wind. Ben hoped he mistook the matter, hoped the mythical beauty who hurried ahead of him into the dark night was not Sophie Harrington. With any other woman, he could ease the ache in his loins and the hollow in his heart tonight.

The bright white octagonal gazebo stood out in the

darkness. Moonbeams glistened on the small pond beside the domed structure.

Sophie's heart hammered a bit wildly as she pulled a willing Ben to the gazebo and up the steps. Plump down cushions softened the benches, and roses blossomed along the lattice of one wall. The scent of roses sweet and strong perfumed the air. Ben tugged at her hand and pulled her to a stop in the center of the gazebo. Sophie turned to him.

"Who are you?" he asked in a soft, deep timbre.

"Tonight it is not important who I am . . . or who you are," she whispered softly, attempting to disguise her voice.

Sophie's father would be furious if he knew she planned to seduce a mere seaman. And Ben would never knowingly risk the admiral's wrath.

"Is it you, Sophie?" Ben asked the question quietly, without emotion.

"I am the goddess of love."

"It *is* you. I feared as much."

"Diana is my name."

"What do you want from me?" he asked.

"I want you to make love to me," she replied without thinking. *Sweet mercy! It was true.*

The jest she had thought to play on him was on her.

Ben did not reply. He stood as still and quiet as a hand on a broken clock.

"Do you not wish to make love to me?"

"I do not wish to be your tool."

Sophie understood his concern. In a more direct effort to persuade the seaman and ease his fear, she rose on tiptoe and kissed him lightly on the cheek.

"You smell as sweet as honeysuckle," he said, yet unmoving, perhaps unmoved.

"'Tis a common fragrance."

She tugged at the rope around his robe.

"Someone will come and find us here," he protested.

"Where is your courage? Have you never made love in the open beneath a spring moon with the scent of roses filling the air?"

If he did not find his courage soon, Sophie would lose hers. She was uncertain how to begin and Ben continued to balk. From the moment she had first seen him tonight dancing with Rosalind, she longed to be in his arms. She yearned to feel his lips upon hers. Sophie knew what she wanted, knew the source of her discontent and restlessness.

These unfamiliar needs had been growing within her for days. Last night when she and Ben had rolled on the floor in the chamber above the saloon, when they lay together with just a breath between them, her heart had been lost. Lost for the moment or forever, Sophie could not be certain. Tonight she might learn the truth.

For who was better than Ben to initiate her in the ways of love? He'd been almost her constant companion since that first day at the dock. The man who had saved her from drowning, held her during the storm, defended her honor in a barroom brawl.

She loved the way his eyes crinkled at the corners when he laughed. She looked forward to seeing his cocky swagger across the room. When his mouth curled up in a lopsided smile, her insides melted like honey in hot tea. Even the scars on his massive chest, stark reminders of battles lost, drew her to him.

Sophie felt quite light-headed. Shamelessly, for just this one night she sought to make Ben's warrior strength, his bruising kiss and breathtaking virility, hers. Her heart beat furiously as she stood before the dark, dangerous-looking man wearing a monk's hooded robe. Waiting.

"No, I have never made love beneath a spring moon," he said at last, his voice thick and uneven. "I have never made love with a woman such as you."

Before Sophie could respond, one of Ben's large warm hands cupped the back of her head, the other framed her face. Her domino slid away as he brought his mouth down on hers.

His lips, hot, wet, and demanding, took hers fiercely. He kissed her deeply. Sophie floated as if suddenly given wings. Her soul soared toward the stars. Her senses alive and tingling, she required more of him. His kiss grew soft and tender. Sophie's knees wobbled, threatening to give way.

Ben was a flesh-and-blood hero. His tall, rough-hewn figure was of legendary proportions, mightier than Neptune, lord and ruler of the sea. The magnificent sailing instructor could command the oceans' ebb and flow, still water or storm, just as he guided the dizzying surge of emotion within Sophie, from sweet serenity to shattering excitement.

The hand that had been cradling her head slipped downward, lightly caressing her bare shoulder. A delicious, warm shudder rippled through her. Complete surrender to this galvanizing man seemed the only and loveliest thing to do.

Sophie savored Ben's masculine blend of lust and spice. She whimpered with delight as his tongue slipped between her lips.

"Sophie Harrington!"

Drat! Flora!

Sophie and Ben jumped apart simultaneously. The most wrenching experience Sophie had endured of late.

"Go to her," he whispered. "She mustn't see me."

Having no choice, Sophie turned away. Good sense suddenly returned. She'd come so close to forsaking her vow of celibacy in Ben's arms—without once considering the consequences.

Fourteen

"Do you know what this is?"

Only Ben's eyes moved, fixing on the dirty sheet of paper the admiral waved above his head.

The Commandant of Midshipmen had summoned Ben to his office at the start of the academy day. Ben and his little traveling band consisting of Sophie, Flora, and Graham arrived in Annapolis the evening before, exhausted by their hurried journey from Georgetown.

Ben stared at the offensive paper, fearing he knew what the admiral brandished about with unconcealed fury—the ransom demand.

Trouble. More trouble.

But as it happened, Ben was almost too tired to care, tired and bothered. Unable to deny for more than a minute that the goddess in his arms was the admiral's daughter, Ben had been torn. The wish to teach Sophie a deserved lesson vied with the longing to love her. Desire warred with honor. Honor had been losing when Flora appeared.

At the time he had not been grateful for the tavern maid's ill-humored interruption. Worried that Sophie might do something foolish, the brazen barmaid had come to the gazebo on a hunch. Although he wasn't certain about Sophie, Ben knew Flora had saved *him* from doing something foolish. She'd hissed at his fleeing shadow like an angry snake, grumbled about men beneath her breath, and whisked Sophie away.

Ben hadn't been the same since. He'd meant only to demonstrate to Sophie where her impetuous actions could lead. He had no intention of falling under the spell of her lips, the wonder of her innocent welcome. But he had.

The sound of a fist meeting hard wood tore Ben from his reverie, hauling him back into the present.

Glaring at Ben, his furious superior leaned across his desk. "Do you know what this is?" he repeated loudly. "While you were off on a wild-goose chase, *this* was delivered direct to Dulany House. The villain tied it to a stone and threw it through my study window, breaking the pane."

Ben knew. The admiral sounded more offended by the broken window than by the ransom demand. Ben directed his gaze at the paper now lying flat on the desk, covered by Wesley Harrington's hand—minus the admiral's pinky finger.

"It appears to be a ransom message from the thief who stole Soph— Miss Harrington's journal," Ben said in the most mild-mannered tone he could muster.

"The scoundrel wants six hundred dollars!" the admiral roared.

"That seems excessive. If you don't mind me saying so, sir."

"My daughter must have written terrible things. Terrible things," the admiral growled. His thick dark brows gathered in a menacing frown.

Ben understood Harrington's fears. He shared them. Ever since Sophie had confessed she'd written about him in her journal, he'd felt an odd sense of doom . . . or was it secret delight?

"With all due respect, sir. Your daughter claims to

have a fertile imagination, but perhaps the journal is not as—"

"Have you learned anything?" Harrington thundered, bringing to an abrupt end Ben's attempt to assuage his fears.

"Abigail Grant is about to give birth and wishes to wed the father of her child. From what I could discover, this fellow, Fletcher Thurman, does not work for a living. The couple are in dire need of finances, which is why I believe that Thurman and Abigail are responsible for taking Sophie's journal."

"Do you know where to find this Thurman thief?"

"Since you have received the ransom, I expect he is somewhere in the area of Annapolis. I have a description of him. I'll find him."

"He demands a response in two days' time!" Admiral Harrington flung the offensive message to his desk at the same moment a knock came at the door.

"Enter," he bellowed. "At ease, Swain."

Andrew Ferguson strode through the door, casting an irritated frown Ben's way before addressing Harrington. "Forgive me, but I did not know you were engaged, Wesley."

The admiral and Ferguson were on a first-name basis.

"My business with Seaman Swain has concluded," he replied, folding the ransom message.

The captain shot a sideways glance Ben's way. "As it happens, my business includes the seaman."

Bilge water stirred in the pit of Ben's stomach in warning.

"I have found that a student, one of yours, Swain, is grossly ill fitted to the academy and naval life. With your permission, Admiral Harrington, I should like to dismiss Midshipman Baker."

Ben stiffened. Anger, hot and sharp, bolted through him. Anger that he dared not show before the pompous captain and the already disgruntled admiral. "Your pardon, sir, but I beg to differ. In my opinion, Midshipman Baker has a great deal of potential. It would be a mistake to dismiss the boy."

"Your opinion is irrelevant. You are no longer instructing basic seamanship, I am," Ferguson noted in his supercilious way.

"But I know the boy. He's been my student for weeks."

"If you would like to resume your duties, then I will concede the decision to you." Andrew shot Ben a condescending smile.

"Swain takes orders from me," the admiral reminded his friend and future son-in-law. "The boy will stay until Ben completes his current assignment."

"Very well." Captain Ferguson spoke tersely as he strode rigidly to the door. "I shall be escorting Sophie to Mrs. Frawley's garden party tomorrow evening if that will be convenient."

Without hesitation, Admiral Harrington spoke for his daughter, a presumption Ben knew would bring Sophie to full bristle. "Certainly, Andrew. Sophie will be delighted to attend with you."

"We must announce our engagement soon as well. I have been put off one too many times."

Patting his rotund middle, Harrington grinned. "You have my blessing."

With a jerk of his head in grudging acknowledgment to Ben, the captain strode from the room.

Alone once more, the admiral addressed Ben. "Find the blackmailer immediately. If anything happens to prevent the marriage between Ferguson and my daughter, you can forget assignment to a ship and

I cannot guarantee that you will retain your position at Annapolis. Do you understand?"

"Yes, sir."

Sophie had followed Ben to her father's office, but unprepared for an encounter with the admiral, she chose not to intrude on their meeting. She had dreaded the day when a ransom note would appear on his desk. And it was only a matter of time before her father noticed that Sophie had returned without the new wardrobe she'd gone to Georgetown to purchase.

Instead, she'd returned to Annapolis with an unrelenting ache and a simmering heat emerging from womanly regions heretofore unknown and unexplored. Sophie would never forgive Flora for interfering with her tryst in the gazebo with Ben. She'd been left with a longing she could not lose.

She had no opportunity to speak with the oddly taciturn sailing instructor on the return journey home. Sophie traveled in the coach; he rode on horseback. She peered out the window frequently as her thoughts flitted from recovering her journal to taking up where she had left off with the splendid seaman.

Ben had known it was Sophie masquerading as the goddess of love. She knew it instinctively. What she didn't know was whether he would have continued making love to her or whether he would have cried off in the end.

Knowing he would be searching for Fletcher Thurman today, Sophie decided to follow Ben. He had an idea what the scoundrel looked like and if he found either Fletcher or Abigail, Sophie wanted to be there. Conducting a search herself would be difficult. If her father discovered her questioning shopkeepers and innkeepers, he might take exception. The admiral embarrassed easily.

After leaving her father's office, Ben did not start out for town, much to Sophie's surprise. He hurried to the dormitory where he fetched Midshipman Baker. As the boy and his instructor walked toward the city dock, Sophie could see that Ben talked and the boy listened. When they reached the dock, before her disbelieving eyes, Ben turned over his beloved, *Nantucket Lady,* to the green midshipman.

Joseph Baker had very nearly capsized a sloop during the stormy day that Sophie would remember for the rest of her life. She'd been in the sloop, clinging to the side for dear life.

From the shadowed steps of the customs house, Sophie watched as Ben then started up the hill. Holding her parasol at a shielding angle, she followed. In front of the Sugarplum Sweet Shop, he stopped abruptly and turned so swiftly that Sophie had no opportunity to duck into the concealing overhang. He'd caught her.

A slow, crooked smile turned up one corner of his mouth. Her heart raced fiercely.

"Would you like a muffin, Sophie?"

"Thank you, but I shall make the purchase myself. I came to town expressly to buy muffins."

He shook his head. "And I thought you were following me."

"Oh, no." She giggled as if the thought were the silliest she'd ever heard.

"You may as well walk with me as behind me, Sophie. People will talk less."

He plainly did not believe her.

"I was not—"

"If you wish me to trust you, you will cease your

foolish fabrications." His narrowed blue gaze bored into her eyes.

Shifting nervously from one foot to the other, she recalled the confidence Ben had shared with her. The girl he wished to marry had not been truthful with him. He'd been deeply hurt although he refused to admit it.

But Sophie's white lies were not the same. She had never hurt anyone. She never would. Still, the slightest fabrication was useless if Ben could so easily determine when she told less than the truth.

Silently, somberly, Sophie nodded her agreement. With this inexplicable fire burning inside her for the sailing instructor, she wished to earn his trust. She wished to earn his admiration, and more. "Where are you going?" she asked.

"To Reynolds Tavern and then for a ride in the country."

"Do you think Fletcher and Abigail are staying in Annapolis?"

"Yes, although I rather doubt they are able to stay in an inn. I expect they are hiding somewhere on the outskirts of town in a barn or abandoned shack."

"Somewhere where they would not call attention to themselves."

"Yes, but someone in town may have seen them."

"I have a feeling you will find them soon. The prospect is exciting."

"And dangerous, likely."

"My only fear at the moment is spending the rest of my life with Andrew Ferguson."

Ben grinned and Sophie's heart swelled to twice its normal size. *Sweet mercy!*

"I understand," he said.

"Did you see my father this morning?"

"You know I did. He's received the ransom note. Your journal will be returned for six hundred dollars."

Sophie gasped. She'd been waiting for the ransom demand, thinking, hoping, she might answer it. But any possibility of retrieving the journal herself with a simple payment vanished. She was at her father's mercy, unless Ben could be persuaded to help.

Sophie spent the better part of the day riding beside Ben in search of Abigail and Fletcher. Although she never said a word about what had passed between them in the gazebo, she regarded him differently. In turn, he treated her with a stilted deference. His cool indifference wounded her. She had been too bold.

Although they had been at cross-purposes from the start, Sophie respected Ben, and believed that they had become friendly adversaries. Her brazen behavior at the masquerade apparently had put him off. Nothing would ever be the same between them again, and she had no one but herself to blame. But his kisses, ah . . . she would always remember Ben's kiss.

Ben questioned two farmers who had seen Fletcher the day before, but a search of the area north of town yielded no trace of Thurman or Abigail.

"I'll start again first thing in the morning," he told Sophie.

"Please, Ben, not yet. There's a barn just down the road, look." She pointed down the hill. "Please, let's look there before we give up."

To Sophie's relief, Ben nudged his horse onward.

The dirt road led to an abandoned barn and the remains of a farmhouse that had burned to the ground months ago. Where the barn's color hadn't faded from red to rust, the paint was chipped. The hinges of one door had come loose, causing the door to remain partially open in a drunken list.

Even though it was growing dark, Ben had been un-able to refuse Sophie's request. When her astonishing aquamarine eyes, darkened with disappointment, met his, Ben's heart reacted with a swift wrenching pain. In that one fleeting moment she appeared sweetly vulnerable, like a mermaid lost in the waves of a strange unfamiliar sea.

As soon as they reached the barn, he dismounted and held out his arms to help Sophie. Her hands rested on his shoulders, his hands circling her waist. Ben lifted her, held her. Unwilling to allow her body to slide against his, at the same time he desperately wanted her body . . . to slide against his.

Immobilized by indecision, Ben hesitated. Sophie's gaze locked on his. His pulse leapt as if he'd been suddenly put in the way of danger. Dragging a deep breath, he whirled her from the horse and away from him, setting her down firmly.

"Don't move," he warned in a hushed tone before turning to tie the horses to a broken buggy close by.

Sophie stared at the barn door as if she were willing Abigail, Fletcher, and her journal to be inside.

"I'll go in first," he said. "Stay behind me."

Ben did not even bother suggesting that Sophie wait until he'd first searched and cleared the barn. Too headstrong to pay attention to any such orders, she'd do as she pleased, which might prove more threatening than if she stayed close to him.

Tension gripped Ben. Muscles taut and mind keenly aware, he feared they might be stepping into a trap and proceeded cautiously. For all he knew, Fletcher might be armed and prepared to shoot. If anything happened to Sophie, Ben would never forgive himself. Yet at her insistence, he was leading her into a potentially life-threatening situation. Years from now he would wonder what madness possessed him that he sought to satisfy the admiral's daughter, thereby ending his naval career in an old abandoned barn.

With two last words of warning, "Quiet, now," Ben stole through the open door.

As long as he could smell honeysuckle, feel the warmth radiating from her body and Sophie's skirts slapping against the back of his legs, Ben felt assured he could protect her. Of all times, this would have been the only good time he could think of for her to be wearing bloomers.

He waited for his eyes to adjust. The shaft of dim light from the open door and a large door-like opening in the loft provided the only light. Quickly enough, Ben could make out four stalls, a loft, and an open area used to store buggies, plows, and the like.

Deciding to investigate the loft first, he moved swiftly to the rickety ladder that led to the top floor of the barn. Sophie steadied the roughly hewn contrivance as he climbed. A thin layer of old hay covered the floor and in the far corner a horsehair blanket was spread over a clump of stale hay. Two small candles, burned to stubs, stood at one corner of the blanket.

"They've been here," Sophie whispered from behind him.

"Someone's been here," he corrected.

"The stalls are empty," she added, in a voice barely audible.

"Don't be discouraged. We have just begun to search."

"But I'm running out of time. My life, the opportunity for life as I've dreamed, is slipping away."

Regarding her anguished expression, Ben forgot what it meant for him to recover the journal. The reassignment he sought seemed less important than saving Sophie's impossible, improbable dream.

He *had* snapped.

"More than likely, Fletcher and Abigail are moving from place to place, choosing abandoned dwellings like this. Look." He grasped her hand and tugged her down, forcing Sophie to sit on her heels as he did, examining the stubs of candles between them. "These candles have been freshly burned."

"Do you think they were here last night?" she asked, a flicker of hope lighting her eyes.

He didn't know, but feeling a misbegotten need to keep her hope alive, he nodded. "We'll find them tomorrow."

"Thank you, Ben." With tears glistening in her eyes once again, Sophie leaned over and brushed her lips against his cheek.

Closing his eyes to savor the moment, Ben didn't realize that Sophie had lost her balance until she toppled over on him.

Oomph. Ben fell back onto the blanket spread-eagle with Sophie on top of him.

Damn, damn, damn. What sort of devil heaped temptation like this on a sailor too long without feminine companionship?

Damn. He was only a man, a lonely Nantucket whaler alone in the dark with a beautiful woman. A woman whose warm body pressed against his, whose dear heart beat against his. Hot silver streaks of desire shot through him like rockets run amuck.

Sophie stared at him, her eyes wide with surprise, her lips just inches away. As she continued to look down upon him, her lips slowly curved upward into a heart-stopping smile. Ben never thought he'd die like this. Her dimple dove to enchanting depths as the surprise ebbed from her eyes, replaced by a sparkle that would put the stars to shame.

His noble attempts to put an end to their deepening attachment by being distant, treating the admiral's daughter with polite indifference, had apparently failed.

Ben dared not move. He should order her to get up at once, to remove her body from his. But he daren't breathe, could barely swallow. His throat had gone dry as old stern rope. His heart thrumped against his chest.

"Ben," she said softly.

Bullet hard, with aching loins and stomach tightly braced against any other unexpected motion, he moved the only body part he presumed safe—his eyelid. He winked.

Ben heard her low, throaty chuckle as she lowered her head. Still wearing a slightly wicked smile, Sophie paused a breath away from his lips . . . and then she kissed him. Lips as sweet as sugar, as soft as silk, met his. Ben groaned.

Sophie's kiss deepened.

He was a lowly seaman. He could not make love to the admiral's daughter. But the man that he was wanted Sophie more than he'd ever wanted a woman in his life. While Ben burned, his conscience shouted for him to go no farther.

Her kisses were like the welcome caress of rain on a dry desert. She ran her fingers through his hair, teased his tongue with hers.

"Sophie . . ." His breath came hard, and his voice broke, thick with the desire that racked him. "I cannot guarantee that you will remain celibate much longer if you do not leave me this instant."

Her puzzled expression gave way to a smile so

radiant that it seemed to light the darkened loft. "I have renounced my vow."

Another thought struck him. "You are not using me, are you?"

"Using you?" she repeated softly.

"This is not your idea of research for whatever you're writing in the new journal, is it?"

"Oh, no. Oh, no," she crooned.

Before he could raise any further objection, her lips were on his again. Sophie's tender, soulful kiss set Ben afire. He'd wanted her for so long, dreamed of her for so many, many nights that he was not certain he could contain his desire. This maddening, delightful, delicious woman brought curious excitement to his life each day. For years, Ben had prided himself on his self-imposed discipline. But just when he needed it most, all self-control had vanished. Normally a man of iron will and strong moral fiber, he had neither the strength nor the will to refuse Sophie's kisses. Needles and pins tumbled to his toes, and he lost himself in the sweet cloud of honeysuckle that engulfed him.

When the dimpled beauty framed Ben's face in her hands, her fingertips felt like the first rays of sun following a storm at sea. Sophie's warmth and eagerness served to silence even the voice of Ben's conscience.

The barn door below creaked as it swung in the wind and finally closed. The enveloping darkness created a safe, sweet velvet cocoon meant only for two.

Gathering her in his arms, Ben rolled Sophie over. He lay to one side of her, sprinkling kisses from her nose to her eyelids to her ears. Sophie hadn't known until now how sensitive an ear could be, or a neck.

Enfolded in Ben's arms, one delicious sensation followed another. His were the only arms meant to hold her. For he inspired Sophie. The swagger in the step, his ready laughter, and seductive wink warmed her, made her smile when she'd wished to either cry or rage.

Her father had set them against each other, but the admiral could not turn her heart away from the sailing instructor. It did not matter that he was not an officer. Ben was everything a man could and should be. Sophie's heart belonged to Ben Swain.

When he fumbled with the buttons of her bodice, Sophie helped, eager to be free and closer to him. Wiggling out of its confining sleeves beneath him, she heard him moan as she tossed the garment aside. Ben drew his shirt above his head and flung it away.

Awed by his masculine beauty once again, Sophie regarded his massive chest, scarred and magnificent, lean and muscular. Her breath slid from her body in a slow, gossamer stream as she gazed upon her glorious lover, a lusty survivor of battles with men as well as with beasts of the sea.

He lowered his head and grazed her lips with his. Slipping her arms over his shoulders, Sophie splayed her fingers against his bare, brawny back. Touching him! Touching him as she'd wished to do for ever so long, since the first time he'd kissed her. She felt the contrasting textures of his flesh, rough and smooth. Her fingertips tingled. She grew warmer still.

Having never made love, she felt uncertain as to what to do next. Reigning in her impulsive nature, Sophie waited for Ben to show her the way. Within seconds, his gentle kiss gave way to a deep, fierce possession. Sophie's heart beat so loudly, she feared it would shake the barn's rotting rafters.

She ached to be still closer to his heart, to his soul. But how?

Her fumbling fingers found the buttons of his

trousers and soon he joined her in a flurry of impatience to remove the clothing that came between them.

Ben kissed her fiercely. The pulse at her throat throbbed with excitement. His palms cupped her swollen breasts. Before she'd recovered from this breath-stealing sensation, the sailing instructor's mouth slid from her lips to cover her taut nipples.

"Oh, sweet mercy, Ben!"

He had so much more to teach than sailing!

Scarlet ribbons of fire and golden streams of molten honey surged through Sophie and settled achingly between her thighs.

Her handsome hero lifted his head. Desire glazed his dark indigo eyes as they met hers. "Sweet, sweet, Sophie," he murmured thickly.

"Don't stop," she cried in a whispered gasp. "Please don't stop!"

A heavy lock of hair fell across his forehead, his brows gathered in a questioning frown. "Are you certain?"

"I have never been so certain of anything," she rasped.

He smiled, the smile of a man who adored his woman. And for the present, Sophie resolved to believe Ben adored her, just as she adored him. In truth, she more than adored him. What she had not dared to admit before, even to herself, she silently declared now: She loved Ben. She loved Ben Swain. She would always love him. No matter what seas he sailed, Sophie's heart would always belong to Ben.

Unable to function with thought any longer, her mind reacted to feelings. The fire in Ben's touch, the delicious goose bumps that rose along her flesh. Sophie felt as if a torch burned within her, no, a bonfire. She could not catch her breath, could not tear her eyes from Ben's striking form, his wondrous manhood.

Crushing her to him, Ben held Sophie for a long silent moment. The solid beat of his heart, the steely hardness of him, aroused her even more. The gritty texture of his skin and the musky male scent of him filled her senses, overwhelmed her, excited her. And when his palms skimmed to her waist along the soft curve of her hip to rest on the sensitive inner side of her thigh, the unfamiliar ache consuming her became unbearable.

"Oh, Ben," she whimpered. "I'm going to die."

"No, you're going to live, Buttercup," he promised, "As you have never lived before."

Smothering her with kisses, gently parting her thighs, Ben fulfilled his promise. Sophie gasped as Ben entered her with the tenderness of a longtime lover. Her gasp was not from pain but from the miracle, the sweet melding of souls. At last she had discovered what it meant to be complete. Like sail to mast, Ben completed her.

United with the only man who could make her feel as if they made love in the Garden of Eden, rather than a derelict barn, Sophie soared, lighter than air, higher than the heavens. Arching her back, she thrilled to each thrust as Ben took her to an extraordinary world known only to lovers. In her most fanciful imaginings, Sophie could not have created, nor duplicated, the fire and passion, the soul-deep joy she felt at being one with Ben. She reached for the sun and the stars meant only for her in this new world.

Laughter, excitement, and the loveliest ache of all bubbled up within her until she reached blissful release. In a golden kaleidoscopic explosion of sight and sound, Sophie cried out.

Floating slowly, softly suspended above their make-shift bed of horsehair blanket and hay, she heard Ben's deep baritone echo in her ear, calling out her name. "Sophie!"

After long moments of silence he repeated her name again in a worried tone. "Sophie?"

She heaved a heavy sigh of contentment. "I am not dead, but I believe I have reached heaven."

Fifteen

A man could be driven just so far! Ben could not be blamed for making love to Sophie. But, dear God, what had he done? And done with the admiral's daughter!

He'd spend the rest of his life confined to a small cell on a forgotten island. But he would always remember the enchanted hour he'd spent with Sophie Harrington.

Ben had never experienced the runaway passion that he'd felt holding Sophie's lithe, loving body. She'd pushed him over the edge. Making love had taken on a whole new and strangely disturbing meaning.

When Ben left the barn, his knees had wobbled like a schoolgirl's. Shaken, confused, and floating on whatever thin slice of air seemingly lifted his feet from the ground, he silently escorted Sophie home.

Up until a few days ago, he'd been an honorable man with honorable intentions. Sophie had rendered Ben incapable of honorable thoughts where she was concerned. Consumed with desire for a woman who vowed to win her independence at any cost, he feared for his sanity.

Thankfully, Sophie appeared lost in her own thoughts and did not demand conversation, or worse, explanations. Ben dared a sidelong glance. She wore a dreamy expression. A small smile played at the corner of her lips, swollen from his kisses. If he were not mistaken, there was a new and different gleam in her eyes.

"Sophie . . . I have taken your . . . your most precious gift, and I—"

"Say no more, Ben. I made my choice, one I do not regret, will never regret." Her gaze locked on his and she cast him a dazzling smile.

Ben sucked in his breath.

Was there any woman more beautiful, more charming?

His heart flopped about in his chest as if he were a lovesick youth. Ben would do anything for Sophie, but what she wanted the most. When he retrieved her journal, he must return it to the admiral or face life behind a landlubber's desk.

Ben parted company with Sophie at the back door of Dulany House. While he felt reluctant to leave her, Sophie, in obvious high spirits, appeared downright luminous as she bid him good night. Damn. He didn't understand. He didn't understand his feelings . . . or hers.

When he returned to his attic chamber, two missives awaited him. With a swiftly beating pulse, he tore open the first with uncharacteristic impatience. A letter from Matt meant his brother was obviously still alive. In the brief message, Matt said he was quitting the gold fields and returning to Nantucket. He promised to come by Annapolis to visit Ben, before going home to take care of their mother.

Poor Matt. Ben could read between the lines. His brother had not fared well in the gold mines and had chosen the one course left to him, taking care of their mother. Ben felt grateful.

The second message contained an invitation to Lieutenant and Mrs. Gilbert Frawley's garden party at twilight on the following evening. The penned invitation noted the faculty gathering was being held to celebrate the completion of the newest dormitories.

He'd never been invited to one of the Frawleys' galas before, and they entertained quite frequently. Ben didn't go to garden parties. He didn't balance china teacups on his knee. He'd had no training in the use of the proper fork. He tossed the invitation away. Ben required only a splash of grog, a rowdy song, and a good cigar. Then again, he had no doubt Sophie would attend with Andrew Ferguson. Perhaps he should be on hand.

Sophie woke up the next morning with a smile. Her body hummed; her heart rejoiced. There could be no question that her sweet, languid state of being had to do with Ben's lovemaking. If only he shared her bed. The next time—and she promised herself there would be a next time—she meant to turn the tables and make love to the sailing instructor.

As much as she longed to stay abed all day, she had much to do. There were any number of abandoned dwellings in the area that must be searched for Fletcher and Abigail.

But first she must make a hurried visit to Flora. Her friend had boasted of possessing a full vial of French female pills that promised to purify the system. The thought of having Ben's baby left Sophie torn. On the one hand, the idea pleased her surprisingly enough; on the other, it frightened her. In this uncertain state she made her way to Flora's hired room above the livery stable.

She was met with a scream.

"Flora! Flora, are you all right?" she cried, rapping furiously on the door.

The scream died, and silence prevailed. The light breeze carried a horsey aroma through the open windows of the corridor.

Pressing her ear to the door, Sophie heard a stumbling sound. The door opened a crack. Flora with damp, fiery strands of hair dangling in her face eyed Sophie through the two-inch gap.

Obviously, Sophie had come at a bad time. Flora was entertaining a gentleman. Graham, more than likely. She fell all over herself apologizing for the intrusion. "Oh, dear. I am so sorry, please excuse me, I'll . . . I'll return at another time."

"No. Come in. Quickly." Flora opened the door and yanked Sophie inside the room. "You're just in time to help."

Anxious, but curious, Sophie slipped through.

Thick velvet curtains were drawn across the two windows. Although it was a bright, light spring day, Flora's chamber would have been in total darkness save for three lanterns, one on each side of the bed and another on the dresser in the rear wall.

Sophie's gaze came to a sudden halt, fixing on the figure in Flora's bed. It wasn't a man.

"Abigail!"

"Hello, Miss Harrington."

"I have been looking everywhere for you!"

Tears slipped down Abigail's flushed and perspiring face as she turned her head from Sophie.

Sophie looked to Flora. "Is Abigail ill?"

"She came into the tavern last night at closing. Her water broke."

"Her water broke?" Sophie repeated, having no understanding what Flora meant.

"Abigail is having her baby."

"No!"

"She's been in labor for the past ten hours."

Bewildered, Sophie hurried to Abigail's bedside. "But it is too early, too soon."

"Four weeks early," Abigail said in a weak voice.

Apparently unconcerned about the early arrival, Flora used the looking glass in the corner to pin back her stray locks. She spoke in a matter-of-fact tone. "Even so, there's every reason to believe Abigail will deliver a strong healthy child."

"Of course." Sophie bobbed her head in agreement although she didn't believe a word. What did Flora know about babies? "I'll go for the midwife," she said.

"No!" Abigail screamed.

Sophie stopped in her tracks. "Why?"

"I have nothing to exchange for the services of a midwife."

"Do not worry," she said, turning back to smooth the hair from Abigail's perspiring forehead. "I shall pay her—gladly."

Abigail clasped Sophie's hand and squeezed it. A bright, raw fear shone in her hazel eyes. "No one must know where I am."

"Certainly a midwife will be discreet. But why? Whom are you hiding from?"

"I am afraid that if Fletcher knows where I am, he will come for me and hurt our baby."

Sophie was stunned. Fletcher? She assumed that Abigail knew that Ben Swain was looking for her. The tall, powerful sailing instructor was truly a man to be feared. But Fletcher Thurman, the father of her baby? Why should she fear him?

"What sort of man would harm his own child?" she asked.

"Fletcher would." Dropping Sophie's hand suddenly,

Abigail gasped then clutched her stomach. Clenching her teeth, she gave out a long, loud moan.

All thoughts of questioning the girl concerning the apparent breach with Fletcher evaporated. This was no time to ask where Sophie's journal might be. She would save her questions for tomorrow. For now, Abigail's pain filled the close room. And to Sophie's untrained ear, her former maid sounded close to death. Abigail screamed. Sophie started.

Staring down at Abigail's extended stomach, quite visible through her thin chemise, Sophie's pulse raced as if she were the one in labor. Something was about to happen, she could feel it in her bones and she did not want to be in the room.

"Oh, sweet mercy," she murmured, attempting to get a hold of herself. She would hate for Flora and Abigail to think her a fainthearted mouse. But she was.

Flora lifted the hem and peeked beneath Abigail's chemise. She blew a strand of hair from her face. "It's coming."

Sophie felt the blood drain from her face. She swallowed hard, over the dirt-dry lump that had formed in her throat.

"Oh, oh, oh!" Abigail cried, each exclamation increasing in pitch and volume.

"Listen to Flora," Flora said to the grimacing mother-to-be. "You've got to start pushing now."

Tears streamed down the young girl's face, but she nodded bravely.

The tavern maid turned to Sophie and issued orders with the stern efficiency of the admiral himself. "Put down your parasol, take off your hat and gloves, and stay with Abigail. Do whatever needs to be done. Flora's going for supplies."

Sophie followed Flora to the door. "I can't stay here by myself, alone with her," she protested beneath her breath. Angry with Flora and frightened for Abigail, Sophie's nerves had all but scattered. "I . . . I can't watch Abigail die."

"Abigail's not going to die," Flora insisted in the same hushed tones. "Push!" she shouted to the girl over Sophie's shoulder, before lowering her voice once again. "All you have to do until Flora gets back is encourage her to keep pushing. And be there if the baby comes quickly."

"The baby might come quickly?" Sophie felt her heart stop.

"Abigail is in the final stage of labor. The babe might come sudden, it depends. Now, let me go, so that I can get back in time."

"Give me the cloth, give me the cloth," Abigail cried out from the bed.

Sophie rushed to do her bidding.

"Wring it out."

Her maid was giving her orders. Sophie did as Abigail requested and the pain-racked girl clamped the cloth between her teeth.

"Push," Sophie instructed with a fair amount of trepidation.

She'd never actually witnessed the birth of a child. Her knowledge and information had ended with the tragic results of birthing within her family.

"I'm pushing, I'm pushing."

Sophie looked about for another cloth and, when she could not find one, tore a strip from her chemise—a habit, of late. Submerging the scrap of linen in the washbasin, she wrung it out and placed in on Abigail's forehead.

"When this is done, I want you to come home to

Dulany House with me," she told the grunting girl. Sophie fervently hoped that Abigail would be one of the fortunate women who survived the rigors of childbirth.

Abigail made a muffled sound.

"Push now," Sophie reminded her gently, wishing she had the experience to sound as authoritative as Flora had. "Push!"

Spitting the cloth out of her mouth, Abigail shrieked and pointed to the end of the bed.

Sophie jumped and scurried to the foot of the bed just in time to see a head emerging. "Sweet mercy!"

Throwing back Abigail's worn chemise, a mixture of wonder and excitement churned in Sophie's stomach.

"Push!" she shouted, forgetting for the moment that the birth of this baby meant certain death for Abigail.

The baby's head face and shoulders emerged.

Abigail howled.

Sophie's heart raced.

"Once more!" she cried out, caught up in the thrill of the impending birth. "Push!"

With a mighty effort that shook the bed and vibrated in the young mother's last whoop, the baby was born with a wail of protest.

Tears of relief and joy spilled down Sophie's cheeks as the tiny infant slipped into her hands. She held the baby gingerly, as if it might break, and with a gentle finger cleared the newborn's mouth, triggering a fresh burst of indignant cries. Unable to control the flow of her own tears, nor the goose bumps that she felt, Sophie cradled the wet and wrinkled infant in her arms.

"It's a girl," she announced. "And she's beautiful."

"Give me my baby, Miss Sophie."

Abigail lived! Abigail glowed! Despite her perspiring body, and the purple globes beneath her eyes, the new mother was alive and well and happier than Sophie had ever seen her.

Sophie carefully laid the baby on Abigail's stomach. "I think that next we must cut the cord," she said, looking around for something to accomplish the task.

As she searched, the door flew open and Flora dashed in juggling a variety of baby items.

Sophie grinned at her. "You have missed a miracle!"

A garden party. If anyone had told Ben that he'd be attending a garden party, he would have laughed. Now, a dart tournament would be another matter.

Mild weather and a star-filled sky greeted the Frawleys' guests at the twilight garden party held on the sloping green lawn with a view of the bay. Cakes and candies prepared by Lulu of the Sugarplum Sweet Shop were served along with fine English tea and old French liquors.

Sophie arrived with her father and Andrew Ferguson, wedged between them like a prisoner.

He had begun to think as she did. Damn!

Sophie moved slowly, her gaze scanning the crowd. Was she looking for him? When she found him seconds later, the answer became clear. As she locked him in her shining turquoise gaze, Ben's heart slammed against his chest.

Resplendent in a lapis blue gown, Sophie was simply the most beautiful woman in the garden, putting even the flowers to shame. Her off-the-shoulder gown of satin and lace shimmered as she moved, moved with a grace that held Ben spellbound. His gaze lingered on Sophie's tawny, sun-streaked hair, parted in the center, pulled to her crown, and gathered with a blue silk bow. A soft cascade of waves fell to her shoulders, brushing her fair skin, where his kisses had been.

When she hadn't appeared, fast on his heels today, he'd worried. First he'd worried that she'd discovered the whereabouts of Fletcher Thurman, then he worried that she'd been kidnapped by Thurman, and lastly he worried that she'd taken ill.

But she looked well, splendidly well.

Vibrant and captivating, Sophie commanded attention. All eyes turned her way but her sparkling gaze remained fixed on his, warming him, exciting him. The blood rushed to his head.

She could not marry Andrew Ferguson.

Ben hadn't liked Ferguson from the start. The pretentious captain had earned his rank through political connections at a time when hardly anyone reached captain anymore. Too many officers with seniority waited for promotion.

But Andrew Ferguson, who had not demonstrated bravery at sea nor a vast store of seafaring knowledge, had achieved a rank that made him Ben's superior . . . but in name only.

Ben strode toward the trio to pay his respects as was expected of him, but his gaze remained on Sophie alone. He hadn't seen her all day, and he couldn't get enough of her. Besides, she had some explaining to do. Where had she been and what had she been up to?

The opportunity to talk with her did not present itself. As soon as salutes and pleasantries were exchanged, Andrew sidled to Ben's side, slapping him on the back as if they were comrades.

"You'll be interested to know, Swain, that in addition to instructing your classes, I have managed time to pursue the rigging of sails and steam in one vessel," he said. "My progressive engineering ideas have not suffered for your reassignment."

He gloated, the pompous ass. And he had bad breath.

"I look forward to touring your vessel," Ben replied, all civility.

"You will not find a more superior ship," the sloping-shouldered captain assured Ben. "I shall be at the helm steering the future of the Navy."

More likely, Ferguson would be stationed aft, looking back into the past.

Ben smiled as if he agreed with Ferguson's absurd notion of sails and steam. In addition to all else, the captain obviously lacked foresight. Steam-powered warships, and perhaps submersibles, were plainly the future of the fleet.

"Have you heard that the Collins line shall shortly be launching a steam ship for transatlantic travel? They wish to compete with Cunard, and I have heard no mention of sails."

"Fine for a commercial endeavor," Andrew allowed, "but sails are an integral part of Navy tradition."

"I shall look forward to boarding your ship," Ben replied. Arguing would do no good. Unfortunately, many naval officers shared Andrew's attitude, an attitude that must change if the Navy were to progress from its current stagnant state.

Before Ben could address Sophie, Admiral Harrington took his elbow, guiding him away from his daughter, who appeared upset with his action. Ben felt the same.

When they were well out of earshot, Harrington's pleasant garden party expression transformed into a menacing frown. "You have not found this Fletcher person yet?"

"No, sir, but I'm close. For the better part of the day I kept watch on an abandoned barn where Thurman's been hiding. He'd already left when I got there at dawn. But he'll return—and I'll get him."

Since Fletcher had already made himself at home there, Ben felt certain Thurman would return to that particular barn. He'd been reluctant to end his surveillance in order to attend the garden party. But he'd had to know why Sophie hadn't joined him today. He'd feared that only a life-threatening condition could keep her from tracking down Fletcher Thurman.

"Time is running out. If I don't make the ransom payment, Sophie's journal will be all over Annapolis and Washington. If a word, just one word, is published in the Annapolis paper, you'll be on a shrimp boat."

"Sir, I don't think you have to worry about making the payment. I'll capture Fletcher and retrieve the journal before he makes good on his threats. Although this attempt to ransom Sophie's journal may be a bluff on his part."

"I'm not taking any chances with my career, Swain. And you hadn't better either."

"Anyone who knows your daughter will understand she is prone to exaggerate the facts."

The admiral hiked a speculative brow. "And how well have you come to know my daughter, Seaman Swain?"

Ben thought his heart had stopped beating for a moment. "Well enough to have learned Miss Harrington's penchant for overstating the truth at times."

Harrington glared at him. "Get on with finding Fletcher. You have no time for garden parties. Sophie will do nothing untoward with the captain and me at her side."

"Yes, sir. I'll say good night to Miss Harrington and be on my way."

"No need. I shall be happy to convey your regrets to Sophie."

Ben dipped his head and saluted his commander. In the guise of a request, Admiral Harrington had ordered him to leave the party. But as Ben reached the edge of the garden, he stopped to look back, lingering for one last look at Sophie.

The Naval Academy's newly formed midshipmen band played on the wide veranda, where several couples danced. Ben wished he could ask Sophie to dance with him. He would gladly dance all night with her, just to hold her in his arms.

The canopy of stars and a full silver moon shining above the Frawleys' garden were so perfect they might have been ordered. Laughter, music, and sweets to eat and drink promised a magical evening. But when Ben Swain turned to leave without so much as a fare-thee-well, the hope of magic died for Sophie.

At her father's insistence, she'd been escorted to the party by Andrew Ferguson. She'd surrendered to the admiral's tyrannical dictates once again. But she knew she could not go on with this particular charade. Before the evening was over, she would put an end to Andrew's suit.

The slow white heat that burned within her for Ben Swain could not be stirred by any other. No other man could ever compare. Sophie had promised Ben no more white lies, no more exaggerations. Giving the ruddy-cheeked captain false hope that she would one day become his wife was worse than a white lie. She resolved to face her father's wrath and end the matter. But after the deed was done, oh, how she wished she could run to the Bailey cottage on Prince

George Street. In her dreams, Sophie envisioned owning the cottage before coming to a final confrontation with her father.

Ben had stopped. He stood on the veranda gazing back at her. He looked wonderful. Taller than most of the officers in attendance, he held himself with great dignity and authority. From his thick shock of cocoa brown hair to his long, muscular legs, the handsome sailing instructor presented a compelling figure. His rugged male magnetism reached across the manicured lawn, reached out to Sophie alone. A shiver of delight rippled through her.

Smiling, she willed him back to the party and to her side.

"Dearest, I have brought you champagne."

Sophie hadn't noticed Andrew Ferguson's return. She hadn't realized that he'd left the area to begin with.

"Thank you." She took the goblet from him, but her gaze remained on Ben.

"Ladies and gentlemen. May I have your attention?" Andrew rapped on his goblet with one of Mrs. Frawley's silver spoons.

The band stopped playing as Andrew rapped on the goblet once again. A shushing began, spreading quickly as word passed among the party goers that there was to be an announcement.

"Andrew? What are you doing?" Sophie snapped beneath her breath. She smiled, but she was nervous, her distress involved a roiling stomach.

"Ladies and gentlemen, your attention, please," he repeated, paying no attention to her.

The admiral strode to the captain's side. Sophie's apprehension deepened. Her gaze locked on Ben's, who stood on the fringe of the party. Hoping he could see her subtle movement, she raised her eyebrows to indicate bewilderment.

Ben stepped down from the porch, sauntering closer.

Sophie's eyes never left his.

Andrew, beaming broadly, made his announcement in sonorous tones. "Mrs. Frawley has done me the honor of allowing me to make a most important announcement at her delightful garden party."

A buzz of speculation rose as the guests questioned each other on what this mysterious announcement could possibly be.

"Without prolonging the suspense," Andrew continued. "I should like to announce my engagement to Miss Sophie Harrington."

Sophie did not hear the remainder of Captain Ferguson's announcement. At once nonplussed, she felt oddly disoriented and then dizzy. Closing her eyes against the nightmare the evening had become, she swooned.

She would have fallen off the bench if Seaman Swain hadn't rushed to catch her.

Sixteen

Ben stormed through the doors of Reynolds Tavern. He needed a stiff drink, maybe several, and a tough game of darts to put him back in any sort of reasonable disposition.

After he'd caught Sophie from what surely could have been a nasty fall, he'd been shoved out of the way by Ferguson, and summarily dismissed by the admiral. While Mrs. Frawley vigorously fanned Sophie and Ferguson pushed a glass of water to her lips, Ben had been forced to leave the garden party. His blood still boiled. He could almost feel the steam shooting from his ears.

Damn them. No wonder Sophie possessed a rebellious streak. Ben would rather scrape barnacles for the rest of his life than have to live with Admiral Harrington. Sophie's ability to withstand her father's rigid insensitivity was testimony to the tawny-haired beauty's strength. Any other woman would have sought an early marriage. Determined to achieve her independence, the admiral's daughter had chosen to endure trials and tribulation.

Ben understood. If Sophie thought she would find herself in the same contemptuous position with a naval officer as her husband, a man used to giving orders and being obeyed without question like her father, independence would indeed seem the only answer.

"Give me a whiskey." Gus, who owned Reynolds Tavern, served up Ben's drink. "Where's Flora tonight?"

"Sick. She says." Gus didn't sound as if he believed her.

Ben couldn't blame him. Flora loved the lads more than she did serving whiskey and grog. The wild redhead had likely taken up with Graham for the evening.

"Better leave the bottle," Ben said, before downing his drink. Turning, he braced his elbows on the bar as he searched the crowded tavern for familiar faces.

In the back, among the dart players, he found a face he did not expect to see.

"Matt!" Ben yelled the name out in surprise, so loudly most of the patrons turned to gawk at him.

Including his brother. Matt looked over his shoulder at the sound of his name. A slow, wide grin spread across his face. "Big brother!"

In less time than it took for a man to make a bull's eye, Ben had crossed the room and swept his brother into a bear-sized hug. It had been four years since he had seen Matt. Years in which he'd worried, fretted, then finally figured his brother had been left for dead in the ruthless California gold fields.

"I've never been so glad to see anyone in my life."

"Yeah. You never said that before." Matt pulled back. The devil still glistened in his light blue eyes, but his boyish face had been darkened by the sun to the shade and texture of old saddle leather.

"I've never felt the way I do now," Ben admitted.

"Damned if you're not a Blue Jacket! Ma wrote me that you'd gone and done it, but it was hard to believe that my big brother would go takin' orders from some government sailor."

"It's tough, but I do it," he replied with a grin. "The California hills have done you no harm, little Matt. You look good, real good."

Although Matt's shaggy brown hair signaled the need for a haircut, he remained a good-looking young man. His appearance had been made more interesting by the ravages of weather and experience.

"I am good." He laughed and swiped a hand through his unruly dark hair. "Came to visit with you for a spell on my way back to Nantucket. Ma told me you were here. Did you get my letter?"

"Just the other day."

Matt made a small snorting sound. "You can cross country faster than the mail gets delivered."

"When did you get into Annapolis?"

"I got in a while ago, on the late afternoon stage. Went by the faculty quarters but you weren't there."

"I was at a . . . uh, garden party."

"Garden party? Did you say garden party?" Matt let out a laugh that rumbled through the tavern and stopped just short of shaking the rafters.

Ben straightened to his full "at attention" stance. "Naval personnel attend the functions we are commanded to attend."

"I think you'd better come back to Nantucket with me, Ben, before the Navy makes a mouse out of you."

"Let's sit down."

With a hand on his brother's back, Ben led Matt to a small table on the side of the room. No sooner had his butt met the chair than one of the tavern's working girls set down the bottle of whiskey Ben had ordered, along with two glasses.

"You don't know how happy I am to see you alive and well," Ben began. He poured a glass and slid it toward Matt.

"I'm gonna make you even happier."

"No, I don't think so. Doubt you could."

Matt leaned toward him until only inches and the whiskey bottle separated them. "I struck gold, big brother."

Ben's head jerked back on its own accord, as if it had come apart from his body. "What?"

"I mined until I had enough to live comfortably for the rest of my life. And that's after I pay you back for everything you gave me to pay my gambling debts."

Ben couldn't believe what he heard. "You're not serious."

"Dead serious. All that I owe you is sitting in the bank down on Main Street waiting for you to collect. I deposited it this afternoon—with interest."

Astonished by this unexpected turn of events, Ben could only shake his head and grin. "I must be dreaming."

"No, you're not dreaming. Your little brother just grew up. Back in those hills of California I realized what a mess I'd made of my life. I was a fool kid who thought he knew everything and I gambled away all the family owned—except the house for Ma, and you saved that."

"You did have a run of bad luck."

"And then I figured out that I missed Nantucket. Up in those mountains, I missed the sound of the sea. I gotta be where I can hear the surf pounding against rock."

"Are you thinking about whaling again?" Ben asked.

"Naw, I don't have to work. But I'm thinking about teaching school, kinda like your doing, but with younger boys. The little ones need to know a lot more than seafarin' skills. They need to know how to read

and write and do their numbers—in case of strikin'
gold." Matt flashed a grin before getting serious
again. "We were lucky to have a ma who knew how to
read and write."

"Yeah." Dumbstruck, Ben could only stare at this new,
mature man who claimed to be his younger brother.

"We're the only two Swains' left," Matt continued.
"Figured, we owe something to the island. I'm gonna
marry me a sturdy Nantucket woman with wide hips
and father a dozen kids."

Ben grinned and raised his glass. "You're going to
make some lucky lady a happy woman."

"I'll drink to that."

"How long can you stay in Annapolis?"

"Now, that I've seen you," Matt said, "I'll be leaving
in the morning after a shave and a haircut. I gotta get
busy and find me that lucky lady."

"You've been away from the island a long time. The
island folks are going to be glad to have a Swain back
among them."

"What about you, Ben? Do you ever think of going
back?"

"No, not yet, anyway."

"Have you found yourself a lady?"

In answer, Ben gave his brother a smile meant to
convey, maybe. But yes, he'd found a woman, although she was no lady. And she wasn't his.

"Swain."

Engrossed in conversation with his brother, Ben
hadn't been aware of Andrew Ferguson approaching
their table. *Damn*. This meant he had to get up and
salute in front of his brother. Matt would be snicker-
ing but Ben had no choice.

"Captain Ferguson."

"I hold you responsible for the incident at the garden party this evening." The captain's ruddy cheeks had taken on an alarming shade of scarlet as he ground the words through his teeth. "I shall warn you once. Stay away from the admiral's daughter."

In the old days—a few short weeks ago—Ben would have decked the hairy blowhard. But while keeping company with Sophie, he'd learned out of necessity to hold his temper in check. Still, he felt a keen desire to let loose with one double-fisted blow to Andrew's belly. Instead, he stared the man down with the ghost of a smile, hoping to further irritate Sophie's unsuitable suitor.

"Yes, sir."

"Or I shall call you out."

"Yes, sir." Hadn't Ferguson heard, the Navy had banned duels?

With a sharp salute and even sharper click of his heels, the captain stalked from the tavern.

"What was that all about?" Matt asked. "And why didn't you knock him into tomorrow? What's the Navy done to you, Ben?"

It wasn't the Navy; it was Sophie.

Several hours later, hunched over to avoid the eaves, Ben stared out of the attic window in his cramped room in Dulany House. No one was awake when he returned. Except for the gas lights in the corridors, all was dark and quiet. He looked toward the Severn but could see nothing in the pitch black night. The shade of night matched his mood. Pitch black.

Matt planned to return to Nantucket in the morning. And when Ben recovered Sophie's journal, as he felt confident he would do tomorrow, she would be lost to him forever. Now, formally pledged to another, the spirited rebel's fate was sealed. When he turned in her journal to the admiral, Ben would be assigned to sea duty and Sophie would be consigned to marry Andrew Ferguson.

His heart ached for her, for what had happened earlier in Mrs. Frawley's garden party, and for the man Andrew had shown himself to be later in Reynolds Tavern. Ben had wanted to comfort her, and the feeling persisted even after a joyous reunion with his brother, several drinks, and a fat cigar.

Sophie had been plainly shocked when Ferguson announced their engagement. What a cruel surprise to spring on her. Sophie was not a frail woman prone to swooning, but she possessed a sensitive soul.

Nothing stirred in the grand old house; not even a candle dripped. Everyone slept, except Ben. And Sophie. Sophie would never be able to sleep tonight. In the firm, undeniably arrogant belief that she needed him—Ben realized his arrogance worked both ways, as a failing and as a strength—he went to her. He stole quietly out of his room, down the ladder, and through the corridor in the hopes that Sophie might appreciate his company for a moment.

She answered the first soft rap, which indicated she'd not been sleeping either. Silently motioning him into the spacious chamber, she quickly closed the door behind him.

The gaslights were off but one lantern burned, its pale golden rays casting enough light for him to see that her eyes were red from crying. The knot in his stomach tightened.

He traced the still wet trail of her tears with a fingertip. Her lips trembled. Ben would trade his life for a sorcerer's power to ease her heartache and banish her melancholy.

Sophie lifted her gaze, awash with tears yet to be shed. He lowered his head until he could not see the sorrow in her gaze, until his forehead rested on the nest of tawny waves twirled to the top of her head. She was barefoot.

Suddenly struck with an astounding desire to kiss her toes, Ben closed his eyes and let out the breath he'd been holding. He'd reached a new level of madness. Never before had he kissed a woman's toes before, nor had the slightest desire to.

Whirling on her heel, Sophie glided away from him. Her pale lavender satin dressing gown flowing behind her. He followed and clasped her hand from behind, pulling her around to face him.

Her lips quivered, and when she lowered her eyes, her long dark lashes caressed her cheeks. A tense, sad silence enveloped them.

Ben searched for a way to tell her how sorry he felt, but became distracted. The plunging neckline of Sophie's dressing gown revealed deep, pearly cleavage, delicate and enticing. The desire to explore the alluring valley once again swept through him swiftly and urgently. What kind of man had he become? Ben silently chastised himself for entertaining such thoughts when he'd come to offer comfort and consolation.

He lifted his eyes from temptation. Yet his heart hammered against his chest like a mast being battered by the wind.

"Are you all right?" he asked her quietly.

"Oh, Ben!" she cried in answer. Sophie flung her arms around his neck with the fervor of a woman about to be shipwrecked.

Ben crushed her to him. "Your father and Ferguson didn't give me the opportunity to speak with you . . . or stay to see how you fared."

"I did not know Andrew meant to announce our engagement. He did not ask me or I would have told him that I could not marry him."

"What are you going to do?" Ben asked the question but feared the answer.

Sophie backed out of Ben's arms. "Give him a reason for breaking off the engagement."

"Like what?"

"I don't know." She twisted the lace hanky in her hand. "I have worn a path in the carpet thinking of it. I've been trying to think of what Fifi LaDeux would do in the same circumstance."

"I beg you not do anything impulsive, Sophie. You are not the heroine in a novel. Your father won't react kindly to your rejection of Andrew after a public announcement."

"He shall probably roar and howl and send me to St. Louis." Her breasts rose and fell as she heaved a great sigh. "But what will it matter? You will be on your ship."

"I see no ship in sight. Fletcher Thurman eludes me still."

"But he is here!" she exclaimed, coming alive with excitement. "I know he is because I have seen and been with Abigail."

"Where? When?"

With a dismissive flick of her wrist, Sophie turned away. "'Tis a long story."

"I have time. Did she tell you where he's hiding?"

"No, she fell asleep before she could tell me. Abigail is not with Fletcher any longer."

"What happened?"

"I don't know." She shook her head, paused, and grinned. "What I do know is that I delivered her child today."

"You?" Ben blurted in surprise. Well aware of how Sophie feared childbirth, he found it impossible to believe she would participate in any way in the birthing process.

He suspected a scheme to divert him from questioning her further about Abigail and Fletcher.

Sophie beamed proudly. "It was not half as dreadful as I'd heard."

"No?"

"Abigail did quite well, aside from being rather exhausted by the end of it."

"Both you and the mother survived?"

"Of course, silly!"

"Apparently, you can't always believe what you hear," he commented. "The dangers of childbirth likely have been blown out of proportion."

"Apparently. And although the baby came early and is quite fragile, she appears to be a healthy infant," Sophie gushed.

"Good. Good for you and good for Abigail."

Ben wondered if this experience had cured Sophie of her fear of childbirth. It made no difference. She could never be his. If she refused to marry Ferguson, her father probably would send her away. And then Admiral Harrington immediately would begin the search again, looking for another officer of rank to marry and subdue his audacious daughter.

"First thing tomorrow I intend to collect Abigail and her baby and bring them here where you may question her."

Sophie would let him question Abigail? "Where are they now?"

"They are staying with Flora."

"It would be better if I questioned Abigail there. That way your father need never know of her complicity if

you don't choose to tell him. Abigail may remain innocent, the victim of evil Fletcher Thurman as much as
you."

"Of course! I should have thought of that. Thank
you, Ben." Sophie slanted him a soft, chagrined smile.
"It seems that I am always thanking you. You are always saving me from imminent disaster."

"I *am* getting quite good at it, aren't I?" he quipped
with a grin.

But his teasing comment masked a heavy heart.
Ben wished that he could save Sophie's dreams.

"And yet you remain so humble," she countered
with a twinkle in her eyes.

"I'll see Abigail first thing in the morning," he said,
resuming a serious tone. "With her help and a little
luck, I'll have Fletcher in custody by the end of the day."

"If I haven't lured him into my net by then."

"What?"

"I have my own plans for the future of Fletcher
Thurman."

"Thurman is dangerous, Sophie. Stay away from
him and let me handle this."

"And then you will be giving my novel to my father
and leaving Annapolis for the first ship to depart its
port."

"You're writing another novel, I've seen the new
journal," Ben pointed out in his own defense. "Perhaps this is the one that will gain you your
independence. In that case, we both shall have won
what we sought."

"In any case, it appears we may not have much
longer together," she said, raising a wistful gaze to his.

"Perhaps not," Ben agreed, feeling a painful stab in
his heart. For a man who'd come to cheer Sophie,
pain was not part of the plan. "But we shall always be

friends. No matter where in the world that I may be, I shall buy and read all of your novels. And I will write you long letters from my ship describing everything in sight. You will be the first to see my designs for the ships that shall take the Navy into the future." He paused, taking both of her hands in his.

"And you shall write to me from the cottage on Prince George Street telling me about your latest escapade."

"Yes. Yes I will," she agreed eagerly.

"We have our memories."

"And we have tonight."

"Tonight?"

Did Sophie mean she wished to make love? How could he even consider making love to the admiral's daughter in her chamber? What kind of fool would do such a bold, crazy thing right under his commanding officer's roof?

He would. At the moment, gazing into Sophie's great luminous eyes, Ben felt that sort of fool.

In the next moment, she erased all doubt of what she had in mind—as well as any lingering good sense left in Ben. Gently framing his face in her soft palms, she slowly drew his head down until his lips met hers.

She tasted of peppermint. She tasted of desire.

His arms slid around her. Ben kissed her fiercely, as if he would never feel her lips beneath his again. He kissed her urgently, as if the moment would end before its time.

More dangerous to him than a legendary sea siren who lured sailors to their doom, the defiant Sophie Harrington had become as necessary to Ben as feeling the roll of the sea beneath his feet.

When he could no longer breathe, when his heart hammered against his chest in an unrelenting excitement, Ben swept Sophie off her feet and carried her to the bed.

"Wait," she whispered.

He eased her down at bedside.

She slipped off her dressing gown. Transfixed, he watched while the delicate lavender fabric pooled to the floor, falling in soft folds around her bare feet.

She was the goddess of love. No one could match Sophie's physical perfection. He stood in wonder of the creamy flush of her body, each rise and fall of her breasts and the taut rosy buds of her swollen breasts, aroused and waiting for his touch.

Tension and desire coiled inside Ben until he thought he would either yell out or take her with loving force.

But he could do neither, not here, not now.

Passion consumed him, heated his blood, quickened his pulse, lodged in his throat. Ben simply shook his head, shaking away the vision of making love to Sophie. Turning on his heel, he strode toward the door but stopped just short of it when Sophie seized his hand from behind.

Ben stood still. Not daring to turn around, to look into her eyes, to be captivated by her lips, seduced by her alluring body.

"If this is our last time alone together, I should like to remember the love that we shared at the last," she whispered. "Lock the door, Ben. Let me make love to you."

He risked everything. If he were caught in Sophie's bed, he'd be locked in irons and thrown in the brig for the rest of his life.

"I understand what I am asking," she said. "And I will understand if you choose to leave."

This did not sound like the defiant, sassy Sophie he knew; nor was it the would-be novelist bent on conducting intimate research. Desire deepened her tone and gave her voice an unfamiliar huskiness. This was a new woman who wanted him.

Ben locked the door.

Abigail cradled her sleeping baby. Although small and scrawny, Flora Sophie Grant was a beautiful baby. She gazed at the newborn, vowing aloud to give Florrie a good life.

Flora had left Abigail and the baby to tend bar at Reynolds Tavern. Night had fallen and with it came fear for Abigail. She cringed with every sound, the sound of owls, the sound of creaking floorboards. Fletcher would be looking for her, and she feared he would find her. Love and marriage would not be on his mind.

Sufficiently recovered from the physical exhaustion of labor, Abigail concentrated on her predicament. After being visited by Sophie and the handsome seaman in Falls Church, Abigail realized the enormity of her mistake.

Unable to go through with Fletcher's ransom scheme, she'd spent her last coins to return to Annapolis. Determined to find and stop him, she'd scoured the countryside until she'd come across an old abandoned barn.

Fletcher, hiding in the loft, answered her call. She spent the night with him, attempting to convince him to give up the scheme. He refused and threatened to kill her and their child if she tried to interfere. She agreed as she always agreed to anything he said. He expected her to be compliant, willing to do his bidding even when she knew it wasn't right. But this time was different. This time he had broken her heart.

Abigail remained with him through a sleepless night, and as the first hazy rays of dawn filtered through the barn door, she stole away. Leaving Fletcher sleeping in the barn, she stealthily made her way back to the city by way of the fields. Her first labor pain struck as she reached Main Street. Acting on instinct, she hastened to Flora Muldoony for help.

Now, an entire day had passed and Fletcher would be looking for her. In the blurry throes of labor, she'd not been able to confess the truth to Sophie Harrington. The admiral's daughter had been all kindness, delivering the baby and promising to provide a home for them.

Abigail had fallen asleep nursing the baby while Sophie explained to Flora what had happened during the tavern maid's absence. When Abigail awoke, Sophie had gone. She'd left a message to expect her first thing in the morning. The admiral's daughter meant to take Abigail and her baby home to Dulany House.

But morning was hours away and Fletcher was out there somewhere looking for Abigail.

Sophie awoke with a start the following morning. She'd meant to rise at dawn but one look told her it was well past that time. Full, warm rays of sun streamed through her windows.

She reached out for the pillow beside her. Clutching it to her, she buried her face in its soft down and breathed in Ben Swain. The virile scent of him lingered on the pillow where his head had rested well into the wee hours of the morning. Sometime during the night, long after Sophie had fallen asleep nestled in his arms, Ben had left her.

The inner serenity that most people knew on occasion, but that had always eluded Sophie, she had found at last in Ben's arms. Engulfed in his arms of warmth and might, she felt lighter than the air she breathed. Her feet no longer touched the ground, Sophie wandered paths of pristine white clouds. She gazed upon calm, glistening blue waters.

Never having made love to a man, a shy uncertainty filled Sophie at the start. Her heart pounded in an alternating rhythm with the staccato beat of her pulse. But then she splayed her palms across his massive chest. Her fingertips tingled at the touch of his corded muscles, crisp dark curls, and pebbled flesh. Within minutes her inhibitions slipped away, replaced by unbounded passion.

Oh, sweet mercy!

As her lips lovingly caressed old scars, liquid warmth, thick and sweeter than honey, flowed through Sophie. With feathery kisses, she'd nuzzled an enlivening trail across Ben's tight muscular belly, until she ached, until he moaned.

Sophie savored the sight, the scent, the sound, and the taste of him. In an astounding turn of events, she discovered that pleasuring the seaman aroused her to a fiery state. She meant to explore every inch of Ben until he cried out for mercy, until she exploded in a burst of flame. Like the stars in the sky, Sophie and Ben ignited the night. She would never love like this again. He touched her soul, Sophie touched his, and all that was wrong with the world was right . . . for one night.

The trail of her kisses led to his manhood. The sight of Ben's magnificent arousal even before she touched him filled Sophie with incredible joy. Delicious waves of excitement rocked her body, leaving her light-headed and aching with a fierce need. A need Ben soon filled with each loving thrust.

But that was last night, and this was the new morning. Reluctantly pushing the pillow aside, Sophie wished she could push her memories of Ben aside as easily. If she could not have the handsome seaman in her life, she would have no one.

But she still had a dream.

After hurriedly dressing, Sophie declined breakfast and set out on a most important assignation, one that might change her life.

"Wait up, Miss Harrington!"

Her father's aide. Drat.

Sophie had been on her way to Flora's intending to question Abigail before Ben reached her. She planned to seek out Fletcher Thurman on her own.

Aware that she might require more than resolve to recover her novel, she carried a Derringer in her reticule. The small revolver was the latest in weapons. She'd borrowed it from the admiral's weapon case reasonably certain it would not be missed for a few hours. Sophie had also stuffed her savings into the small bag. Over the course of a year, she had squirreled away thirty dollars from her monthly allowance. In her opinion, that was a vast amount of money, more than the information contained in the journal was worth. The villain simply would have to be satisfied with less than he'd asked for in the ransom note or she might be forced to shoot him.

Determined to recover her novel, Sophie would do most anything. Although she had never fired a weapon before, she'd watched the acting midshipmen at practice.

Her frustration knew no bounds as she followed the admiral's aide into her father's office. Her head buzzed as if a horde of bees nested there. Needles and pins prickled at her from within and without. Brows furrowed, she fairly bristled with impatience at this unexpected order . . . and that's what it was, an order. Her father never asked for her presence. He demanded it, just as if Sophie were still a schoolgirl.

Ben would be way ahead of her. If her father delayed her for any amount of time, she would have no hope of finding Fletcher Thurman before the handsome seaman.

The admiral sat at his desk stroking his Vandyke. Andrew Ferguson, as rigid as one of her whalebone corsets, stood at his side.

Oh no, more trouble.

Seventeen

The admiral's pinched lips and stern countenance appeared more intimidating than usual as he regarded Sophie from behind his desk. From her earliest recollections, it seemed she always stood on the opposite side of the desk from her father. One type of wall or another always stood between them.

Andrew Ferguson stood beside the admiral wearing the stoic expression of a martyr. "Are you feeling better today, dearest?"

"Oh, yes, much better, thank you. I am not in the practice of swooning when taken by surprise."

"Too late, I realized my mistake," he said. "I should have discussed what I'd planned with you, Sophie. But having waited so long to announce our engagement, with one delay following another, I decided to take matters in hand rather than hear still another objection."

As he surely would have.

"Also, as you might remember, I did have your father's blessings," the slope-shouldered captain added.

"And once again you embarrassed me, Sophie," the admiral snapped.

"Father, I did not swoon to embarrass you. It just . . . happened."

Her explanation did nothing to soften her father's formidable expression. Sophie glanced at the grandfather clock in the far corner. Precious time ticked away. Ben would be way ahead of her. While he confronted Fletcher Thurman, she must soothe Captain Ferguson's wounded pride. Sophie chafed at the unfairness of it all.

"Andrew had already offered for your hand," her father grumbled. "His public announcement should not have been all that shocking."

"Exactly so," she agreed hurriedly. "I am at a loss to explain what came over me, but I should be glad to take up the matter later. You see, I am already late for an appointment in town."

Her father's gaze narrowed on her. His flat ash gray eyes held no light, no forgiveness. "No appointment that you have made can be as important as arriving at a mutual understanding, and setting a course for the future."

"Yes, sir." *No, sir.*

"Since Captain Ferguson has announced his intentions to make you his wife, I felt it only honorable to tell him about the humiliating situation in which we find ourselves."

Sophie hoped her father didn't mean what she thought he meant. "Which humiliating situation would that be, Father?" she asked, attempting to make light of her predicament.

Her father's scowl was fearsome. He could fell enemy forces with that look—no gun deck was required on Admiral Harrington's ship.

"Andrew has generously agreed to pay the ransom to recover your journal. He remains firm in his commitment to marry you. All the captain asks in return is that I reassign Ben Swain at once and that you give up writing your journals."

"No!" Sophie blurted. Trembling with outrage,

unable to catch but the shallowest of breath, she turned to Andrew, who had raised his gaze to the ceiling. "Begging your pardon, but I cannot marry you. I do not love you, Andrew. Further, I . . . I do not wish to marry . . . anyone!"

"You will marry Captain Ferguson or I shall send you to Saint Louis," her father thundered.

"I shall pack my bags and send my aunt a message that I will be arriving soon," she bristled. Whirling on her heel, Sophie stormed toward the door, but stopped midway. "You are a good man," she said to Andrew. "And you will make some woman the perfect husband. I do not mean to embarrass or humiliate you by ending our engagement. But if you had only told me beforehand, I should have explained. I have long wished to be an independent woman."

"But every woman wishes to wed," he protested.

"Most women, but not all," she corrected him, before being struck with a wonderful idea. "My friend Rosalind is looking for a husband and she prefers him to be a naval officer. I shall introduce you to Miss Montrose before I leave for Saint Louis."

Andrew appeared bewildered. She moved too swiftly from one thought to another for him. "If you do not marry, what will you do with your life?"

"I wish to be a writer."

"A writer!" The stodgy captain rocked back on his heels. "How foolish, Sophie. Haven't you caused problems enough with your writing?"

She angled her chin proudly, as high as it would go. "Not nearly."

While Andrew sputtered, the admiral exploded up from his chair. "That's enough, you incorrigible . . . insolent girl. Go! Return to Dulany House at once. You are confined to your room until further notice."

"Father, please—"

Recovering his composure, Captain Ferguson interceded. "Tempers are flaring. Perhaps we should continue our conversation this evening."

The admiral drew a deep breath and settled into his stiff military bearing. "I expect you are right, Ferguson."

"In spite of her flight of fancy, I still wish to marry Sophie," Andrew said quite graciously, and stubbornly, given the circumstances.

Sophie marveled at his tenacity until he addressed her in a rather supercilious manner. "I am certain that you will come to your senses shortly, dearest. In the meantime we shall forge ahead and take care of the ransom matter and Seaman Swain."

Sophie opened her mouth to object but did not speak out in time.

"Go!" her father bellowed, pointing to the door. "Back to Dulany House and to your bedchamber."

He ordered her about as if she were a child. Stung by his high-handedness, Sophie straightened her shoulders, lifted her head, and marched from the room without a backward glance.

She knew her history. Many a sailor had met his death for refusing to obey an admiral's order. Still, Sophie could not return to her bedchamber when all of her dreams tumbled down about her like a rain of soot.

Ben saw his brother off on the stage at daybreak. Being with Matt again had been a boon, and not because his brother had made him a wealthy man again. To know his brother had triumphed and thrived over the odds gave him a great deal of pleasure. To see firsthand that Matt had become a mature young man with plans to put down permanent roots in Nantucket lifted a ship's ballast of guilt from Ben's shoulders. No longer would he be solely responsible for his mother; no longer did he need to concern himself with populating the world with little Swains.

Great gray and plum clouds rolled across the sky, promising stormy weather before day's end. The humidity left Ben feeling warm and sticky as he hurried to Flora's room above the livery stable. If luck were with him, and it was about time for luck to arrive, he would make swift work of questioning Abigail. Bent on finding and capturing Fletcher Thurman before midday, Ben figured he just might have his deployment papers by dinner.

He took the stairs to Flora's flat two at a time. Positioned at the side of the building, the steep wooden steps were imbued with the aroma from the livery stable.

Making no attempt to hide his eagerness, Ben banged on the door. After waiting a decent amount of time, he realized that no one was going to let him in. He listened. No baby wails. No baby sounds at all. Damn. If Abigail had bolted already, he'd be too furious to be reasonable when he finally did catch up with Thurman.

Folding his arms across his chest, Ben stared at the closed door as if it held the answers he needed. He heard the muffled sound as he weighed his options and did not hesitate. Leading with his shoulder, he threw his weight against the door and broke the lock.

"Flora!"

Poor Flora lay bound and gagged on the floor. Her green eyes flashed with anger; her red hair fell in a tangled mass. Wearing only her chemise, she appeared to have started the morning off on the wrong side of the bed—not that Ben would dare mention it to her.

Squatting beside the obviously livid woman, Ben untied and removed the faded red bandanna gagging her. Instead of thanking Ben, she shrieked, "If I ever get a hold of that weasel, I'll kill him!"

Her arms had been tied behind her back, her legs bound at the ankles. Ben worked quickly to free her.

"Does this mean you've met Fletcher Thurman?"

"He took Abigail and the baby. What kind of man threatens to kill his own child?"

"No man I've ever met."

"He's holding the baby to make sure Abigail doesn't give him up before he gets the ransom this afternoon."

Had the admiral agreed to pay the ransom without letting Ben know? "Do you know where Fletcher took Abigail and the baby?" he asked.

"No."

"Can you remember how he was dressed, what he looked like?"

"He's wearin' baggy trousers, and a checkered shirt. And one of those big, floppy felt hats that mostly hid his face," she added. "But Flora could see he had a mustache. His boots came up to his knees."

"Anything else?"

"He looked like a dirt-poor farmer. Only the saints in heaven know what Abigail ever saw in him," she declared.

"Can you think of any place where a man might hide that's not too far from the Graveyard Creek Bridge?"

"There's an old abandoned mill out that way, northeast of the academy grounds."

"Thanks."

"Bring Abigail and her baby back in one piece, Ben. Flora knows her men, and I'm as certain as the sun will set tonight that Fletcher Thurman won't give Abigail and her babe anything but misery."

"I'll do my best, Flora." Ben started down the stairs. "And if Sophie comes by looking for Abigail, don't tell her what's happened. I don't want her getting involved and getting hurt."

"You think she'll give chase to Thurman too?"

"Don't you?"

Flora nodded her head. "Flora may have to tie her down."

"If you need more rope, you'll find plenty on my sloop."

Trusting Flora to keep Sophie from following him, Ben made it to the academy stable in record time. He hadn't seen Sophie this morning and didn't know if her absence from this melodrama should worry him or not. She might have seen Thurman abducting Abigail and her infant and followed. Damn. He hoped Sophie wasn't in danger.

Hurriedly saddling the first horse available, he rode off before anyone knew he'd returned. While he could walk to Graveyard Creek Bridge from the academy grounds, he wasn't sure of the mill's exact location. Riding seemed the wiser and speedier course.

It was almost over. Shortly he'd be back aboard a ship, anchors aweigh, sails full, and feeling the salty slap of the wind. In the evening he'd be at work designing the ships of the future. The thought that hit him next knocked the air from his lungs.

Sophie. He would miss Sophie Harrington. He would never again hear her laugh, look into her remarkable eyes, or taste her soft, sweet lips. He would hear no more tales of the exciting adventures of Fifi LaDeux.

But perhaps with Sophie out of sight, she would be out of his mind as well. Perhaps.

Without warning, his high spirits crashed. The ebullience of a moment ago escaped him, leaving Ben feeling dead in the water.

Sophie arrived at Flora's flat in a high state of agitation. The aroma of horses did not settle her nerves . . . or stomach.

When her frazzled-appearing friend opened the door, she flounced past her, and then stopped in her tracks. "Where's Abigail? Where's the baby?"

"Gone."

Sophie spun on Flora. "Did Ben Swain take them?" she demanded. "Has he been here?"

"Yes, Ben's been here, but it was Fletcher Thurman who took Abigail and little Florrie."

"Oh, no!"

"The scoundrel tied up Flora as well."

"Were you hurt?"

"Only my pride. Came to my place and took what he wanted. I hope Ben kills the weasel."

"Ben's gone after him?"

"What do you think?"

Sophie turned on her heel. She didn't expect Flora to tackle her. The body blow came as an unpleasant surprise.

Whumph. Sophie fell on the hard wood floor with a thud. Her stomach prickled with pain. Her nose flattened against the hard, plank floors. "What are you doing?" she gasped.

"Ben said to keep you here."

"Flora, if I don't recover my journal, I'll be married to Andrew Ferguson before you can blink. Either I marry a man I cannot like, or my father will put me on the stage to Saint Louis. Those are my choices."

Flora placed her bare foot on the small of Sophie's back. "No one can force you to marry or leave town."

"My father has his ways."

Flora sighed. "Ben's doing this for your own good. He doesn't want you to get hurt."

Bracing herself on her elbows, Sophie strained to look over her shoulder and up at the well-meaning redhead holding her captive. "Ben doesn't know what's good for me. Flora, Andrew has agreed to pay the ransom if my father signs the redeployment papers for Ben. Andrew will have my novel and Ben will be gone to sea. Admiral Johnson will not be looking at his ship designs and I will not be living an independent life."

"Captain Ferguson is jealous."

"He has no reason to be."

"Of course he has. He must have noticed the way Ben looks at you. The whole town knows Ben Swain's mad in love with you."

"No!"

"They're not talking about your bloomers anymore. They're talking about what a handsome couple you and the sailing instructor make."

"'Tis only gossip. Must I forever be plagued by gossip?"

"For once, it's true."

As much as Sophie wished to believe Flora, she found it impossible. Ben had never said he loved her, never indicated he'd rather be in Annapolis with her than out at sea. While she prided herself on a well-formed imagination, Sophie could not afford to allow her daydreams to run rampant. Ben Swain had already stolen her heart and caused her to renege on her vow of abstinence. She could not allow him to interfere in her last remaining resolve.

"I have no time for gossip, Flora. If Fletcher Thurman gets to the bridge and collects the ransom, my novel will be destroyed. My father and Andrew will throw it into the fire. Months of writing will end as ashes and I shall have no opportunity to live the independent life I've dreamed. Someone else will be living in the cottage on Prince George Street."

Sophie did not mention what might happen if her father or Andrew read her journal. If he recognized himself, her father would disown her and Andrew would learn who had captured her heart.

After a long moment of silence, the tavern maid drew a deep breath and straightened her shoulders. "Flora had better come with you."

"Hurry, we have no time to waste."

Leaving his horse tied to a tree near the road, Ben approached the abandoned mill cautiously. The wooded area surrounding the mill gave him ample protection to make his way sight unseen. He dodged from tree to tree, keeping low, going slow.

Ducking behind a large boulder, just yards from the mill, he listened. Except for the insects and birds who dwelled in the woods, he heard no other sounds.

Fletcher might not be hiding in the old mill at all. Ben had taken a gamble but one he must play out. Tension coiled in the pit of his stomach like a hot cable. Staying low, Ben dashed to the building, pausing behind the thick trunks of ancient oaks to make certain he hadn't been detected. When he reached the gray, deteriorating building, he plastered his body flat against the wall and edged toward the open door.

A baby cried.

A slap echoed.

A woman yelped in pain.

After a few minutes, the baby quieted.

Ben withdrew his prized personal pistol, one of the new Colt police revolvers. Eyes focused in continuous scrutiny, he slowly eased into the mill. Once inside, he lurked in the shadows, waiting for his eyes to adjust to the dim light.

The first thing that Ben saw clearly was at the opposite end of the mill. On a raised platform he could make out the Thurman family tabloid. Abigail nursed her baby, while Fletcher watched from the south window. If someone were to approach the mill from the vicinity of the Graveyard Creek Bridge, Thurman would see the interloper. He'd completely discounted any other approach to the mill, including the one from the north, which Ben had just used. Fletcher Thurman had failed as a farmer, and apparently, he didn't have the makings of a successful thief either. He lacked the intelligence required for his chosen profession.

Ben kept to the shadows, quietly approaching the platform until he was only yards from Fletcher. He hoped that Abigail had not experienced another change of heart and had freely reunited with the father of her child. If that were the case, she might come to Thurman's aid. It was a risk Ben had to take.

Stepping out of the shadows, Ben quickly climbed the short ladder leading up to the platform. The third rung creaked. He stopped.

"Didja hear that?" Fletcher asked Abigail.

"What? I didn't hear anything."

Fletcher grunted.

Ben counted to ten and scrambled up the remaining three rungs, leaping on the platform with his revolver drawn.

He aimed his weapon at the farmer's head. "It's over, Thurman. Turn around, real slow."

"Seaman Swain!" Abigail cried.

Fletcher whipped around quickly, losing his balance in the process.

"Down on your knees," Ben ordered.

"Don't shoot. I ain't done nothin'. Don't shoot," Fletcher begged in a shaky voice as he obeyed Ben's command.

"You've done plenty," Ben growled. "Lay flat, spread-eagle."

Button-sized tears spilled from Abigail's eyes. Her pale left cheek bore the scarlet imprint of Thurman's hand. "He took me. Fletcher took me and the baby from Flora's. I didn't want to go with him. But I had no choice."

"It's all right. You're safe now," Ben assured her.

Abigail backed as far away from Fletcher as she could while Ben searched the sniveling piece of fish bait.

He kept his revolver pointed at the villain's head. Two outside pockets were sewn into the oversized jacket Thurman wore. Slipping his hand inside the left pocket, Ben found a gun, which he tossed out the window. In the right pocket he found Sophie's journal. Clutching it tightly, he withdrew the black leather-bound book.

"Get up," he barked at the crook who had begun to curse worse than any sailor.

"I ain't goin' to jail." Fletcher said, glaring at Ben in shifty-eyed hostility.

"Just get up."

Ben didn't expect what happened next. Halfway to a standing position, Fletcher appeared to have lost his balance. In the confusing, senseless scrambling, one hand reached down into the back of his trousers. As the thief lurched toward him, Ben caught a flash of silver and realized what it was too late. The blade of Thurman's knife was raised to slash him in the chest.

Reeling in surprise and pain, Ben dropped the coveted novel as he staggered. Fletcher's form blurred before him as Ben grew dizzy. Swaying like a drunken gunner, he swayed and fell forward. When he heard Fletcher's scream of fury, he knew. Ben's last conscious thought was that he had fallen on top of Sophie's journal.

Flora drove the rented buggy as if it had wings. But the buggy had neither wings nor springs. Sophie clung to the bench for dear life as they jolted over every bump. The team of young horses raced down the dirt road leading to the mill as if the devil were after them. Deciding the back road was best in case Fletcher attempted an escape, Sophie and Flora headed directly into the oncoming storm.

Sophie spotted the first crack of lightning in the distance. The jagged bolt lit up the sky and more than likely the length and breadth of the Severn River. But she couldn't turn back now.

"There's a storm headin' for us!" Flora cried as she pulled up the horses.

"Don't stop!" Sophie cried. "We have to go on."

"Flora can't drive through mud and ruts, it's too dangerous."

Clutching her somersaulting stomach with one

hand and gabbing at the reins with the other, Sophie remained undaunted. "We have to go on."

"No, no we don't," Flora declared, "The sky is dark as night."

"You head back, but let me out first," Sophie demanded, sounding a good bit braver than she felt.

"It's gonna start raining soon. The storm will be overhead before you make it to the mill."

But Sophie refused to be stopped. "I have to find Fletcher before he turns my novel over to Andrew and picks up the ransom."

Jumping from the buggy, Sophie winced as another lightning bolt split across the sky. An ominous rumble of thunder caused her to feel weak in the knees. She sucked in a ragged breath. Her heart pounded against her chest. If she did not retrieve her journal, all hope for the life she dreamed of would die.

The admiral had struck a bargain with Sophie. If she changed the names in her novel, she could publish the book under a pseudonym and live the life she'd dreamed in the Bailey Cottage on Prince George Street.

"Go back," she called to Flora before turning and running into the woods toward the mill.

Sophie ran as if her life depended upon her speed, and in more than one way, it did. Her skirts tangled in her legs, causing her to stumble. If only she had worn bloomers! Her hat caught on a branch and tore away, and before she had traveled another twenty feet, her hair came tumbling down. The wind blew the silky strands in her face and mouth. Burrs caught at and ripped her dress.

She slowed as she approached the mill. The door stood open, blowing in the wind, which gained in strength by the minute. The first sounds Sophie heard were the wail of the baby and Abigail's sobs. Fearing the worst for her former maid and the newborn, she curbed the impulse to dash headlong into the mill. Instead, she carefully and quietly made her way through the open door.

When her eyes adjusted to the dimness, Sophie reacted with a horrified gasp. Ben lay on the floor. Abigail, holding her baby, crouched down beside him pleading, "Get up, Ben. Please, God, make him get up."

Rushing to Ben's side, without any thought of danger to herself, Sophie fell to her knees. "What happened?" she cried.

"Fletcher . . . Fletcher had a knife," Abigail sobbed. The baby wailed louder as Sophie's former maid laid her down on a mound of hay in the corner.

Sophie crooned in Ben's ear. "Ben, Ben are you all right?"

Without waiting for a reply, she rolled the unconscious seaman over with Abigail's help. The first thing to meet her eyes was her journal. Her precious novel had been lodged beneath Ben's chest and bore his blood. Blood!

Blood stained the unconscious seaman's open blue jacket and the white shirt beneath. Sophie quickly ripped a strip of linen from her petticoat. Her fingers trembled so badly she could barely unbutton his shirt. As she pressed the cloth to his wound, Ben's eyes fluttered open.

"Sophie?"

"Don't talk. You'll be fine. We'll get you back to town and to a doctor as fast as possible."

He spoke slowly, breathing laboriously. "Take your journal. Go, Sophie, go."

Unbidden tears gathered in her eyes. "But, but what about your ship assignment, your ship designs?"

"Like you said, I'll be deployed to a ship eventually."

"You don't know what you're saying." Hot tears trickled down Sophie's cheeks. "You've lost a great deal of blood. You're delirious."

"This is no time to argue, Sophie."

"Say no more, save your strength," she urged in a hushed, insistent tone. Her heart drummed wildly against her chest while her pulse skipped in fear.

He smiled weakly. "Go, Sophie. Fly while you have the chance."

But Sophie felt numb, completely unable to fly. Pressing the cloth against Ben's wound with greater force, she did not even look up when Flora rushed through the door.

"What happened?"

"Ben's hurt," Sophie said.

"Fletcher stabbed the seaman," Abigail added. "Seaman Swain is dying."

Rain pounded on the roof, lightning cracked the sky, and the rumble of thunder shook the ground. The deluge had begun.

Was he dying? Ben struggled from the black curtain that kept enveloping him. He likened the throbbing pain in his chest to the bite of a whale. Once more he forced his eyes opened. A blur of women's faces looked down upon him, Sophie, Flora, and Abigail. The women regarded him anxiously, as if he were about to draw his last breath.

This is not the way he'd expected to die.

Eighteen

Sophie thought her heart would break. Immobilized by pain so palatable she could barely catch a full breath, she brushed back the thick chestnut locks that had fallen across Ben's forehead.

Torn between fleeing and staying at the seaman's side, Sophie applied still more pressure against his wound. Unable to stanch the bleeding, she pressed an ear to his chest and listened to the faint, weak beat of his heart. A bone-deep chill ran through her.

If Sophie was to claim the future she had dreamed of for so long, she must run. She had no choice but to venture into the oncoming storm to save her dream . . . or to save Ben.

"There was nothing I could do to stop Fletcher from hurting Seaman Swain," Abigail sniffled.

"He's had his comeuppance. The swine is out there in the woods bleeding from his butt right now," Flora announced.

"From his butt?" Abigail's eyes widened.

"He ran past Flora in the woods. A man who's running in the woods is up to no good. Figured it must be the Thurman weasel so I took aim and fired. I didn't have time for questions."

"Look." Sophie had barely listened to the exchange between Flora and Abigail. Her attention was riveted to the spot where Ben had fallen. She picked up her bloodstained journal. *The Romantic Adventures of Fifi LaDeux, An Unmarried Woman.*

Abigail lowered her eyes. "Please, please forgive me. I never should have taken it."

"You have what you wanted. Take your novel to New York City," Flora urged. "If you leave now you can catch the afternoon stage."

Leave? Sophie lived among the students and instructors at the Naval Academy, all held to high moral standards. They did not steal, they did not lie, they did not cheat. In every matter they strove to be fair. She could do no less than honor their strict code of conduct.

Ben had recovered her journal and paid a dear price. His life was at stake. Under no circumstances could Sophie take advantage of a wounded man, or disregard the bargain she'd made. She listened to the thoughts tumbling about in her mind, and then she listened to her heart. Ben needed her.

"No," she said, shaking her head. "I can't leave. I can't leave Ben now."

In the tight-lipped manner of a disapproving school mistress, her redhead friend wagged a finger at her. "Flora and Abigail will take care of the sailing instructor. You go on to New York. No one can stop you now."

"Ben needs a doctor," Sophie replied, motioning for Flora to take her place at his side. "I'm going for the doctor."

Abigail immediately objected, "But it's a full-fledged storm out there."

"There's no time to wait." Sophie pushed to her feet. "Apply as much pressure against the wound as you can, Flora."

"Flora knows how to nurse a man!" she replied indignantly.

With a roll of her eyes, Sophie turned and made for the ladder. "I'll be back as soon as possible."

Summoning more courage than she ever would have believed she possessed, Sophie ran from the building and into the storm. The onslaught of pelting rain stung her face and blurred her eyes. The lightning cracked like a sharp whip, lashing across the sky. The ground shook beneath her feet at each deep, ominous roll of thunder.

Leaving the buggy near the mill to transport Ben if the doctor thought it wise, Sophie ran toward the Naval Academy grounds through the empty fields of Saint John's College. If luck were with her, Dr. Collins would be on duty. The hospital stood by itself between the superintendent's residence and Recitation Hall.

Sophie's heart hammered against her chest until it ached. Her body started and trembled with each new lightning bolt. But she never stopped running. Holding her skirts as high as she dared, she dodged trees and rocks and fallen limbs in her path. Knowing that at any moment fate could deal a lethal blow, a lump of fear the size of one of Lulu's cinnamon buns lodged in Sophie's throat. She could be killed in an instant by one lick of lightning, just as her schoolfriend Mary who had died so many years ago.

When Sophie neared the Graveyard Creek Bridge, she saw a man hunkered down behind a thick copse of hawthorn bushes. She slowed for a better look. Andrew Ferguson clutched a sack, no doubt the ransom money. He was waiting for Fletcher, a meeting that would never take place. But Sophie dared not stop to tell the captain. He would soon realize he waited in vain. Sooner or later he must come in out of the rain.

Fearing Ben's life depended upon her making good time, she ran on through the driving rain. Out of breath and with a painful stitch in her side, she refused to slow down. Her tears mingled with the rain pouring from her eyes, streaming down her face. Sophie did not pause even for a glance at Dulany House as she ran by. She gave no thought to being followed.

Bursting through the door of the hospital at last, Sophie shouted in the glistening, empty corridor, "Dr. Collins! Dr. Collins!"

The old doctor answered her call at once. Drenched to the skin, and dripping all over the shiny new floor, she described Ben's condition and where he lay mortally wounded.

"I'll come with you, I'll show you where—"

"There's no need for you to go out in the storm again," the balding physician soothed. "Don't worry, Miss Harrington, I know the mill. I can find it."

Sophie would have argued but the hospital door slammed open with a whoosh of storm wind. The admiral stomped toward her, obviously furious.

"Is my daughter ill?"

"No, sir," Dr. Collins replied with a calm, cordial smile. "But a warm bath and bed would be in order for Miss Harrington."

"Come, Sophie."

Sophie did not dare protest. The dark cold anger lurking in her father's eyes threatened to erupt at any moment. Confident the doctor would go to Ben at once, she lifted her chin and preceded the admiral from the hospital.

The sailing instructor would live and her journal was his to do with as he pleased.

* * *

Ben felt as if he had been sleeping within a dark fog. He drifted slowly through the damp haze. Even more slowly the fog finally dissipated, replaced by a misty light from above. Struggling to get past the light, he opened his eyes, blinking.

Where the hell was he?

Damn! His chest felt as if it had been lanced by a hot poker.

"Seaman Swain?"

Ben turned his head.

"Midshipman Baker?"

The tall, gangly young man smiled and jumped out of the chair in the corner where he'd been sitting and stood at attention. He greeted Ben with a formal salute. "Yes, sir. How are you feeling, sir?"

"I feel like a man who's been floundering at sea without a sail for several months. Weak, in other words. And I have a pain in my chest. Has someone removed my heart?" he quipped, attempting to make light of his condition.

Joseph offered a sheepish smile. "No, sir. Doc Collins stitched you up but he wasn't certain what your condition would be when you regained consciousness."

Ben looked about the small, white room. "Where am I?"

"The new hospital, sir."

Of course. Although he'd never been inside the new infirmary, it made sense for him to be here considering his pain. And then Ben remembered. Fletcher Thurman's knife.

"I have a knife wound."

"Yes, sir. But you're going to be as good as new," the boy assured Ben. "All of the fourth classmen volunteered to take care of you. We've been taking shifts since the beginning when you were brought in."

"The beginning? Who brought me to the hospital?" Before he passed out, the last thing Ben remembered seeing were the faces of Flora, Abigail and Sophie. The women had hovered over him, regarding Ben with varying degrees of horror.

Joseph poured a glass of water from the pitcher on the bedside table. "As far as I know, Doc Collins found you."

"Well, I can thank Dr. Collins, but I don't know how I am to thank an entire class of midshipmen."

"By coming back as soon as possible," the midshipman said, handing Ben the glass of water. "Captain Ferguson doesn't know as much about sailing as you do. And I don't think he likes us much either. We've missed you."

Ben smiled. "And I've missed you."

As he said the words, he realized he spoke the truth. He'd enjoyed the excited expressions of the boys as they sailed solo for the first time. He'd gotten a kick out of the dreamy-eyed looks when his students first turned their faces into the wind, their gazes out to sea. He'd been buoyed by their eagerness and quick minds. He'd enjoyed taking green young men and molding them into what he hoped they would be, the finest sailors on the seas.

Sipping the tepid water, Ben asked, "How long have I been here?"

"Two days. The doc says the wound could have killed you, just a half-inch either way and you would have been a goner."

"That's comforting." The odd thing was, Ben had felt no fear when he saw Thurman's knife. The only emotion he could recall was the determination to deflect the blade, and the overriding need to reclaim Sophie's property from Fletcher.

"The doc has taken good care of you."

"I'm sure he has. Do you know what happened to the man who knifed me?"

"Thurman is his name, sir. Miss Flora shot him in the rear. He's in the brig waiting for the Falls Church sheriff to come and get him. Seems he stole a horse to get to Annapolis and that's just one of the charges against him. The man is an out-and-out criminal."

"That he is."

"I heard with those charges and his attempt to kill you, Thurman will be an old man before he gets out of jail."

Distracted, Ben rubbed his wound in a light, circular motion. "Poor Abigail. She and her babe will be feeling the results of Fletcher's deception long after I am healed."

"What was the fight about?" Joseph asked. "If you don't mind me asking," he added hastily.

"I was attempting to regain stolen property, a journal."

"There's a journal stashed in the sack with the clothes you were wearing. Is that the one you mean?"

Ben straightened up in the bed—and grimaced from the pain the movement brought. "Let me see it."

Baker pulled a sack from beneath the bed, and after a quick rummage, stood up again holding the journal. Sophie's journal.

Taking it from the boy, Ben held the bloodstained journal and stared at it in wonder as he turned it over in his hands. There could be no mistake. This was Sophie's novel. Why hadn't she taken it? Had she not seen it?

"Is that what you were fighting over?" Joseph asked, with an expression that plainly reflected his opinion that the small object couldn't possibly be worth a life.

Ben nodded. Puzzled that the journal would still be in his possession and unable to come up with a satisfactory explanation, an edgy feeling crept under his skin. "This is the journal I recovered."

If he asked the young midshipman to leave, he could read *The Romantic Adventures of Fifi LaDeux, An Unmarried Woman.* He could discover what the beautiful Sophie had written about him. But some how it didn't seem right. Reading the novel without the dimpled beauty's permission would be like invading her innermost thoughts. He couldn't do it.

The curly-haired fourth classman nervously shifted from foot to foot at Ben's bedside. His hazel eyes fixed on the journal. "It's covered with your blood."

Ben looked up at Joseph. "You know, although I recovered it, this journal doesn't belong to me. Would you mind putting it in a fresh sack and giving it to Miss Sophie Harrington?"

"The admiral's daughter?"

"Yes. Don't give the journal to anyone else but Miss Harrington. Bide your time until you are able to catch her alone."

"Yes, sir." Joseph saluted Ben as if he'd just received an order from the admiral himself.

"And Joseph, as soon as my sea legs are solid again, I'll be back to teaching."

The young man broke out into a wide grin. "Yes, sir."

After the boy had left, Ben fell into a deep, contented sleep. His next visitor came later that evening.

Ben steeled himself as the unsmiling admiral marched briskly into his room.

"I heard you were recovering," he announced from the foot of the bed.

"Yes, sir. I shouldn't be hospitalized for very much longer."

"Am I to assume that you did not recover Sophie's journal from Thurman?"

"He knifed me and ran."

Heaving a weary sigh, the admiral removed his spectacles and commenced to absent-mindedly wipe them on the corner of his jacket. "A thieving farmer has outwitted us all. Captain Ferguson waited four hours in the pouring rain to give Thurman the ransom and the yellow-bellied thief never showed his face."

"Perhaps I scared him off."

"Very likely. Still, the scoundrel has bested us," he said, returning his spectacles to the bridge of his nose. "You lie wounded, and Andrew is confined to bed with near pneumonia."

Ben suppressed a smile. Who but Andrew would wait four hours in the rain? "Please extend my wishes to Captain Ferguson for a speedy recovery."

"In light of the missing journal, he has decided not to marry Sophie."

Coward.

"I cannot blame him," Admiral Harrington added. "Andrew has also requested a transfer to sea duty as soon as he is fully recovered."

"The captain must be disappointed," Ben ventured. He attempted to present a grave expression despite the pleasurable news of Ferguson's imminent departure gave him.

Admiral Harrington stroked his graying Vandyke beard. "I can only transfer one of you, and Andrew has seniority."

Astonishingly enough, Ben felt not a twinge of disappointment. "I understand," he said quietly.

"Until Sophie's journal is retrieved, my position is tenuous. I may yet find my naval career in ruins."

"Your daughter is extremely resourceful," Ben pointed out, offering what little comfort he dared. "In the end, she may recover her novel. I cannot believe Sophie has given up."

"She has no choice but to give up. I am sending my daughter to live with my sister in Saint Louis. God knows I've tried, but I cannot approve nor understand her strange ideas and behavior."

The pit of Ben's stomach dropped. "May I be so bold as to suggest that perhaps Sophie's sometimes unpredictable behavior has been to gain your attention? She may feel as if you do not love her."

He had indeed been too bold.

A fearsome scowl deepened the crevices of the admiral's face. "Not that this is any of your affair, but I refuse to wear my emotions on my sleeve, Swain."

"Yes, sir. Naturally, sir. But I have discovered that women do not understand a man's reluctance to express his feelings. If you talked with—"

"Out of the question," the admiral snapped. Without another word, he turned on his heel and strode to the door. But as he reached the passageway, he paused and looked back at Ben. Although his frown seemed permanently etched, his mind apparently was not set in stone. "But I might write my daughter a letter."

"Yes, sir."

"As soon as you're fit, Seaman, you are ordered to return to your regular duties as sailing instructor."

"Yes, sir," Ben replied in a stronger tone.

Saint Louis had much to recommend it, Sophie felt certain. The great Mississippi must be a marvelous sight. After a week, the admiral had lifted her restriction to her bedchamber, which Sophie likened to a stint in the brig with bread and water. He'd given her orders to prepare for the journey to Saint Louis. She had shred so many petticoats in the past several weeks, ordering new ones to be made topped her list.

As she shopped along Main Street, her gaze returned repeatedly to the *Nantucket Lady* docked at the city pier. Just yesterday, Sophie had waylaid Dr. Collins and learned Ben was recovering well. She felt some relief. But oh, how she longed to see him.

She would give anything to see his smile, to hear him sing the grog song and listen to his deep, lusty chuckle. He would have another scar on his chest—Fletcher Thurman had seen to that. But Sophie would never brush her lips against the new scar. She would not be healing Ben's wound with her love.

She had considered then dismissed a dozen possible methods of slipping into the hospital without her father knowing. She could hardly do so unnoticed. Still, how could she leave Annapolis without saying goodbye to Ben? Resolving to find a way, she turned down Prince George Street for a final look at the Bailey Cottage.

In the middle of the narrow cobblestone street, Sophie came to a dead halt. What little spirit she had left plummeted. The cottage was no longer for sale. The sign in the window had been removed and the cottage appeared vacant. Her eyes filled with tears.

"Miss Harrington!"

Hastily wiping away the evidence of her distress with the back of her hand, Sophie turned to see Midshipman Baker hurrying toward her.

Sophie forced a smile. "Good day, Joseph."

Nodding curtly, in proper midshipman fashion, he returned the greeting. "Good day."

"What brings you to Prince George Street?"

He held up a sack. "I've been following you. Seaman Swain asked me to give you this."

Ben! Ben was thinking of her! He'd sent her a gift from what might have been his deathbed!

Sophie's heart beat a swift tattoo as she took the sack from the dark-haired boy. She drew in a breath as she peeked in the sack. "My journal!"

Appearing ill at ease, Joseph adjusted his cap. "Seaman Swain wanted you to have it as soon as possible."

For the first time in days, Sophie felt alive. Excitement bubbled through her. Once more her dream was within reach. She could flee to New York and pass her novel among the publishers. She could be living an independent life before summer's end. Although she'd had her heart set on living in the Bailey Cottage, she would find another home, perhaps one even more charming.

But why? Why had Ben given up his opportunity to turn her journal over to the admiral and receive the orders that he so desperately coveted? Why had the tall, dark, blue-eyed whaler traded his dreams for hers?

Sophie's heart fluttered wildy within her chest.

"Midshipman Baker, tell me, how does Seaman Swain fare?"

The midshipman adopted a rigid stance, focusing somewhere above and beyond her. "The sailing instructor is still weak but claims he shall be back teaching our class shortly," he reported in clipped tones.

The news served to elate Sophie even more. Just a few short minutes ago, all hope seemed lost, and now the world seemed almost right. The good earth spun on its proper poles.

"I wish I could see Seaman Swain and thank him personally," she mused aloud.

"Yes, ma'am."

She smiled at Joseph, studying him. Under Ben's guidance, he'd made great strides. She had no doubt that Joseph would become a skilled sailor and exemplary naval officer. He appeared to have gained a new degree of confidence without the cockiness of many midshipmen.

"Thank you for bringing my journal to me."

"Yes, ma'am. My pleasure, ma'am."

Since the sailing incident in Annapolis Harbor, when she'd convinced Joseph to take her sailing, the boy seemed nervous in Sophie's company.

"Is that all, ma'am?"

"Yes." But as he raised his hand to salute her, which was not at all necessary, Sophie was struck by a brilliant scheme.

"Midshipman Baker, would you mind if I borrowed your uniform for a brief time this evening?"

He paled.

Nineteen

Ben couldn't quite believe his eyes. At first, he suspected a relapse complicated by an onslaught of
delirium. A noise, a cultivated clearing of a throat,
wakened him from a light sleep. When he opened his
eyes, he did not immediately recognize the midshipman who stood at the foot of his bed. But after
blinking the silent figure into focus, he realized that
only one person in the world possessed turquoise
eyes.

"Sophie?"

She winked as if he were in complicity. "How are
you feeling, Ben?"

Appalled.

"Sophie, what are you doing here?"

With the exception of the mothers of sickly midshipmen, female visitors were not allowed in the new
hospital.

The woman who seemed to believe that most rules
weren't meant for her simply smiled. No, she beamed.
Sophie's dazzling smile purged the last of Ben's pain.
In the warm light of her smile, Ben felt his strength
return. He could bound out of bed and take her in
his arms, crush her to him, smother her with kisses.

What it had taken the doctor almost a week to
achieve, Sophie had accomplished in an instant. She

had healed him, but not of the smoldering ache he felt for her—that, too, had returned incredibly swiftly with double the intensity.

"I came to make certain you were well," Sophie replied, apparently unaware of the effect she had upon Ben. "And to say goodbye."

Although he knew this time would come and thought that he'd prepared himself for it, the sharp pain that suddenly pierced his heart was far worse than that caused by the blade of Fletcher Thurman's knife.

"You're leaving for New York," he stated. He knew. He didn't have to ask. Sophie had long waited for the opportunity to sell her novel to a New York publisher.

A spectacle he never imagined to see distracted Ben momentarily. A woman dressed in full uniform sashayed to his side. A female figure clothed in the Naval Academy uniform was shock enough; one that sashayed added a disturbing element to the astonishing sight. Obviously, Sophie had been spending too much time with Flora. He figured the tavern maid had been born swinging her hips.

"I could not go without saying goodbye," Sophie said quietly.

"Your disguise is better than the last," he said, giving her as much of a smile as he could muster. "You do wonders for the uniform. Will it replace your bloomers?"

Laughing softly, Sophie perched on the edge of his bed.

If Ben wasn't feverish, he soon would be. She was too close. He couldn't stop her, wouldn't if he could.

Come closer.

His mind willed her. He'd lost all control.

"Thank you for returning my journal." Her glistening green-blue eyes met his, tropical pools of ever-changing light. "But I would not have had you risk your life."

"Getting stabbed was my own fault," he answered, attempting to ignore the unnatural quickening of his heart. "If I had been using my head, I would have been prepared for a trick like that. Crooks like Fletcher Thurman carry concealed knives as a matter of course."

"You are a man of great courage."

He shook his head. "I did what had to be done, what any man would do."

"You are not any man." Sophie reached out and ran her fingertips lightly over his jaw, seemingly oblivious to the tough stubble of his beard. "You are a man of great courage and loyalty."

Needles and pins pricked at his skin. His blood warmed. Tension swirled in the silence that fell between them. Ben could think of nothing to say, he could think only of what he would like to do to Sophie, do with her. He sucked in his breath.

"I am indebted to you, Ben." Her gaze fell to his lips.

Ben wet his lips. His throat felt as dry as gravel. "No."

She leaned closer, enveloping him in a slightly intoxicating cloud of honeysuckle. "You have come to my rescue time and again."

Damn. He was on fire.

Averting his eyes, Ben replied hoarsely. "I've simply protected you as the admiral asked me to do."

"My father acted unfairly by assigning you to watch over me as if you were a nursemaid."

"In the beginning, I resented the assignment," he admitted. "And then I came to enjoy . . . your company."

The admiral's daughter seemed headed for dangerous territory, and she would take Ben with her if he wasn't careful. It would serve no purpose to confess his feelings now, when she was about to leave Annapolis.

"You have acted above and beyond the call of duty," she said softly.

"What has happened to Abigail and her infant?" Ben asked, lowering his head and swiping both hands through his hair. A brisk change in conversational course was needed or he would be lost.

"She is once again serving as my maid, and I have been helping her care for the baby. Little Florrie is a lovely baby." Sophie's eyes sparkled as her full, rosy lips parted in a wide smile.

The taste of her lips, like the sweetest summer berries, still lingered in Ben's mind, in his senses. "Does the admiral know that Abigail played an important role in Fletcher Thurman's plan?" he asked.

"I explained to my father that Fletcher forced Abigail to steal the journal. In a manner of speaking, he did. Abigail was just as much a victim of Thurman's villainy as me. And after swallowing a good deal of pride, which I have learned to do," Sophie added with a rueful smile, "I begged the admiral to allow Abigail to return to her former position. She was not meant to be a washerwoman, after all, and her baby deserves a good life."

"And the admiral agreed?" Ben asked, tearing his gaze from her mouth to the long, graceful column of her neck. "What . . . what of Flora?"

Sophie shot him a teasing smile. "Flora is giving up her wicked ways to marry Graham."

The amazing news took Ben completely by surprise. His mouth fell open. "I never expected to see Flora Muldoony settle on one man, much less marry," he said when he had recovered his composure.

"She loves Graham . . . and she is with child."

"What?" Incredulous, he could hardly believe that he had heard Sophie correctly. While he lay bedridden, the impossible had happened.

Sophie only nodded and smiled. And to his immense pleasure, her dimple dove to beguiling, heart-skipping depths.

"I guess being with child is as good a reason to marry as any," he allowed.

"Ah, but I can think of a better reason," Sophie said.

Ben feared to ask. As it happened, he did not have to supply the question.

"Love is the best reason to marry," Sophie declared, and cast him a smile that glowed with triumph.

"Unless you desire the independent life."

Instead of replying, Sophie took Ben's hand in hers and raised it to her lips.

Before Ben knew what she was about, the beautiful, outrageous admiral's daughter gently kissed his open palm. The warm, feathery brush of her lips against the soft pad of his sensitive palm sent white-hot fire racing through his veins. Her touch conveyed a tenderness he'd never known, never felt.

His heart roared.

Taking his hand in both of hers, she nestled it to her cheek. "Once I thought I wished to live a celibate life, but recently, I have discovered that I am quite unsuited for such a cold existence."

Hauling in a deep ragged breath, Ben closed his eyes. How much more could he endure? He wasn't made of steel, yet she tested his willpower. What was she saying? And why was his body trembling as if he were a boy about to lie with a woman for the first time?

Ben's rambling thoughts evaporated with the first bounce of the bed.

He blinked his eyes wide open. "Sophie! What are you doing?"

"I wish to be close to you one more time," she said, snuggling up to him.

Before Ben had time to explain how it might look if someone walked into the room, someone did.

"Hell and damnation! What is the meaning of this?" Dr. Collins sputtered. "Hell and damnation, what are we coming to when a midshipman and an instructor share the same bed?"

Sophie jumped from Ben's bed so swiftly the cap fell off her head and a cascade of long tawny locks fell to her shoulders.

The old doctor's horrified expression slowly transformed to one reflecting disgruntled relief.

"Dr. Collins. I am so sorry. I know that I have disregarded your rules and I have no business being here," Sophie apologized in a rush of words. "But if you would look the other way, just this once, I shall leave right away and no one shall be the wiser. No one shall ever know that I was here."

The doctor's gaze narrowed on her. "You are the young woman who ran through the storm to get help for Seaman Swain, aren't you?"

Sophie had run through the storm, through thunder and lightning, to save him? Ben felt the blood drain from his face.

Lowering her eyes, Sophie nodded. "Yes, I am."

Her voice was but a whisper.

"All right, young lady," the doctor said. "You had every right to visit. But go now, before you get us both in trouble."

"Thank you, sir." Misty-eyed, Sophie turned to Ben. "Goodbye, Seaman Swain."

The pain that tore through Ben was unbearable. It felt as if some wild animal gnawed his bones.

"Goodbye, Buttercup."

Later that evening, after Sophie had cried her heart out, calmed her reddened eyes with cold compresses, and donned a suitable gown to make herself the picture of propriety, she knocked on the door of her father's study.

"Come in."

The admiral sat at his desk, writing.

She halted midway. "Good evening, Father."

Looking up, he laid down his pen. "Good evening, Sophie."

"I do not mean to disturb you but I have pressing business that I would like to discuss before I leave for Saint Louis. Are you busy? Should I come back at another time?"

"I was, was just writing a letter. Sit down."

Gingerly perching on the edge of one of the wing-back chairs facing his desk, Sophie felt more nervous than she had ever been when approaching her formidable father. Twisting a lace hankie in her hands, she began. "Father, if you remember, you and I entered a bargain several weeks ago regarding the novel that I had written in my journal."

"How could I forget?"

"No, of course you never would." Without success, Sophie attempted to still the nervous twitch at the corner of her lip. "If I recovered my journal, you agreed that I might establish an independent life if I was fortunate enough to sell *The Romantic Adventures of Fifi LaDeux, An Unmarried Woman.* "

"Yes, I agreed to your terms."

"And I offered to change the names of the characters in my novel to protect any living, actual person that they might be based upon—that is, loosely based upon," she added. "I also promised to publish under an assumed name."

The first signs of a frown appeared at the bridge of her father's nose. "I remember. Where is this leading?"

"Further, we agreed that should Seaman Swain recover the journal, he would be rewarded by receiving immediate deployment to ship duty and you would forward his steamship designs to Admiral Johnson at once."

"Yes, Sophie." The admiral removed his spectacles and rubbed the bridge of his nose. "But the bargain we struck is meaningless without the journal."

Sophie inhaled deeply, raising her chin as she did so. "I have the journal in my possession."

Her father leaned across the desk so quickly he almost smashed his spectacles. "Where is it? How did you recover it and when?"

Holding her hands up as if to hold him back, Sophie took another deep breath. "I shall explain, but first, I would like to change the terms of our agreement."

If thunder took human form, her father would be the model. He spoke her name as if it were a dire warning. *"Sooophie."*

"If you approve, I shall turn the journal over to you."

Before replying, the admiral silently contemplated the ceiling. "My own daughter bargains like a Baltimore merchant," he lamented.

"Are you at least willing to listen to what I propose?"

Sophie asked, forging boldly ahead despite the churning of a nervous stomach.

"I'm listening."

"If you will see that Seaman Swain is given deployment to a ship and forward his steamship designs to Admiral Johnson, I shall give my journal to you and leave for Saint Louis without a whisper of protest."

Her father inclined his head as if he hadn't heard her correctly. "Why would you do such a thing? What are you up to? You have been yammering about independence for months and now you throw the opportunity away so that Seaman Swain may have his steamship designs considered?"

Sophie would have stood, but she feared her legs would fail her. Her knees felt like the Sugarplum Sweet Shop's fudge looked before it hardened.

"I am not up to anything. The truth is, Seaman Swain deserves a turn at good fortune more than I do. He will make a fine naval officer one day, and you will be acknowledged as well for any recommendation you might give him."

The admiral angled his head, regarding her suspiciously. "Have you formed an affection for the seaman?"

Could he see the answer shining in her eyes? Sophie swallowed hard. "My feelings have nothing to do with this bargain. 'Tis the just and honorable thing to do."

"I have just deployed Captain Ferguson to ship duty."

"Andrew has left the academy?"

"Yes."

"He did not say goodbye."

"Can you blame him?"

Yes, Sophie could.

"I think a farewell would have been the proper thing to do. I should have liked the opportunity to set things right with Andrew."

"Perhaps. Or perhaps I did not choose wisely for you."

Amazed to hear her father's admission, Sophie offered a soothing remark, "But you made the attempt, and I do appreciate your trying to find me a respectable husband."

Pressing his lips together, the admiral nodded. "In any case, when I sent Andrew off, I used the only deployment available to me at present."

"Oh, no!" Sophie jumped from her chair. "There must be something you can do."

"I could courier Swain's ship designs to Admiral Johnson at once, if that will satisfy you."

"Yes, thank you. It would. And when another opportunity for deployment arises?"

"I shall sign transfer orders for Seaman Swain."

With a grateful sigh and a happy smile, Sophie turned on her heel. "I shall fetch the journal for you."

"Wait!"

Sophie turned. The negotiation had gone well with her father. For once she was not leaving his office feeling frustrated, and he did not appear exasperated with her. Had it been too good to be true? She held her breath.

"Before you go, Sophie, I would like to read you the letter I have been writing."

How strange, she thought, and curious. Her taciturn father had never asked for her opinion in the past. Sophie's world had been turned upside down of late; nothing had gone as she expected. Shooting the admiral a nervous smile, she nodded and returned to her chair.

He put on his spectacles, cleared his throat, and focused on the page before he began to read.

My dear Sophie,

Upon the death of his beloved wife, a Naval Officer of my acquaintance was left with a beautiful, intelligent daughter. But a man who has grown up on the seas has no knowledge of what to do with a little girl, or how to treat her. She remained a mystery to him, and he kept his distance. While unafraid of battle he feared raising his precocious little daughter.

He decided upon a strict hand, the way he had been brought up. He provided the best care he could find and the finest education available for females. But the daughter took on notions ahead of her time—more than likely as a result of her education. He had no one to blame but himself. She did not grow into a docile, simpering miss, she blossomed into a young woman of spirit.

Soon she was of marriageable age and the officer sought to find her a good husband, someone who would take care of her after he was gone. He failed. He has been a dismal failure with his daughter from the beginning. Nevertheless, he loves her. He loves her with all of his heart.

Transfixed, Sophie stared at her father. His hands had trembled as he read her the letter. The letter had been about her . . . and him. Sweet mercy! It seemed that all Sophie could do was cry and shred her petticoats of late. Her cheeks burned with tears.

"That's as far as I've written," he said in a soft rasp.

Sophie knew it was not polite to stare, especially to regard your father as if you were seeing him for the first time. But she was. The admiral dropped the letter on his desk, lowered his head, and removed his spectacles.

Freed from inertia by his movements, Sophie hurried to his side. Kneeling beside him, she clasped his hands. "Thank you. Thank you for reading your letter. You are an excellent writer, you have written with your heart," she said, grinning through her tears. "You have let me see within your heart."

"Sophie—"

"I know I have tried your patience in the past and I apologize for those times. But I have always loved you too, Father. I promise never to cause you embarrassment again."

"And will you stay?" he asked, standing, lifting Sophie to her feet so that they faced each other, eye to eye. "I, too, often speak in anger. Despite my grumbling, I shall miss you dearly if you go to Saint Louis. We have a lot to learn about each other, Sophie. Say you will stay in Annapolis."

Sophie felt as though the sun had dawned within her, spilling light and warmth through her entire being. Momentarily unable to speak, torn between tears and laughter, she planted a firm kiss on her father's cheek.

"I thought you would never ask . . . but," she added with a saucy smile, "there is one condition."

The next night, following his release from the infirmary, Ben lounged on his sloop. He'd spread a blanket on deck and rested his head back against a plump down cushion. Tonight he would sleep aboard the *Nantucket Lady* beneath a star-filled sky.

Grateful to be alive and back on his vessel, he softly hummed the grog song. But he couldn't shake the sadness that permeated him. Ben doubted that even a moonlight sail about the bay would restore his spirits. Losing Sophie was like losing his heart, relinquishing his soul.

The rebellious beauty didn't even know that he'd fallen in love with her. He hadn't told her. Instead, he'd returned her journal with hope that she could make her dreams come true. Ben had demonstrated his love in the only way he could. Even if the admiral would consider allowing his daughter to marry a mere seaman, Ben couldn't hold Sophie back. He loved her too much.

A flutter of footsteps on the pier ended his musings. Frowning, he lifted his head to listen.

The footsteps stopped close by.

"Ben! Ben, are you here?"

There could be no mistake. The soft singsong whisper belonged to Sophie. The unrelenting admiral's daughter had come after him again, chasing him down in the dead of night to the dock. Ben thought she would be in New York by now.

His heart hammered against his chest in a rapid, breath-stealing beat. He did not think he could bear another goodbye. Perhaps if he lay very still, she would give up and go away.

She took several more steps. Dear God, she'd stopped. Ben looked up. Sophie stood above him, peering down onto the deck.

She wore a wide, satisfied smile. "I thought I'd find you here. May I join you?"

If Ben had learned anything by now, it was that he could not stop Sophie Harrington. Pushing himself to his feet, he extended a helping hand. With a single light bound, the ever-smiling Sophie boarded *Nantucket Lady*.

Ben turned away, quickly putting distance between them. He turned away from eyes that mesmerized and away from the scent of honeysuckle that tempted him so and weakened his resolve. Attempting to project a calmness and indifference he did not feel, he sat on the blanket and wrapped his arms around his knees.

"Have I interrupted your stargazing?" she asked softly. "Should I come back at another time?"

"No, I'm . . . I'm just surprised to see you."

"Is something wrong, Ben?"

"No. I expected you would be in New York by now."

"My journey has been postponed," she said, sinking down beside him. "Oh, this is lovely. The moon is almost full and there's not a spot in the sky without the sparkle of a star."

"Lovely," Ben repeated, gazing at Sophie. Weeks of mounting emotions, intense feelings he could not express, reduced his voice to a husky croak. He wanted her.

He closed his eyes, but what he could not see he could sense. Her warmth, her light, her spirit. "Why have you delayed leaving for New York?"

"You have not taught me to sail yet."

Startled, his eyes blinked open. "What?"

Turning her gaze from the sky to Ben, she smiled.

"Your humor escapes me upon occasion," he said.

"Do you know how long ago it was that I first asked you to instruct me?"

"Weeks."

She nodded, returning her gaze to the great golden moon that hovered above them. "Earlier this evening, Father read me a letter that he'd been writing. And when he finished, I understood the admiral a bit better. By mutual agreement, we decided that I would remain in Annapolis."

Once again Ben was taken by surprise. He hiked an eyebrow but kept his mouth firmly closed. When Admiral Harrington had visited him in the hospital, Ben boldly suggested that the commandant talk with his daughter. At the time Ben felt he had little else to lose and risked being sent to the brig in irons for speaking in such a forthright fashion to his commanding officer. But Harrington appeared to consider the suggestion, and then replied that he would write a letter. Other than his being docked half a year's pay for insubordination, Ben believed that was the end of it.

He'd been wrong. He'd not lost a penny of pay. And now he could hardly conceal his astonishment. The Commandant of Midshipmen had indeed written a letter to his daughter, a letter that apparently had had the power to initiate a new understanding between the admiral and Sophie.

One piece of astounding news followed another. Sophie's journey to the New York publishers had been put off. Ben had the eerie feeling that something was going on here that he should know about and didn't.

"Are you happy that I shall be staying in Annapolis?" Sophie asked, lifting a questioning gaze to him. Her eyes looked directly into his, as if she would find his answer there.

Ben fell into the dazzling pools of her blue-green eyes. He took a tumble. Like a drowning man, he descended through warm, tropical waters, unable to breathe, unable to stop his fall. He wanted her.

"Only if you are," he said, waiting to hit the sandy bottom.

"Yes, I am."

Perhaps the vision beside him, inching closer by the moment, did not truly exist. Perhaps he had conjured her out of the stars. "Does the admiral know you're out?"

She wasn't wearing her disguise, or one of her feathery- fruity bonnets.

"Not exactly."

It was the real Sophie.

"But neither did I tell my father that I was retiring for the evening when I left his study."

"Oh, Sophie." He could not prevent the sigh that escaped him. Ben knew what to expect by now. Tomorrow morning, he would be standing beside her in the admiral's office, attempting to explain this evening's accidental tryst.

"I have something important to discuss with you, Ben. I could not sleep otherwise."

He had something important on his mind as well, but it had little to do with talk. The tantalizing nearness of her, the rosy fullness of her mouth, beckoned Ben.

Damn, he wanted her.

She appeared to be contemplating the moon and star-spangled sky. After several silent moments passed, Sophie drew a deep breath and exhaled slowly before beginning. "When you returned my journal to me, you sacrificed the deployment you wanted so desperately. Not only did you give up on returning to sea, but Ben, you knew your steamship designs would never be sent to Washington. No one with the power to help you would ever see them. You gave me my novel knowing that you might remain a sailing instructor for the rest of your life."

What could he say?

Sophie turned wide, imploring eyes to his. "Why, Ben, why?"

Ben's heart swelled to a size too large for his chest.

The white-hot ache in his groin flamed, threatening to overpower his restraint. He was only flesh and blood, a man whose desire for one woman had grown all out of proportion. Ben knew without question that it would take the rest of his life to tame his passion for Sophie.

He twisted to face her, gazed into her luminous beauty. Ever so gently, he brushed the pad of his thumb along her satiny cheek.

"Don't you know?" he asked. His tone was hoarse, unrecognizable.

Her gaze never left his as she shook her head.

With his thumb and forefinger, he tilted her chin, raising her lips closer to his. "Because I love you, Sophie. I love you."

Ben brought his mouth tenderly down on hers. His heart slammed against his chest. Again and again.

She parted her lips and drank him in. And when, at last, she raised her head, Sophie's smile took Ben's breath away.

"Oh, Ben, sweet mercy!" she declared in a whisper. Tears streamed from her eyes. "I love you too. I've loved you for ever so long."

Without another word, he crushed Sophie to him, breathing in the honeysuckle that made him weak, the wondrous, sweet scent of the woman who enchanted him. And when he'd kissed her, tasted her, felt the need in him approaching the point of a heavenly explosion, Ben set Sophie back from him.

"I'm just a seaman," he began to explain. "Your father—"

"My father and I have come to a new agreement," she interrupted, her creamy complexion glowing pink and flush. "I may marry whomever I choose."

Damn. She wanted to marry him!

Ben's heart felt close to bursting. He dared not move or speak.

"And when your steamship designs are seen in Washington, you will be recognized as a leader in the new Navy," she continued, excitedly predicting Ben's future. "You shall be a lieutenant before the year is out."

She'd confused him again. "But how are my designs to reach Washington?"

"My father is sending them."

"How? Why?" Ben had begun to sound like Midshipman Baker during his first days of sailing instruction. Confused. Doubtful. Amazed. Ben's mind reeled.

"Because tonight I gave my novel to my father." Her eyes sparkled with delight. "'Twas a clever exchange."

"But Sophie, you could have sold your novel."

"Perhaps, though I doubt it." She spoke earnestly but with a wry, disparaging smile. "The novel I am writing in my new journal is far superior. By penning the first, however, I learned a great deal."

Dazed, Ben could only stare at this bright, beautiful woman he loved with all of his heart. She'd filled his life with surprise and excitement; she'd given him a love deeper than any ocean, more exhilarating than any unexplored harbor. His heart drummed and his head whirled with unexpected possibilities. "I am at a loss . . . a loss for words."

Sophie burst into a peal of laughter. "But I am not."

"Of course not."

"I shall always write but I will not have as much time as I'd planned."

"Why is that?" he asked dutifully.

"I want to have babies, your babies, Ben."

Damn!

Now he knew for certain that he was dreaming. Ben reached out and pulled Sophie into his arms, to feel the lush curves of her body against his, to bring his mouth down on her lips, to make certain the woman was real. She curled into him, soft as silk, warm as the summer sun. She was real.

Ben had subdued mighty whales and warring men, but he'd met his match in Sophie Harrington. He hoped that for the rest of their days he would possess the insight and wisdom to honor her as an independent woman, with a mind and a voice that should be heard. But at the moment, the desire to make love to her surpassed all other thought and emotion. He longed to feel Sophie's round, bare breasts in the palms of his hands, to feel her moist and waiting for him. The admiral's daughter, the goddess of love at last unmasked, was willing and wanting him.

"You are the only woman I've ever wanted to have my babies."

"When can we start?" she murmured.

"Have you ever been on a moonlight sail?"

Twenty

Ben and Sophie stood side by side in her father's
study in Dulany House. From his rigid stance, Sophie
knew the splendid man towering over her suspected
that she'd landed him in trouble again. But this command appearance had nothing to do with Sophie.
And the admiral did not appear to be angry, only
mildly preoccupied.

"You may be wondering why I have called you here
this afternoon," he began.

"Yes, sir," Ben replied.

"Admiral Johnson has sent word he wishes to see
you at once, Seaman Swain."

"Oh, Ben!" Sophie exclaimed, clapping her hands
together. "I knew it!"

After shooting Sophie a quelling glance, her father
continued, addressing Ben alone. "The admiral is impressed with your steamship designs and would like to
discuss them with you."

Ben's full-out grin and twinkling eyes managed to
set Sophie's heart to pounding.

"Yes, sir," he said. "Thank you, sir."

"My pleasure. You're an asset to the Navy and I
could not wish for a better son-in-law."

Sophie glowed.

"Thank you, sir. Sir, if I may speak freely?"

"Certainly."

"When you first ordered me to watch over Sophie, I must confess that I resented the assignment—"

"My father *ordered* you to—"

Sophie cut short her retort as both men turned to her. She smiled. "I knew."

"Of course you did." Ben chuckled and turned his attention to her father. "I got over my resentment. You gave me the best order I ever received, sir. It was the luckiest day of my life."

"Of course it was." Sophie beamed.

"When do I leave for Washington, Admiral Harrington?"

"Directly after the wedding. You must marry my daughter before anything else, or we shall both be plagued."

"I understand."

From the corner of her eye, Sophie thought she saw Ben wink in a decidedly conspiratorial fashion at her father. As she wondered if he would take such a liberty, Ben saluted the admiral, turned sharply on his heel, and strode to the door.

Before joining Ben on the porch, where he waited for her, Sophie gave her father a hug. The admiral still blanched at her small demonstrations of affection. In time, he'd come around—Ben had.

A gentle breeze from the harbor cooled the early summer afternoon. She greeted Ben with a proud smile. "You will be an admiral someday, Seaman Swain."

"If I am so fortunate as to reach the distinguished rank, I shall owe it all to my clever wife," he said, bussing her on the nose. "Sophie, I have something to show you."

"What?"

"It's a surprise. You have surprised me often enough.

Now it is my turn." Grinning, he clasped her hand in his. "Come with me, my Buttercup."

Her heart melted. She could feel its liquid warmth pouring through her soul. Sophie could not resist the twinkle in Ben's eyes, nor the mischievous smile on his lips. The galvanizing combination acted to seduce her as quickly and surely as when passion burned in his gaze and his sensuous lips brushed against the tender hollow of her neck.

Ben had escorted Sophie to the parade ground for a concert by the fledgling academy band and later to wave goodbye to Midshipman Baker as he departed on his first cruise aboard the *U.S.S. Preble.*

With her father's blessings, Ben had given Sophie her first sailing lesson and just last night she and her dark-eyed hero had attended the lyceum for an enlightening lecture by Miss Lucy Stone, a college graduate and advocate of women's rights.

Sophie enjoyed being part of a couple. She could not imagine the independent life she'd once dreamed of could give her the pleasure she took in being with Ben. Soon they would be wed in the garden of Dulany House. Sophie counted the days. It mattered little where Ben must work or live, as long as they were together.

At the moment, she found it difficult to keep pace with him as he hurried past the gate and up the street. After only two blocks, she came to an abrupt halt. "This is Prince George Street."

"I know, come."

More curious now than ever, Sophie shrugged her shoulders and followed. Ben stopped in front of the Bailey Cottage.

"Oh, Ben, the cottage was sold weeks ago."

He nodded. "Sophie, do you remember me telling

you that my younger brother went to California to search for gold?"

"Yes." But what, she wondered, did that have to do with the Bailey Cottage?

"Matt found his gold and repaid me. He restored the family fortune. We made a great deal of money in the early days. I'm not a pauper who must get along on a seaman's pay—or a ship designer's salary." He dangled the keys before her. "I bought Bailey Cottage."

"Oh, Ben!" Sophie's pulse jumped and raced at double its normal speed.

"I feared someone might buy it before you sold your first novel."

"I love you!" Throwing her arms around him, she kissed Ben as if it might be their last embrace. She planted a long, deep, wet kiss on his mouth.

When at last Sophie raised her lips from his, Ben swayed momentarily as if he might lose his balance. "Inside, inside," he drawled, "before you have the whole town talking."

"Keeping the whole town talking is what I do best!"

The corners of his mouth turned up in a delicious crooked smile before her handsome husband-to-be pressed the keys of Bailey Cottage into Sophie's hand. "This will always be our home, Sophie. No matter how far we may wander, we'll always return to our home on Prince George Street, henceforth to be known as the Swain Cottage."

Laughing through her tears, Sophie opened the door with trembling hands and was met with the inviting fragrance of oranges and cloves, a fresh and delightful blend.

She stared in wonder. "How did you do it?"

"It wouldn't have been possible without Flora and Abigail to help me. They are nesting women, full of baby talk and what makes a comfortable home. And they know your tastes."

Sophie could barely see her husband for the tears in her eyes. He towered above her, a droll smile upon his lips, his dark indigo eyes alight with anticipation.

"It's beautiful," she sighed, scanning the parlor before moving into the indoor kitchen with its spacious brick hearth and large round oak table. On the center of the table, a plate of mouth-watering cinnamon buns from the Sugarplum Sweet Shop awaited them. "You've thought of everything, Ben!"

He led her from room to room until they reached the second floor. The rear bedchamber overlooked a small rose garden. Awestruck, Sophie surveyed the room from the plump down bed covered with a rainbow quilt to the fireplace, bookshelves, and a writing desk complete with paper, pencils, and quills.

"I hope you like it," Ben whispered at her side.

"Even a skilled writer would have no words to thank you well enough."

Sophie crossed to the bed, dove her fingers deep into the mattress, and then perched upon it. "I'm testing," she explained, gently bouncing. "Have you sampled it?"

"I've been waiting for you."

His simple words triggered a needling desire. Hot liquid sugar swirled between her thighs. Sophie stood. With her eyes on Ben's, she slowly and deliberately peeled off her clothes. As she tossed her bodice, Ben began to hum the grog song.

To the rhytmn of his husky baritone, Sophie shed her powder blue skirts, her slippers, and finally her lace chemise in the same unhurried manner. When the layers of her garments pooled at her feet, the evidence of Ben's arousal was clear—and startling.

His dark eyes, glazed with desire, fixed on her as he

approached. He came to a stop but a breath away. She could feel his heat.

Sophie unbuttoned Ben's jacket and his trousers.

Her heart thrummed and her breath came in shallow gasps, tasting of ecstasy. Ben loved her for the woman she was. He would never constrain her. He would always be her champion, the man who protected, loved, honored, and adored her.

And she would love him to the end of her life. She would give him sons and daughters, and days and nights of unparalleled bliss.

With loving abandon, Sophie eagerly, delicately skimmed Ben's long muscular frame, corded arms, and flat, iron-hard belly. The scars that stood out beneath her splayed fingertips felt smooth in contrast to the rough male texture of his skin. Hot, insistent waves of desire skipped down her spine.

He moaned when she brushed his steely erection, gasped when she sank to her knees and loved him.

"Oh, I must write about this," Sophie murmured later, much later. "I surely must write of this."

Thrilling Romance from
Lisa Jackson